Reforming LORD RAGSDALE

CARLA KELLY

SWEETWATER BOOKS
AN IMPRINT OF CEDAR FORT, INC.
SPRINGVILLE, UTAH

ISBN 13: 978-1-4621-1224-1

Published by Sweetwater Books, an imprint of Cedar Fort, Inc.
2373 W. 700 S., Springville, UT, 84663
Distributed by Cedar Fort, Inc., www.cedarfort.com

LIBRARY OF CONGRESS CATALOGING-IN-PUBLICATION DATA

Kelly, Carla.
Reforming Lord Ragsdale / Carla Kelly.
    pages cm
Originally published: New York : Penguin, 1995.
ISBN 978-1-4621-1224-1 (mass market)
1. Man-woman relationships--Fiction. I. Title.
PS3561.E3928R43 2014
813'.54--dc23

                                    2013034837

Cover design by Kristen Reeves
Cover design © 2014 by Lyle Mortimer
Edited and typeset by Melissa J. Caldwell

Printed in the United States of America

10   9   8   7   6   5   4   3   2   1

To my sisters, Karen Deo and Wanda Lynn Baier—
Family isn't just anything; it's the only thing.

KEEP MY COUNSEL LEST THOU SLIP.
IF LOVE OR HATE MEN OFFER THEE,
HIDE THY HEART AND HOARD THY LIP.
WED NO MAN. REMEMBER ME.

—from the Irish, seventeenth century

Chapter 1

I WONDER WHY IT IS THAT MY MISTRESS IS *so ignorant,* Lord Ragsdale thought as he took a sip of morning brandy and gazed at the heavily scented letter spread out before him on the breakfast tray. *Could it be that no one ever taught her the difference between "there" and "their"—and what on earth is this word?*

He held up the paper closer to his good eye. "Hmm, it appears that I am either thoughtless, thankless, reckless, or feckless, and I don't think Fae knows that word."

He felt a tiny headache beginning from all that scent, so he crumpled the letter into a ball and threw it across the room toward the wastebasket by his desk, which was over-flowing with other correspondence. As usual, he was wide of the mark. "Fae, why so much musk on one letter? Do you think I am an otter?" he asked her miniature, which resided, smirking, on his night table.

He took another sip and then slid down to a more comfortable level in the bed. *Of course, you didn't take on Fae in the first place because she was a grammarian,* he reminded himself. *You acquired her services because of her other splendid talents. Fae Moullé might not be able to string a coherent sentence across a page, but she knows her way to a man's heart.*

It was a thought that only a week ago might have propelled him from his house on Curzon Street to her little

1

love nest (paid by him), only a brisk walk away. As he closed his eye, he asked himself what had changed in so brief an interval. Perhaps it was the rain. That was it; too much rain always made him restless and dissatisfied.

He opened his eye and stared at the ceiling. "Fae Moullé, I do not love you," he told the plaster swirls overhead. "No, Fae, I do not love you."

Lord Ragsdale sighed and jerked the pillow out from behind his head. He lay flat on the bed and almost returned to sleep again. The room was cool and silent, but some maggot was burrowing about in his brain now and wouldn't let him doze. Of course, it was well past noon too.

Perhaps it was time to send a letter to Fae, severing all connections. He could sweeten her disappointment with a tidy sum and offer to provide excellent references. The thought made him grin, in spite of his vague discomfort. A woman like Fae Moullé ought to have no trouble snaring another marquess or earl. *England is full of dilettantes*, he thought, *and we recognize what we like.*

He thought back to Fae's letter, and the one the day before, teasing him for a new wardrobe to peacock about town in. While he liked the way she looked when she strolled about town with him, her hand resting lightly—but so possessively—on his arm, he was already dreading the mornings that would be taken up with modistes and models. Fae would not buy anything he did not approve of, so he would have to accompany her to the salons. She would coo and simper over each dress trotted out on display and then look at him with her big blue eyes. "Whatever you want, my dear," she would say.

"Whatever you want, my dear," he mimicked. *Honestly, Fae, don't you possess a single stray thought of your own? What do you like? Do you know?*

He sat up then and left his bed, thoroughly disgusted with himself. He glared into the mirror and pointed a finger at his nightshirted facsimile. "Johnny Staples, you are a spoiled one," he told himself. "You pay Fae's bills, and she must jump through your hoops. You should be ashamed."

He regarded himself another moment and then looked about for his eye patch. No sense in disturbing the maid, who was due any moment with his shaving water. He found it and grinned to himself again, wondering how loud she would scream if she came into the room and found him leering at her with his patch over his good eye.

Too bad it was the Season now. He would have happily traded it all for a week or two on a friend's estate, if he had any friends left. He could take off that stupid patch and let the cold winds blow across his dead eye too as he rode the land. But this was London, and really, his eye didn't look too appealing, all milky white, perpetually half-open, and with that nasty scar. *I could scare myself if I were drunk enough*, he observed as he pulled his robe about his shoulders and gave the coals in the fireplace a stir.

He grunted when the maid knocked, and she entered with his hot water. When she left, he sat at his desk, staring glumly at all the correspondence before him. This was the overflow from the book room too, and he wondered again why he had fired his secretary last month. He ruffled through the letters, many of them invitations that should have been answered weeks ago. "Well, Johnny, maybe it was because your secretary was robbing you blind," he reminded himself. "Which is true, but the man could keep up with my business and knew how to write letters that sounded just like I had written them. What a pity the wretched cove could also duplicate my signature."

Ah, well, the little toad was cooling his heels in Newgate now, awaiting transportation. Maybe if he survived the seven months in the reeking hold of a convict ship, he could find someone to bamboozle in Botany Bay. Lord Ragsdale sighed and looked at his frazzled desk. *I suppose now if I want to cancel my liaison with Fae through the penny post, I'll have to write my own letter.*

Nope, no letters to Fae, he reminded himself as he took off the patch again and lathered up. *She thinks I'm thoughtless, thankless, reckless, or feckless. And besides that, it's too much exertion. I suppose a new wardrobe won't kill me. It's a lot easier than explaining to Fae that I'm tired of her.*

Lord Ragsdale was not in a pleasant frame of mind when his mother knocked on the door. He knew her knock; it was just hesitant enough to remind him that he paid her bills too. He tucked in his shirttails and buttoned up his pants, wondering at his foul mood. *Maybe I should pay Fae a quick visit,* he thought.

"Come in, Mother," he said, trying not to sound sour. It wasn't his mother's fault that he was rich and she was bound to him by his late father's stupid will. *I really should settle a private income on her,* he thought as he reached for his waist-coat. *I wonder why Father didn't? He never did anything wrong.* Lord Ragsdale sighed. *And death came too suddenly for him to say, "Oh, wait, I am not ready."*

As his mother came into his room on light feet, he felt his mood lifting slightly. How dainty she was, and how utterly unlike him. *She doesn't look old enough to have a thirty-year-old son,* he thought as he inclined his head so she could kiss his cheek. True to form, she patted his neckcloth and tugged it to the left a little.

"Am I off-center again, madam?" he inquired. "Funny how one eye gone puts me off, even after . . ." He paused a moment. "Let's see, is it ten years now?"

"Eleven, I think, my dear," she replied. "Oh, well. Two eyes gone would be worse."

He nodded, wondering at her ability to cheer him up. She was so matter-of-fact. Why couldn't he have inherited that tendency instead of his father's leaning toward melancholy?

"I suppose," he agreed as he allowed her to help him into his coat. "Curse the Irish, anyway."

She frowned at him, and he took her hand.

"Yes, Mama. That was rude of me," he said before she

could. "Didn't you teach me not to kick dogs? For so they are. I apologize."

He kissed his mother, and she smiled at him. "Accepted. Now, hurry up and put on your shoes. They are belowstairs."

He looked at her and then rummaged for his shoes. "Mama, who are you talking about?" She sighed loud enough for him to pause in his exertions.

"What did I forget this time?" he asked.

"Your American cousins, John. They have arrived."

He paused a moment in thought, embarrassed to have forgotten something that obviously had meaning for his mother. "My cousins," he repeated.

"John, you are the dearest blockhead," she said, taking his arm and pulling him toward the door. "My sister's children from Virginia! Don't you remember?"

He did now. In fact, he remembered a winter's worth of bills to refurbish the ballroom and downstairs sitting rooms. And wasn't there something about Oxford? "Let's see if I remember now, Mama," he teased. "Someone is going to Oxford, and someone else is attempting a come out under your redoubtable aegis."

"Excellent!" she commended him. "Sometimes you are the soul of efficiency."

"Not often, m'dear," he murmured as they descended the stairs. "Will you begin reminding me on a regular basis that I must engage a secretary, and soon?"

"I have been," she said patiently. "And I've been reminding you about a valet too, and while we're at it, a wife."

He laughed out loud at the seriousness of her expression. "Which of the three do I need worse, madam?" he quizzed as she steered him toward the gold saloon, reserved for unpleasant events, formal occasions, and, apparently, little-known relatives.

"A wife," she replied promptly as she allowed Lasker to open the door for her. "Ah, my dears! Heavens, are you drooping? Let me introduce your cousin John Staples, Lord

Ragsdale. John, here are Robert and Sally Claridge, your cousins from Richmond, Virginia. Come forward, my dears. He won't bite."

Of course I will not bite, he thought as he came forward to shake cousin Robert's hand. He thought he might kiss Sally's cheek, but she was staring at his eye patch as though she expected him suddenly to brandish a cutlass and edge her toward a plank. He nodded to her instead. "Delighted to meet you," he murmured automatically, wondering how soon he could escape to White's and bury his face in a pint of the finest.

He had to admit that they were a handsome pair, as he stepped back and allowed his mother's conversation to fill in any awkward gaps before they had the chance to develop. Sally Claridge had his own mother's ash-blonde good looks. If the expression in her blue eyes was a trifle vacant, perhaps a good night's rest on a pillow that did not pitch and yaw with an ocean under it would make the difference.

On the other hand, Robert's dark eyes seemed to miss nothing as he gazed about the room, looking like a solicitor totaling up the sum of each knickknack and trifle. *I certainly hope we measure up*, Lord Ragsdale thought as he cast an amused glance in Robert's direction, indicated a seat on the sofa to Sally, and then turned his attention to the fifth person in the room.

She should have taken up no more than a moment's flick of his eyes because she could only be Sally Claridge's servant, but he found himself regarding her with some thoroughness, and his own interest surprised him.

Lord Ragsdale enjoyed a shapely woman, and this female before him was no exception to his admiration. She was still covered with a rather shabby cloak, but the slope of it told him that she was nicely endowed. His attention was drawn to her regal posture. She stood straight and tall, her chin back, her head up, as poised a lady as ever favored the gold saloon. Her air fascinated him.

He knew she must be tired. Sally Claridge had sunk herself onto the sofa with the appearance of one destined never to rise again, while Robert leaned heavily on a chair back. The servant before him made no such concession to exhaustion. She bore herself like a queen, and he was intrigued in spite of himself.

"And you are . . . ?" he began.

John threw himself into one of the dainty chairs, and he heard his mother suck in her breath as it creaked. "That's Emma, Sally's waiting woman. Emma, I wish you'd take my cloak. And see here, there's Sally's too. I don't know why we need to remind you."

Without a word, the woman came forward and took the cloaks.

They were both much heavier than the one she still wore, but she draped them gracefully over her arm and retreated into the background again, her back as straight as a duchess's.

Lord Ragsdale looked around at his butler, who stood in the doorway. "Lasker, take the cloaks. Yours too . . . Emma, is it?"

She nodded and showed the barest dimple in his direction.

"You are such a dunce, Emma! Can you not at least say, 'Thank you, my lord'?" Robert burst out.

"Thank you, my lord," the woman whispered, her cheeks aflame with color.

"That wasn't necessary," Lord Ragsdale replied mildly to his cousin.

There was an awkward pause, which his mother filled adroitly, as he knew she would. "Robert, Sally, tell me how my sister does. I know you are both tired, but I must know." With a shy look in Lord Ragsdale's direction, Sally murmured a response to his mother, and Robert rummaged in his waistcoat for a letter. Lord Ragsdale clasped his hands behind his back and took another look at the waiting woman, as Robert called her.

It was a quaint expression, one he had not heard before, but it fit her exactly. She stood patient and still as his mother forged ahead with conversation, looking like someone used to waiting. He thought her eyes were green, and her expression told him that her mind was miles distant. For a brief moment, he wondered what she was thinking, and then he laughed inwardly. *Really, Johnny, who cares what a servant thinks?* he told himself. *I am sure you do not.*

"Well, son, is it agreed?"

Startled, he glanced at his mother, who was observing him with that combination of exasperation and fondness he was familiar with.

"I'm sorry, m'dear, but I was not attending. Say on, please. Tell me what it is I am about to agree to."

It was the merest jest. Out of the corner of his eye, he noticed that fleeting dimple again. Sally registered nothing on her face, and Robert just looked bored.

"John, sometimes I think you are certifiable."

Sally goggled at that. "Aunt Staples, he is a marquess!" she gasped.

"A title never gave anyone brains," his mother remarked, her words crisp. "Bear that in mind, Sally, as you begin your own adventure here this Season." She looked at her son again. "My dear, I was merely suggesting that we all drive down to Oxford to install Robert. It will give your cousins the opportunity of seeing their Grandmama Whiteacre, whom they have never met."

"Then brace yourselves," he murmured, wondering what the waiting woman was making of this family talk. "I think it an excellent idea. Once you have met the family Gorgon, you will only be too grateful for Charon to row you across the River Styx and into the quad of Brasenose."

The blank stare that Robert returned made Lord Ragsdale sigh inwardly and long for the comforts of his liquor cabinet. Obviously his alma mater would be suffering one more fool gladly.

"Provided Mr. Claridge can find the coin necessary for the boat ride."

It was said in such a low tone that he doubted Emma's words carried much beyond his own ears. He grinned appreciatively. "A hit, a palpable hit," he whispered back and was rewarded with that fleeting dimple again. *What have we here?* he asked himself. *A servant who knows her Greek mythology and Shakespeare too?*

But there was something else about her softly voiced reply that set off a bell in the back of his brain. He knew the lilt in her voice.

"Emma, where are you from?" he asked suddenly, his voice too loud in the quiet room. He knew his question was inappropriate, and a rude interruption to his mother, who was saying something to Sally about Grandmama White-acre. Besides that, he could not think of a time when he had ever asked a servant anything that personal. And here he was at his most strident, demanding an answer.

She was as startled as he was. The dimple disappeared, and she looked in dismay from Robert to Sally, as though waiting for a reprimand.

"Come now. It's an easy question," he said, egged on by some demon that seemed to be amplifying his voice until he sounded almost like he commanded troops again. He could see his mother coming toward him, alarm on her face. He held up a hand to stop her. "I want to know where you are from and what is your name."

The servant's face had drained of all color now. She swallowed several times, and if anything, her carriage became even more regal. She looked him right in the eye, something he had never seen before in a servant. She spoke quite distinctly.

"My name is Emma Costello, sir, and I am from County Wicklow."

"Well, curse you, then, and all your bog-trotting relatives," he said, and he turned on his heel and left the room. In another moment he slammed out of the house, ignoring his mother, and hurried down the sidewalk. He was too upset for Fae. It would be White's and a bottle of brandy. Maybe two.

Chapter 2

EVEN THE RELATIVE SERENITY OF WHITE'S in midafternoon could not assuage Lord Ragsdale's curious combination of vast ill-usage and shame of the dreariest sort. After a brief appearance in the main hallway, where the billiards players lounged between games and laid outrageous wagers on the evening's activities, he eased himself into the reading room. He sank with a sigh into his favorite old leather chair (wondering all over again why ordinary homes didn't have such simple pleasures), snapped open the *Times*, and burrowed behind it.

There were several articles that should have interested him. Napoleon had left the French Army under the tender mercies of Marshal Soult in Spain, and Soult had cat-and-moused General John Moore all the way to La Coruña in swift retreat.

"Bother it!" John Staples growled as he turned the page. And here was Napoleon in Paris again, enduring another diplomatic minuet by the lame but adroit Talleyrand. "Spit on all Frenchmen!" the marquess muttered and buried his face in the announcements of weddings and engagements. *Yes, spit on the French*, he thought as he perused the closely written lines to read of friends about to succumb to one stage or another of matrimony. If the French had not nosed about the Irish in the last century and given them cause to revolt, he would still be looking at the paper with two eyes instead of one. And he might still have an army career.

He folded the paper and rested it on his chest, allowing reason—or a close cousin to it—to reclaim him. *John, you idiot, you have made a scene in front of a servant,* he chided himself. He winced at the memory of the shock on his mother's face and Robert's frank stare. Like all good butlers, Lasker had developed sudden amnesia, irreversible until the evening meal belowstairs in the servants' dining room, Lord Ragsdale was sure.

Lord Ragsdale knew that once Lasker spread the word belowstairs about the master's rudeness (probably with raised eyebrows and then the sorrowful pronouncement that the late Lord Ragsdale would never have exhibited such rag manners), he would suffer several days from a slowdown in domestic efficiency. Until the staff recovered from this attack on one of their own, the maid who delivered the morning coal while he still slept would rattle it a little louder in the scuttle; his shaving water would be only lukewarm; there would be scorch marks on his neckcloths; and the béarnaise sauce would be soupy. Such were the subtle punishments handed out by powerless people.

He had only managed the barest glance at Emma Costello when he flung himself out of the gold saloon and was rewarded with a look of bewilderment. If he had suddenly struck her with his fists instead of his words, she could not have looked more surprised. He thought about Emma Costello and County Wicklow and doubly swore at himself for being a fool. He had spent his lifetime upstairs and far from servant gossip, but he knew enough about the hierarchy belowstairs to assure himself that Emma would not be treated well there, either. No one liked the Irish. He should never have shouted at her.

He sighed again and rubbed his forehead above his dead eye. It seldom pained him now, but he massaged the spot out of habit. When his eye was still a raw wound, some imp—was it too much laudanum?—twitted his agonized brain until he began to think that if he rubbed hard enough, his sight would return. It never happened, of course. When the pain lessened, he could only wonder at his foolishness.

So much self-flogging made him restless. With an oath, he got up, listened to the leather chair sigh for him, and moved to the fireplace, where he stood staring down at the flames. Rain scoured the windows again and matched his melancholy.

As soon as the rain let up, he would return to Curzon Street and apologize to his mother and Robert Claridge. An apology to Robert's sister probably wasn't necessary. Sally had watched his brief explosion with the wide-eyed stare of someone destined always to be a fraction late with the news. One didn't have to apologize to servants, of course, so he needn't say anything to Emma.

He returned after dinner at White's and a brief visit to Fae Moullé. She had opened the door to his two-rap knock with her usual cheerful demeanor and helped him out of his overcoat, chattering half in French and half in English about some neighborhood happening. In the early days of their relationship, her bilingual patter had amused him. Now as he allowed her to unwind his muffler, he felt only a certain irritation that she couldn't confine herself to one language or the other. Hot words rose to his lips, but he forced them back. No sense in tempting another work slowdown among those he paid; one from Fae would be much more uncomfortable than lukewarm shaving water. He kissed her instead, allowed her to lead him toward the bedroom, and then changed his mind.

He sat next to her but placed her hands carefully in her lap. "No, Fae."

Her lower lip came out in that familiar pout. He looked at her and wondered why he had thought that expression so attractive. *Grow up, you silly widgeon*, he wanted to shout. He took her hand instead, noting how shapely it was, how each nail was filed to a softly rounded tip. Such effort was probably the work of an afternoon for Fae.

He turned slightly to face her. "Fae, my love, what do you think about when I am not here?" he asked.

A number of expressions crossed her face, but the one that kept recurring was a vague puzzlement that sank his spirits even lower. She just looked at him, as though wondering what he wanted her to say.

"Really, Fae," he plunged ahead, warming to his topic. "When we're not together, what thoughts cross your mind?"

Again that silence. *I don't pay you enough to think, do I?* he considered, and the realization made him rub his forehead once more.

"Do you ever read?" he asked, his voice gentle.

"Read, John?"

"Yes, Fae. That's when you open a book and examine its lines from left to right with the object of interpreting the words on the page. Some do it for enlightenment; others for entertainment," he explained patiently, his insides writhing.

She was silent as she took her hand out of his and gave him her profile. "I think about what I am going to wear and how I should arrange my hair." She brightened then. "When the delivery boy comes with food, he always jokes a bit and asks what I think about politics."

"And what do you tell him?"

Fae turned back to regard him, her eyes wide in her flawless face. "Oh, I just laugh." She gave him a demonstration, her tinkling laughter as lovely as her features.

He grinned then and pulled her up. "Fae, well, it was a stupid question, wasn't it?"

Her hands went to his neckcloth then, but he removed them and put on his coat again. "Some other time, m'dear." She was starting in again in her Anglo-Franco babble as he closed the door quietly behind him.

The evening sky was spitting out snow as he hurried

along the street. If he didn't feel any worse for his encounter with his mistress, he also felt no better. When he returned home and allowed Lasker this time to help him out of his overcoat, he suddenly realized that it wouldn't take much to send him off to Norfolk finally, to an empty estate and a full wine cellar. *I have avoided it too long*, he thought. He stood indecisively in the hall, wondering where his mother was.

"She is at cards, my lord," Lasker pronounced.

"Lasker, you are amazing," Lord Ragsdale murmured. "I don't even have to speak to get an answer from you."

"Just so, my lord," Lasker agreed as they walked along together. He opened the door to the morning room and closed it quietly behind him.

Lady Ragsdale looked up from her solitaire and patted the chair beside her. John shook his head and stood over her, looking down at her hand.

"Mother, you're cheating again," he commented.

"Of course I am," she agreed equably. "How do you expect me to win at solitaire unless I cheat?" She took his hand suddenly and kissed it. "My dear, whatever is the matter with you these days?"

He sat down then and, leaning back, stuck his long legs out in front of him. "I don't know, Mother."

She smiled, glanced sideways at him, and then cheated again. "You remind me of someone on the verge of something."

He smiled back and returned the card she had just laid down to her hand. "If I had uttered such a nonsensical bit of illogic back at Brasenose in my Oxford years, my don would have kicked me down the stairs!" He tipped his head back and stared at the ceiling. "As it is, you are probably right."

"Very well, then, son. Go to bed."

"Yes, Mama." Lord Ragsdale stood up and stretched. "By the way, it is snowing again."

While he watched, she put the offending card back in its place before her. "We are still going to Oxford tomorrow."

"Yes, Mama," he repeated, smiling slightly. He may not have apologized in words, but she understood. *How dear you are to me*, he thought as he admired her calm beauty. *Perhaps if I am extremely lucky, one day I will have a daughter who looks like you.*

She blew a kiss to him as he stood in the open door. "Son, you have a chance to redeem yourself tomorrow."

"Hmm?"

"My dresser is not feeling good enough to travel. Emma Costello will travel in her stead and look after Sally and me."

He sighed, started his hand toward his forehead, and then dropped it. "Then I will be on horseback, madam," he replied crisply as he left the room.

Robert Claridge was still up, but only just, when Lord Ragsdale knocked on his cousin's door. When he opened it to Robert's sleepy "Come in," his young cousin sat up quickly in bed, as though trying to appear at attention.

"For heaven's sake, relax!" John admonished as he closed the door and sat himself down beside his cousin's bed. "I am only your cousin, and by the eternal, I am a stupid one. Forgive me for my outburst this afternoon, Robert," he apologized simply.

Robert scratched his head and lay back down again. He punched his pillow into a comfortable ball and looked at his cousin. "Don't trouble your head about it, my lord," he said. "My aunt Staples explained why you haven't much love for the Irish."

"No, I haven't," he agreed, grateful to his mother all over again for smoothing his path with his young relative. "But that's no excuse for such rudeness to your servant."

Robert's eyes were closing. "I can't see how it signifies. It's just Emma, and I know there are times when she would try a saint."

"Of which I am not one," Lord Ragsdale said with no

regret, grateful down to his boots to be so easily out of that mess. He crossed his legs and settled back in the chair. "Tell me, cousin, how did you get a servant from Ireland?"

Robert opened his eyes. "I was fourteen or fifteen when Papa bought her in the Norfolk sales."

"Bought her?" Lord Ragsdale sat up straight again. "Surely you don't mean that."

"I do, cousin. She's indentured. I was with him at the wharf when the ship's master led the lot of them into the sale shed."

Lord Ragsdale closed his eyes. He had heard of things like that, but the reality was never closer than a column in the *Times*. "Were they . . . were they chained together?" he asked.

"Heavens, no," Robert said. He sat up in bed, wide awake now. "You've never seen a more harmless lot of lice-ridden, scraggly men and women. Everyone was so thin." He paused. "My lord, that's the way things are in America. We buy, sell, and indenture, and don't ask too many questions." He reflected a moment, as though groping about in his memory. "There was something about a rising in Dublin. Papa could tell you."

If that's the way things are, good riddance to the colonies, Lord Ragsdale thought. He was spared any comment on the hypocrisies of American government, because Robert was warming to his subject.

"Papa was looking for a clerk who could cipher. He stood there with the other buyers, calling out what he wanted. You know, someone was yelling 'Seamstress,' and someone else, 'Blacksmith,' and another, 'Cordwainer.' Quite a racket in that barn," Robert explained. "Anyway, they must have been an ignorant lot of bog-trotters, because no one responded to any trades."

"Were they all Irish?"

"Yes, my lord."

"Then that explains it," Lord Ragsdale said. "You've never

seen a more illiterate bunch of popish bead rubbers than the Irish. The only exertion they are capable of is breeding like rabbits."

"Well, I wouldn't know that," Robert said. "Anyway, Papa called out 'clerk,' one more time, hoping for a miracle, and Emma stepped forward." Robert smiled at the memory. "I thought she was daft, and Papa even more daft for considering her." He sighed and lay back down again.

"Well?" John prompted.

"She wasn't wearing much more than a shift, her hair was nasty-looking, and her feet were bare, but Papa snapped off a string of figures, and she added it all in her head." His cousin's eyes closed again. "Papa wouldn't let her ride in the carriage because she had lice, so she walked behind the carriage all the way home."

Lord Ragsdale shook his head. The Emma in his best sitting room this afternoon was a woman with an unmistakable air of elegance, no matter how shabby her clothes. What a strange day this was. "She was your father's clerk, then?" he prompted.

Robert was a moment replying, and Lord Ragsdale resisted the urge to give his shoulder a shake. "No. Mama wouldn't hear of it. Said it was indecent for any female, servant included, to tote up figures and do bookkeeping in the tobacco barn, and besides, she wanted a maid for Sally. So there you are. She's been with us five years. I could check her papers, but I think she has two years to run on her indenture."

Lord Ragsdale chewed on those facts for only a few moments, but it was long enough for Robert to begin the steady, even breathing of sleep. His questions would have to wait. "How odd," he murmured out loud as he watched his cousin another moment and then snuffed the candle with his fingers. He sat there another moment and then left the room quietly.

Lasker, keys in hand, met him in the hall. He bowed.

"Good night, my lord. Is there anything else you will be needing?"

Lord Ragsdale shook his head. He almost asked the butler where they had found room for Emma but changed his mind. Such a question would seem presumptuous, as though Lasker didn't know his own business well enough to make arrangements, no matter how cramped things were belowstairs. And if Emma ended up sleeping next to the coal chute, what concern was it of his?

He retired to his room, tugged off his boots, and settled on the bed with a full bottle of brandy in his lap and another on the night table. He avoided even a glance at his overflowing desk, hoping it would go away. The late hour, followed by a swallow or two of brandy and then another, permitted philosophy to override misanthropy. While he could not overlook entirely the desire to bolt the metropolis, he decided that he could tolerate the remaining few months of this London Season.

There was no question that he owed his mother and cousin the favor of an escort, he thought as he drank steadily. And while he was doing his duty, he could peruse the females who frequented Almack's and other venues of quality, find a lady not wanting in too many particulars, and make her an offer. He had money enough to make Croesus a loan; barring his absent eye, his parts were all present and easy to look upon; he was healthier than most of his acquaintances. "Ah, yes, I will do well enough in the marriage mart," he told the ceiling. "I doubt this will require overmuch exertion."

He took another swig or two from the brandy bottle and then set it carefully on the floor. To his surprise, the bottle fell on its side; to his further surprise, nothing spilled out. He leaned off the bed and regarded the bottle. *I must advise Lasker not to be taken in by the vintner,* he thought. *It seems that he is buying smaller bottles than he used to.*

The next bottle went down faster than the first. Lord Ragsdale considered an expedition down the stairs to the wine cellar for more but discarded the notion. The room seemed to be shrinking, and he did not think he could get out of the door before it disappeared altogether. *Such an odd phenomenon,* he considered as he unbuttoned his trousers, loosened his neckcloth, and closed his eye.

Chapter 3

*T*O SAY THAT LORD RAGSDALE AWAKENED with a big head would be to mince words. His stomach was as queasy as though he was sailing an ocean with mountain-high waves. When he sat up, he whimpered at the pain in his skull. He lay back down again, hoping with all his heart that it had snowed ten feet last night and they would be unable to travel today.

But the gods were not smiling on Lord Ragsdale this morning. When the maid who brought in the coal noticed that he was awake, she screamed a cheery, "Good morrow, my lord," which filled the room and echoed back and forth inside the sorely tried empty space between his ears. After she thundered at least a ton of coal onto the grate, she threw open his draperies on runners that shrieked like banshees.

"It's a good morning for a trip, my lord," she offered with the voice of a boatswain in a hurricane.

He could only force his lips into a weak smile and put his hand over his eye against the glare that threatened to blind his one remaining orb. *If you say another word, I will die,* he thought. To his relief, she said nothing more but slammed the door on her way out so loud that his guts quivered. He gritted his teeth and moaned.

He had progressed to dangling his legs off the bed when his mother banged on the door with a battering ram and opened it a crack.

"John, we want to leave within the hour," she reminded him and then took a closer look. "Oh, John!"

Three hours later, he groped his way downstairs and onto his horse, which waited patiently by the front stoop. Lasker had sent the footman in to help him pack and also to rescue him from his own razor when he attempted to shave his pale face. A splattering of bay rum was more than he could bear. It sent him lurching back to his washstand, where he vomited his toenails into the basin, vowing, as he gagged and retched, never to drink again.

The cold February air was a relief. He breathed as deep as he dared of the icy blast and then pulled his hat low and his riding coat tight around him. He carefully shook his head over his mother's attempts to get him inside the carriage and waited, reins held in slack fingers, while Emma Costello carried in the last bandbox.

As she went to climb in, her cloak caught on the door handle. Her hands full, she struggled to free herself and then glanced in his direction, as if to ask for help.

Embarrassed, he shook his head, knowing that if he dismounted, he would disgrace himself again. To his further chagrin, she quickly lowered her eyes and turned away as if humiliated, continuing her efforts to free herself until Robert dismounted with an oath and lent a hand. Lord Ragsdale watched as she hurried inside the carriage, closed the door, and made herself small in the corner.

Merciful heaven, I am off to such a start with this one, he thought as he regarded Emma another moment and then gently eased Champion into the street. *Please, please let this London Season go by quickly.*

They traveled steadily into a dreary afternoon, the clouds gray and threatening, the wind coming in puffs of blasting cold from all directions at the same time. Robert kept him company for part of the journey and proved to be an amiable companion. He was one of those persons who, if given free rein to talk, would carry on a merry discourse that required little comment or addendum from another. John was content to listen to his cousin. He learned all he ever wanted to know about tobacco farming, the growing slave trade, and the trouble with Federalists without having to respond beyond the occasional "Hmm," or "Indeed." Robert's mellow voice with its soft drawl was soothing in the extreme. By the time Robert succumbed to the weather and begged a seat inside the coach, John was almost sorry to see him surrender.

As soon as Robert retreated to the relative comfort of the family carriage, Lord Ragsdale realized that the next few hours of travel would hang heavy. The day was no warmer the farther they traveled into it, and he felt ill unto death. Had he traveled by himself, Lord Ragsdale would have stopped at the first hostelry that appeared to offer clean sheets and quiet premises. His head began to throb again.

He was about to stop the coachman, admit defeat, and plead illness, when Sally Claridge came to his unexpected rescue. He was swallowing his pride and rising bile when his mother lowered the glass and rapped on the side of the carriage with her umbrella. The coachman reined in and peered back at her. Lady Ragsdale opened the door and leaned out to speak to her son.

"John, Sally is experiencing some distress from the motion. I know this will irritate you, but could we stop early tonight?" she asked.

It was all he could do to keep from bursting into tears of gratitude. *Dear Sally, can it be that you are as estimable as your brother?* he thought as he faked a frown and then nodded, hoping that he did not appear too eager.

"If we must, Mother," he responded after a suitable length of time had passed. He sighed heavily for the effect and then wished he hadn't as his stomach heaved. "Let me ride on ahead and find the nearest inn," he offered, hoping that the inmates of the carriage would see his act as a magnanimous gesture rather than a desperate attempt to get out of their range of vision before he disgraced himself.

Lady Ragsdale nodded and spoke to Sally, who raised her pale face to the window and blew him a kiss. He glanced at Emma, but she studiously ignored him. *Ah, well*, he thought as he tipped his hat and spurred ahead, eager to outdistance the carriage. *I can puke in peace.*

When the carriage arrived at the Norman and Saxon, Lord Ragsdale was in control of his parts again. The inn was full of other clients who must have had second thoughts about the weather, but he was able to secure a private parlor and two sleeping rooms. While he waited for the carriage to arrive, he tested his nerve on a pint in the tavern and watched a card game that, from the unkempt aspect of its patrons, appeared to have been in progress since shortly after Moses brought down stone tablets from Sinai. The ale went down smoothly, settling what, if anything, remained of his stomach's contents. The card game tempted him not at all.

He helped his mother from the carriage, quick to notice that she was not in the best of spirits either. "Poor dear," he murmured as she leaned on his arm. "Too many bumps in the road?"

She nodded. "I always forget what a poor traveler I am. Please tell me there is a bed close by, John."

He kissed her cheek, happy to play the competent son. "There is even a warming pan between the sheets, m'dear. You and Sally can keep each other company, snoring to your heart's delight."

He helped her upstairs and then returned to retrieve Sally, who drooped on Emma's arm in the hallway outside the public room's entrance.

"Can I lend a hand here?" he asked, suddenly shy, and rendered more embarrassed when Emma nodded, relinquished her hold, and tried to disappear against the wall. He took a firm grasp on Sally's shoulder and pointed her toward the stairs, but she surprised him by stiffening up. "Yes, my dear?" he inquired, curious about her resistance.

She didn't say anything, but he followed her gaze into the taproom, where Robert was standing over the gaming table, a pint in his hand. "I wish you would not let him play," she said.

He laughed. "I am sure it is only a harmless game."

"I mean it," Sally replied, and he could almost feel her gravity. He took her by both shoulders then. "Sally, I'll get you upstairs, and Emma can make you and Mama comfortable. I promise to keep an eye on your brother. I am certain I can keep him from sitting down at a gaming table. How difficult can that be?" He attempted a joke because her anxiety disturbed him. "I am certain I outweigh my cousin, if it comes to that."

She regarded him with a wan smile and allowed him to lead her up the narrow stairway and into the room where Lady Ragsdale still sat on the bed, the effort to move beyond her. Emma followed with the luggage. In another moment, the servant was skillfully, quietly in charge. He paused in the doorway until he was sure that all was well.

"I'll order dinner, Mama," he said. "What would you like?"

"Soup and bread for the ladies, my lord," Emma said firmly. "Nothing more."

"And you?"

She seemed surprised that he would ask. She looked up from the floor where she was untying his mother's shoes. "Whatever you wish, my lord," she replied, still without looking him in the eye as if she feared she was too much trouble.

He went downstairs to order dinner and noticed that Robert had not moved from his position by the gaming table. He watched the play intently, and Lord Ragsdale had to call his name several times to get his attention. Even then, he left the room reluctantly, with several backward glances.

"Faro is my favorite game," he confided to his cousin as he allowed himself to be led from the room. "But vingt-et-un will do. Cousin, do you play cards?"

"Never," Lord Ragsdale replied firmly. "I hate cards. I thought tonight that you and I would discuss your coming matriculation at Brasenose. It's my college, you know." He looked at his cousin virtuously. "I went to some trouble to arrange your attendance at this juncture in the term, let me assure you."

He could tell that Robert was disappointed to leave the game, but to his relief, his cousin followed him into the private parlor. Lord Ragsdale poured two glasses of sherry, but Robert was pacing between the windows. "Do sit down, cousin," Lord Ragsdale advised. "We still have a half day's drive tomorrow, and you'll need all your constitution to meet your grandmother. Come, come now. Here is dinner."

They ate in silence. Robert was no longer the attractive conversationalist of the afternoon, and Lord Ragsdale could only wonder at his cousin's restless air. *Well, if I must exert myself, I must*, he thought as he launched into a description of Brasenose and its illustrious traditions. Through it all, he harbored a very real suspicion that Robert's mind was elsewhere.

He was interrupted by a soft tap on the door. It was Emma come to fetch the soup. "Let me help you," he insisted as she struggled with the heavy tray.

"I can manage," she replied, even as he took it away from her. "Truly I can."

He nodded, feeling oddly useful, even though it was only a dinner tray. "Well, perhaps you will allow me to redeem myself."

Emma looked at him quickly and then looked away. "I don't mean to be trouble," she said softly as she opened the door for him.

He could think of no reply to such honesty, so he made none and was rewarded with a second frightened glance and a perceptible drawing away from him, even though they stood close together at the room's entrance. As he came through the doorway first, carrying the tray, he experienced the odd feeling that perhaps Emma Costello cared no more for the English than he loved the Irish. It was a leveling thought, and one that he had not considered before.

He left the tray, kissed his mother good night, and started for the door. He thought Sally was asleep, but she called to him, her voice hesitant, as though she, like Emma, wondered what he would think.

"Cousin, please. Please make sure that Robert does not play cards tonight," she urged.

He smiled at Sally and then bowed elaborately, winking at her on the way up.

"She means it, my lord," came Emma's distinct brogue. Her voice was firm, hard even, as though she spoke to a child, and not a bright one either.

He stood in the doorway, his hand on the knob. "I can't say that I care for your impertinence, Emma," he snapped.

"Then I apologize for it," she replied promptly. "But please, sir . . ."

He closed the door on whatever else she was going to haver on about and returned to the parlor to find it empty. His mind filled with odd disquiet, he hurried downstairs in time to prevent Robert from sitting at the gaming table.

"Come, lad, we're off to an early start in the morning, remember?" he said, nodding to the other gamesters. "You'll excuse us, I am sure."

"Really, cousin, I think that wasn't necessary," Robert protested as Lord Ragsdale followed him up the stairs. "I was only going to sit for one hand." He stopped on the stairs, and his voice took on a wheedling tone. "I promise to be in bed before you get to sleep if you let me go back down."

"No, and that's final," Lord Ragsdale insisted. His head

was beginning to ache again, compounded by the uneasiness that grew on him as he regarded his cousin Robert. *So you will be no trouble*, he thought as he removed his clothes and pulled on his nightshirt. *I think I begin to understand your parents' eagerness to get you out of America. How deep in gambling debt were you there? And why is this my problem now?*

It was a subject to ruminate on. Tight-lipped and silent, Robert undressed and threw himself into bed alongside his cousin. He broke the long silence finally. "I think you are perfectly beastly to deny me one last game before I enroll at Brasenose."

"I think I am nothing of the sort, cousin," John replied. "Go to sleep."

He lay in silence then, wondering if Robert would respond. He stared at the ceiling, listening to Robert's breathing turn regular and deep. Relief settled over him, and he relaxed into the mattress. He hung on another half hour, listening to Robert, and then allowed sleep to claim him too.

⁓

If he had been under oath in the assizes, he could not have told a jury what woke him up early that morning. One moment he was asleep, dreaming of nothing, and the next instant he was wide awake and sitting up in bed. The room was in total darkness. Holding his breath, Lord Ragsdale listened intently for Robert's breathing. Nothing.

Cautiously, he reached out his hand and felt the other pillow. "I could strop that boy," he said out loud as he fumbled for the candle, more alert than he had been in years.

He was the room's sole inhabitant. After the moment of panic passed, his next thought was to return to sleep. Robert's spending habits were none of his concern. He had promised to accompany his mother and cousins to Oxford, and surely that charge did not involve wet-nursing a young man of some twenty years. His own mother had assured him that the cousins would be no trouble, and truly, they would not be if he lay down again and returned to sleep. Besides, he reasoned, half the world's troubles were caused by people too eager to meddle in others' affairs. So what if Robert gamed away all his money? How could that possibly concern him? He blew out the candle.

His eyes were closing again when an ugly thought tunneled through the fog of sleep. *What if it is your money he is gaming, you idiot?* He sat up again and lit the candle once more, holding it high as he looked around the room. Everything looked as he had left it. He glanced closer at his overcoat, slung over a chair back. He was certain he had placed it around the chair before taking off his clothes.

He was on his feet in a moment, pawing through his overcoat. His hands clutched his wallet, but it was much thinner than he remembered. He swore as he opened it and found nothing beyond a couple directions and a toll chit.

Lord Ragsdale looked at Robert's dressing case. It had been rifled through too, as if the owner were looking for something tucked away. He found a leather case containing a variety of legal papers that looked as though they had been crammed back inside in a hurry.

This is going to be a nasty scene, he thought as he shoved his nightshirt into his trousers and pulled on his boots. He didn't stop to look for his eye patch as he ran his fingers through his hair and wrenched open the door.

To Lord Ragsdale's surprise, the innkeeper stood before him on the landing, breathing hard as though he had taken the flight of stairs two or three at a time.

"What on earth is the matter?" Lord Ragsdale said, wincing as the landlord took one look at his ruined eye and gulped.

"My lord, you had better come downstairs at once. I don't think you'll like what's going on. I know I don't, but it's not something I can prevent."

"What can you be so lathered up about?" Lord Ragsdale said as he followed the man down the stairs. "I think my young cousin is spending my money, but that's my business. I intend to give him quite a scold, rest assured."

The landlord stopped on the stairs and looked him in the eye. "He's gone beyond your money, my lord, way beyond. Please hurry."

If anything, the taproom was more crowded than before, even though it was hours after midnight. The same group of gamesters sat at the table, with the addition of Robert and the waiting woman.

Lord Ragsdale barely noticed his cousin, who waved him a greeting and moved to pull up another chair. His eye went immediately to Emma Costello, who stood in her nightdress behind his cousin's chair. She was as pale as her flannel shift, her auburn hair flaming around her face, her eyes burning like coals into his own. She swallowed once, and he thought she would speak, but she said nothing and did nothing but stare at the opposite wall. Her face was wiped clean of any hope, or of any expression at all.

He wrenched his glance away from her and stared hard at the gaming table. There was a document on it, with a seal and ribbons and folded in half as though it had just come out of the leather case upstairs. He looked at Emma again and back at the document, and he was filled with more anger than he would have thought possible, considering that this whole affair was probably none of his business.

He was so angry he could not speak. The man sitting next to Robert nudged him. "Your draw, laddie," he said, and then grinned at Emma and smacked his lips.

"Touch that card, Robert, and I will thrash you until your backbone breaks through your skin."

Did I really say that? Lord Ragsdale thought as he crossed the room in two steps and stood leaning over his cousin's chair.

To his further amazement, Robert merely looked at him and shrugged his shoulders. "Cousin, I am in debt and nothing else will do but Emma. I have her papers here, and I can do as I like. It's legal. Everyone's agreed."

He turned back to the table and reached for the card. Lord Ragsdale slammed his fist down on his cousin's hand, shoved him out of the chair, and sat down in Robert's place, his face inches from his opponent. "I'll make you a better deal," he said, each word distinct in the suddenly silent room. He picked up the indenture papers. "Look here, did he show you how this indenture has less than eighteen months to run?"

The other men at the table crowded close. The smell of rum breath and tobacco made him want to flee the room, gagging, but he looked at each man in turn, hoping for a measure of intimidation from his unseeing eye. "How much was he going to ask for?"

"Two hundred pounds to settle up."

"Against an eighteen-month indenture?" Lord Ragsdale leaned back in his chair to escape the fumes, and laughed. "Well, I have . . ." He paused. *Absolutely no money*, he thought as he stared daggers at his cousin.

The gambler shrugged. "I can take your money as well as his," he offered.

"I don't have any," Lord Ragsdale said.

"Well, then, we play for the wench," said the gambler. "You can go back to bed."

I could, he thought. *She is not my chattel.* He looked at Robert. *And you are not my problem.* He started to get up when he heard the smallest sound from the servant. He may even have imagined it, but suddenly he knew he could not leave her there to the mercy of these men, no matter how much he disliked her. He sat back down again.

"I have something better than that testy Irish wench." He leaned forward again, his voice conspiratorial. "Two horses out in the stable. One a chestnut and the other a bay. The chestnut won at Newport last season. That cuts the debt, and Emma goes back upstairs where she belongs."

I am giving away the best two horses a man ever owned for an Irish bog-trotter who can't stand the sight of me, he thought as he glared at the other men around the table.

The men looked at each other. The hostler by the bar spoke up. "I curried them two bits of bone and blood this afternoon, and he's right, lads." He stopped then and looked around, filled with the pride that comes from being the expert.

Lord Ragsdale stood up, ignoring his cousin, who still sat on the floor where he had pushed him. "Does that clear my cousin's debt, then? Two of the best horses in London, and I take back this paper."

The men nodded. "We'll call it even," the dealer said.

Even, my dead eye, Lord Ragsdale thought as he watched his cousin get to his feet, sway a moment, and then reach for the paper.

Lord Ragsdale was quicker. He snatched the document from Robert so fast that his cousin leaped back in surprise and toppled onto the floor again. "Robert, the only way you can get this paper back is to pay me the two thousand pounds you now owe me."

Emma gasped. Lord Ragsdale looked around in amazement of his own. *I just bought a woman,* he thought as he took her hand and pulled her from the taproom, *an Irish woman I don't like too well, and who doesn't like me at all.*

She sank to her knees in the hall and covered her face with her hands. His first instinct was to leave her there and just go back to bed. He started up the stairs and then returned to kneel beside her in the passageway.

"Don't cry, Emma," he said.

"I'm not crying," she murmured, even as the tears streamed down her cheeks and she savagely wiped them away.

"Thank goodness for that," he replied, keeping his tone light. "'Pon my word, Emma, I hope you are worth two thousand pounds."

Chapter 4

I WONDER WHAT HAS HAPPENED TO THE *simplicity of a good night's sleep*, Lord Ragsdale thought to himself as he fumed in his bed and watched morning gradually overtake the Norman and Saxon. Sleep was out of the question; the more he thought about the disaster of the night, the more put-upon he imagined himself.

Never mind that Robert Claridge lay on the floor of the room, noisily sleeping off a prodigious amount of rum. John Staples rose up on his elbow to give his cousin a particularly malevolent glare. The effort was wasted. Robert slumbered on, wrapped in peaceful sleep that he, Lord Ragsdale, could only wish for.

The nerve of his aunt and uncle Claridge to foist such a problem off onto an English relative they had never met. Lord Ragsdale punched his pillow savagely, trying to find a spot without a lump, and considered that the whole affair must be yet another way for Americans to wreak vengeance on their late antagonists. *I have done nothing to deserve this cousin*, he reflected.

He thought of Emma Costello, standing so quiet as Robert prepared to sell her on the drawing of a card. He groaned and stuffed his pillow over his face, as if to shut out her calm face that seemed to stare at him still. He had never seen anyone so totally without hope and yet so brave in the face of it. He removed the pillow and sat up so he could stare daggers at his sleeping cousin.

"One thing is certain, Robert," he said, making no effort to lower his voice. "Only a truly wicked master would try what you tried. And I don't care if she *is* Irish. It was a low blow."

Beyond the smacking of his lips and a rude noise, Robert made no comment. Lord Ragsdale sighed and looked away toward the window, urging dawn to forget that it was February and appear sooner.

By seven o'clock he was dressed and pacing the floor, stepping over Robert on each trip across the room and resisting the urge, each time, to kick him. Finally, his baser instincts triumphed. He kicked Robert in the ribs with enough force to waken his cousin.

Or, perhaps at that moment, Robert had decided to wake up on his own accord. He sat up, making no comment on ill-treatment, and regarded his cousin beatifically. "Ah, Cousin John," he said. "Did you sleep well?"

Cousin John could only stare in amazement at his relative and open his mouth once or twice like a fish hooked and tossed onto the shore. Lord Ragsdale looked down at Robert, certain in his heart of hearts that if he murdered his cousin on the spot that no jury of twelve men just and true would ever convict him. He sat down on the bed and glared at his relative.

"Don't you remember anything of last night?" he began and then stopped. The conversation sounded familiar to his ears, and he almost smiled in spite of himself. That hoary question, probably asked since caveman days, was the preamble to many a morning's argument when his father was still alive. *This will never do*, he thought as he stared hard at his cousin. "Robert, you are a certifiable scoundrel," he stated firmly. "You have been through your money and my money. You nearly sold your servant to a man I wouldn't trust a saint with and forced me to give up two thousand pounds' worth of horse to redeem her and to keep you from a knife in the ribs and a trip to the river, I don't doubt."

Robert burped, winced, and sat up. "All that happened last night?" he said as he clutched his head with both hands.

"It did. We happen to be dead broke now, and if my mother doesn't have any yellow dogs on her person, we will be making beds and cleaning the *pissoir* to pay for our lodging!" Lord Ragsdale gave an unpleasant laugh. "Or rather, you will be doing that and we will watch!"

He regarded his cousin a moment more and then stood up. "Wash your face and come to the parlor. I think you and Sally owe the Staples branch of the family some enlightenment."

He slammed the door behind him and was rewarded with a groan from Robert. Lord Ragsdale smiled in satisfaction and resisted the desire to slam the door again. *Life is suddenly full of exertions*, he thought as he rapped lightly on his mother's door.

The inmates were dressed already, and two out of three were regarding him with some anxiety. Sally Claridge was easily the more agitated of the two. She gave a start when he came in, and he wondered for a second if he had forgotten to put on his eye patch. No, it was carefully in place. As he watched, Sally's face turned bright red as she reached for her handkerchief and began to sob. The marquess groaned.

"Sally, it is much too early for tears," he assured her. Sally sobbed louder into the already soaking scrap of lace in her hand. In desperation, he gestured to Emma. "Tell her that nothing was ever solved with tears," he pleaded.

"I have always found tears to be singularly valueless," she agreed and handed her mistress a more substantial rag. "Dry up, now, miss, or your eyes will swell and you will look quite twenty."

Lord Ragsdale smiled in spite of himself, charmed—if against his will—by the lilt of Emma's brogue and her common sense. Lord Ragsdale was grateful. One woman in tears would suffice, especially before breakfast. He regarded his mother, who smiled back at him from her seat by the window.

"Troubles, John?" she asked, her voice hearty enough to make him suspect that she was enjoying this domestic tempest.

"You needn't appear so cheerful, Mama," he insisted. "I think my cousins are a great lot of trouble."

Sally burst into louder tears, edging on the hysterical. He felt the hairs rise on the back of his neck and his temper shorten perceptibly. He looked to Emma Costello for help, and to his amazement, she glared back at him.

"Must you make a situation more difficult, Lord Ragsdale?" she asked.

No servant had ever addressed him like that. Hot words rose to his lips, but to his further astonishment, he stopped them. She was absolutely right; there was no sense in tossing another log onto the blaze. He bit his tongue, glared back, and turned his attention to his mother again.

It may have been his imagination, but Lady Ragsdale seemed to be enjoying the whole affair. "You needn't take such pleasure in all this," he snapped, coming as close to pouting as he cared to admit. "It may put some sand in your eye when I tell you that Beau Rascal in the other room gambled away all my money too. My dear, unless you have some pounds sterling tucked somewhere to pay the innkeeper, we're going to have a hard time avoiding the constable. Oh, Sally, cut line!" he ordered when his cousin increased the volume of her misery.

Lady Ragsdale blew a kiss to her sorely tried niece. "John, dear, you know I always travel with cash. I have enough to pay our receipt here."

"Well, thank heavens for one piece of good news this morning . . . Now if you could only produce enough for me to reclaim my horses."

"That I cannot do," she said and gave her head a sorrowful wag.

He sighed, the martyr again. "Mama, they were prime goers," he began and then stopped himself, because it sounded like he was whining.

"I'm sure they were, my dear," she agreed as she reached out to clasp his hand. "But I want you to tell me something, son."

"What?" he asked in irritation when she continued to look at him.

"Tell me if all this will matter in even a week or two."

"Of course it will!" he shot back.

"Why?" she asked softly.

He had no answer. Of course it mattered, he wanted to shout, but for the life of him, he couldn't think why. He had plenty of money, and there would be other horses. He looked at Sally, who was hiccupping through her tears now, and then at Emma. *Why the deuce do I wonder what you are thinking?* he asked himself.

He was spared the pain of further analysis by the arrival of Robert. It was a soft tap on the door, as though sound was painful to his cousin. *I can appreciate that*, John thought grimly. He opened the door quickly, hoping that his cousin might be leaning on it to support himself.

"Robert!" he exclaimed, noting with a certain malicious pleasure that his cousin winced at his loud greeting. "Grand of you to join us. Sit down, please."

Robert sat, after looking around at Sally as though for help. His sister was deep in a handkerchief and unlikely to be of any assistance. No one spoke. To Lord Ragsdale's supreme annoyance, everyone looked at him as though expecting leadership. He could have told them that was a waste of time, but since they seemed to expect him to take charge, he did.

Lord Ragsdale clasped his hands behind his back and strolled to the window. He stood there a moment, rocking back and forth on his heels, and then regarded his cousins. "I would like one of you to tell me exactly what is going on."

Sally tunneled deeper into her handkerchief; Robert merely looked around. Lord Ragsdale sighed and tried again. "Your parents have solicited us to see that you, Robert, are located at Oxford, and that you, Sally, participate in some part of the London Season."

Neither relative said anything. Lord Ragsdale paced away from the window and then back again. "I know there are several excellent, if provincial, colleges in America." He looked at Sally. "And I suspect that Virginia society is lively enough to provide for a spring's entertainment. I must ask myself, then, why you have inflicted yourself upon us."

"Really, John," his mother murmured as Sally began to sniffle again.

"Yes, really," he insisted and paced some more. "Can it be possible that you are no longer welcome at home, Robert?" Lord Ragsdale asked. "Could it be that you have ruined your family?"

A long silence followed, but Lord Ragsdale did not leap into the void. He walked back to the window and looked out, waiting for an answer. *And I will wait until the end of time*, he thought grimly. *We may all grow old in this room.*

"I really don't think it is as bad as all that," Robert said at last, his tone sulky. His mouth opened to say more, but Sally leaped to her feet and hurried to the window to face her cousin.

"It is worse than that," she said, her voice low and fierce. "Robert's gaming debts have mortgaged our home right to the attics. Papa has had to sell half his slaves, and the next two tobacco crops are already lost to repay Robert's creditors."

Lord Ragsdale whistled in spite of himself. "My word, Robert," he exclaimed. "Can't you resist a wager?"

Once started, Sally was ready to contribute in abundance. "He cannot!" she exclaimed, deeply in earnest, tears forgotten now. "There are whole counties where Robert dare not show his face." Her own face clouded over again. "And no one will even consider a marriage arrangement for me with Robert ready to sponge."

She looked so sad that Lord Ragsdale put his arm around her shoulders, drew her close to him, and provided her with his handkerchief. "I appreciate your candor, Sally," he said when he could be heard over her tears.

Sally looked at him, her wide blue eyes so like his mother's. "What will you do to us?" she asked.

He smiled at her. "Exactly what your parents wished, my dear."

He leveled a less-pleasant look in Robert's direction. "You, cousin, will go to Oxford. And if I hear of a single card being turned, you will be on your way to Spain, to serve in the ranks. I know a colonel of foot who will have you flogged regularly if I ask him to."

"Oh, cousin!" Robert exclaimed, getting slowly to his feet. "I am sure that if you will let me bargain with Emma's indenture one more time I can . . ."

"Don't you ever learn?" Lord Ragsdale shouted, oblivious to what the other clients of the Norman and Saxon might think. "She belongs to me now, and I am more careful of my property! Sally, we will attempt to provide you with a come out of some sort. There must be someone of my acquaintance who prefers a pretty face to a large income." He released Sally and turned to his mother. "And now, my dear, if you will fork over some of the ready, I will spring us from this inn."

She handed him some money and then patted his arm. "Well done, John," Lady Ragsdale said in a low voice.

"Someone had to do something," he said pointedly. He started for the door and then turned suddenly and shook his finger at Robert. "I mean what I say about serving in the ranks, you idiot!" He yanked open the door, looked at Emma standing there so quietly beside it, and pulled her out into the hall with him, slamming the door behind him.

"I want a word with you, Emma Costello," he snapped.

She said nothing but pulled her hand from his and clasped them in front of her. She looked him directly in the eye, something servants never did, and he found himself unable to bear her level scrutiny.

"Dash it, Emma," he whispered furiously. "Why did you allow Robert to take you downstairs last night? Why didn't you wake my mother or pound on my door? He could have sold you to one of those ugly customers. Don't you care?"

She was a long time answering him. The servant looked down at her hands, her eyes lowered, and he noticed how absurdly long her eyelashes were. He was standing close enough to see that her skin was as beautiful up close as across a room, and with the most disarming freckles on her nose. She wore no scent but the honest odor of soap. Finally she looked at him.

"I did not dream that you would raise a hand to stop him, my lord," she replied.

Almost bereft of speech, he stared back. "You ... you think I would have allowed him to *sell* you?" he demanded, his voice rising to a higher pitch not heard since his younger years.

"I was sure of it," she said, her voice soft.

If she had calculated for six months or more to devise a way to cut him to the marrow, she could not have hit upon a better plan. He stared at her another moment and felt shame wash over him like a sudden cold spray. It was the most alarming thing anyone had ever said to him, and it came from a servant. He regarded her another moment, and the thought struck him that she was probably right.

"Oh, Emma" was all he could say.

"With your permission, sir, I'll go back inside and help the ladies pack."

He nodded and walked down the hall to his own room. He turned at the door, his hand on the knob, and glanced back at the servant, who had not moved. She regarded him in silence another moment and then went back into his mother's room, closing the door quietly behind her.

～

Lord Ragsdale thought the ride to Oxford would never end. He felt the loss of his horse sorely. A restless person by nature, he chafed at the inactivity of sitting still in a carriage. If he could have paced inside, he would have. As it was, he was forced to endure Sally's snufflings into a long succession of handkerchiefs and her occasional frightened glances in his direction. Robert sulked in his corner, suffering a hangover of monstrous proportions, brought on by bad rum, drunk in immoderate quantities. He opened his mouth several times to speak, but nothing ever came out.

Lady Ragsdale seemed to enjoy the ride. She settled comfortably into the opposite corner, her nose deep in a novel. The only sound in the carriage beyond Sally's sniffles was the regular slitting and turning of pages. Emma Costello stared out the window, occupied with her own thoughts. Her face was blank of all expression, the perfect servant's face.

Except that I know you have not always been a servant, he thought as he watched her. As the miles and hours dragged by, he remembered a fairy tale from the nursery about a princess forced into servitude by a wicked maid. *Absurd*, he thought, wishing that he could fling open the carriage door and trot alongside. *Ireland has nothing but a cursed population that stinks and breeds. I wonder how soon I can get rid of her*, he thought.

As they approached Oxford, Emma Costello claimed his attention again. Sally and Robert were both asleep, leaning against each other, but Emma sat forward and grasped a strap by the window, surprised into exclamation. He glanced over idly to see what was capturing her notice.

"It is Magdalen Tower," he said, following her gaze. *Come, come, John*, he thought, *try for a little conversation, even if she is Irish.* "You should see it in high summer, with the trees all leafed out." There. That was a respectable volley of dialogue. *I can't have her thinking I am a dog of a fellow.*

Emma nodded, her eyes still on the scene before her. "I thought it would look like that," she murmured.

He smiled at her, feeling the hypocrite because of his dislike, and unable to resist the vantage point of superiority. "I had no idea that Magdalen was a subject for the servants' hall in America."

It was a shabby remark, and he knew it. She looked him in the eye, and he felt the urge to squirm again under her scrutiny.

"My father went there," she commented and directed her gaze to the window again, effectively shutting him out of all further conversation.

Lord Ragsdale felt himself blushing. *By all that's imaginable, I have been set down,* he thought in amazement. His embarrassment worsened when he noticed that his mother watched him over the top of her spectacles, her eyes merry. He glared at her, and to his further discomfort, she winked at him.

"That's enough," he said, his voice too loud. He rolled down the glass and leaned out the window. "Stop the coach."

The carriage stopped. His mother watched in amusement, her finger marking the place in the book. Emma's emerald-green eyes measured him up and down and found him wanting.

He flung himself out of the carriage. "I will walk to Grandmama's," he told his mother.

"Very well, John," she said. "Take your time."

He swore out loud as the carriage left him, and stood there a moment, wondering why he was walking and not Emma.

Lord Ragsdale took his time getting to his grandmother's house. At first he walked fast in his anger, but as his rapid stride carried him along through narrow, favorite streets, he found himself slowing down, glancing about even as though his friends from former years might reappear to walk with him, to commiserate, to cajole, to suggest alternatives to duty, to demand that he share notes or a pint. He sighed and stood still, staring up at Magdalen Tower, almost like Emma. "To remind me that life had a purpose once," he said out loud.

Others were passing by. He reminded himself also that at Oxford no one stared at people who talked out loud to themselves. The colleges cherished their eccentrics, and even after ten years and more, he felt himself under that same protective umbrella. It was a pleasant thought, and oddly soothing. He strolled along more slowly now. True, he could not recall what the purpose of life was anymore, but at least it was a comfort to be there.

He thought about lifting a pint at Walsingham's again, but the moment passed. Instead, he let himself into the Brasenose Quadrangle and walked about until he pronounced himself ready to face his grandmother. *I wonder that anyone ever leaves Oxford*, he thought as he sauntered along the outer corridor, his eyes on the dark beams close overhead. He stopped, the first smile of the day on his face. There it was. He reached up and traced "John Staples," carved at the end of his second year. The smile left his face. *I was different then*, he considered. *I was better.*

Chapter 5

*D*USK WAS APPROACHING WHEN LORD Ragsdale arrived at his Grandmama Whiteacre's house. He stood for a long time outside the building, admiring the stonework as he always did. The façade had been quarried from the same rockworks as many of Oxford's buildings, and it glowed with that same otherworldly honey color of late afternoon. But the ivy was dead on the stones now, drooping in the drizzle that had begun as he crossed the Isis and hurried past her neighbor's homes.

He never could think of the place as a home, no matter how hard he tried. There was none of the rest within that he ever associated with his own home. "And precious little of that on Curzon Street either, nowadays," he mused out loud. He wished he understood what had happened to his own home. True, Lady Ragsdale kept it beautiful and timely as always, but he felt no peace there anymore. And there was none here.

As he stood in the rain, several lights came on. He didn't want to go in. Grandmama would be there to pounce on him and scold him. Heaven knows she probably had plenty of charges in her arsenal. Sally would probably cry some more, and there would be Robert, pouting and looking ill-used. Mama would smile at him as though she knew something he didn't. And Emma? Oh, dear.

At what point did I lose control of my life? he thought as he started toward the front door. *When did everything become an exertion?* He rubbed his forehead and wished that the rain did not slither down his clothes and onto his back. He knew that he could not face his grandmother.

He stared hard at the house again, and there was Emma standing in the window. She stood as he was already used to seeing her, with her hands folded in front of her, the very stillness of her impressive to him, for all that he disliked her. He could not make out any of her features, but he knew it was Emma.

As he watched, he thought she raised her hand to him in a small gesture of greeting. He could not be sure, because the light was so dim, so he did not return the gesture. Besides all that, she was his servant.

My servant! he chided himself as he lifted his hand to the knocker, and Applegate—grayer but supercilious-looking as ever—allowed him to enter. *Why on earth didn't I just let Robert lose her at the turn of the card? He might even have won, and either road, I would still have my horses.* "Yes, what, Applegate?" he asked in annoyance.

"I merely wished you good evening, my lord," Applegate repeated, sounding, if anything, even more disdainful than Lord Ragsdale remembered.

"Oh, very well," Lord Ragsdale snapped. "Applegate, am I in my usual room?"

"Of course, my lord," the butler replied as though he addressed a dim-witted child. "My mistress wishes to see you first, however. If you will follow me, my lord?"

"I'd rather not," John said honestly as the footman grasped the back of his coat and helped him out of the wet garment.

It was Emma. "She especially requested that you visit her in the blue room, my lord," she reinforced as she held out her hand for his hat.

He handed it to her. "No relief for the wicked, eh, Emma?" he asked, no humor in his voice.

"Not in your case, my lord," she replied promptly.

Applegate coughed and looked away as Lord Ragsdale nailed Emma with a frown. John slapped his gloves in her hand. "I should have left you at the Norman and Saxon," he murmured.

"It's a mystery to me why you did not," she responded, the lilt in her voice so prominent.

He shook his finger at her, ready to give her a share of what remained of his frazzled mind. Applegate coughed again, so he swallowed his angry words and followed the butler down the hall. He looked back at Emma once to give her another evil stare, but there she stood again, as calm as usual. *Curse me, but you are irritating,* he thought.

To his infinite relief, only Grandmama waited to pounce on him in the blue room. He was spared more of Sally's tears and Robert's distemper. He would have liked a pitcher of whiskey, but his grandmother handed him a cup of tea.

"Well, John, what do you have to say for yourself?" she demanded after the maid fled the room.

He took a sip of the tea and pronounced it insipid. In silence for a moment, he gazed back at his relative, wondering what imp was suddenly at work in his brain. "Grandmama, why do you always greet me that way?" he asked, determined not to be afraid of her this trip. "I cannot remember a time since I was out of short pants that you addressed me otherwise." He sat down beside her. "It is not my fault that our American relatives are sadly wanting."

There, he thought, *I have counterattacked.* He took another sip and regarded his relative, noting that all the females of the Whiteacre side of the family were blessed with pretty faces, from Grandmama to Sally. *I wonder why I never saw that before,* he thought as he took another sip, winked at the old lady, and set down the cup. *Of course, they don't have Emma's high looks, but*—what *is in this tea? I must be losing my mind. Emma has put an Irish curse on me.* He stared into the tea, his hastily acquired aplomb in serious danger already.

If he was going insane right there in the blue room, Grandmama did not appear to notice. She choked over her tea and glared at him. "It is ill-bred to wink, John," she reminded him.

Recovering, he smiled to himself, happy to have set her off guard. "Tell me what you think of the Claridges, my love," he said, delighted to watch her choke again at his unexpected endearment.

She scowled at him. "Pathetic!" She wagged a heavily ringed finger in front of his face. "And so I told my daughter it would be when she insisted on marrying that American." She snorted in disgust. "Sally cried until my ankles started getting wet, and Robert could only say how ill you had treated him."

"Silly of me, wasn't it?" he commented. "I wouldn't let him gamble his servant away to a lecher." He paused and took a thorough, if covert, look at his grandparent. It was always hard to measure her mellowness, but Lord Ragsdale turned on his most blinding smile and ventured. "By the way, Grandmama, how would you like another maid around the place?"

Grandmama let out a crack of laughter. "Not so easy! She's all yours, John! I hear from my daughter that you spent a fortune in horseflesh for her."

"I didn't have any choice!" he shouted, his desperation returning. "Grandmama, what am I going to do with Emma Costello?"

"Buck up, John," she retorted. "I never would have taken you for a whiner."

She finished her tea, refilled it half full from the pot at her elbow, and handed the cup to him, gesturing with her head to the cherrywood cabinet against the far wall. "Put in a drop of brandy before your mother returns," she ordered. "I expect you'll find some use for Emma, if you're any grandson of Lord Whiteacre. Besides all that, she's prettier than your mistress."

He stopped at the sideboard, his hand on the brandy, and then poured in more than a drop. "Madam, pigs will fly before I would even consider kissing Emma Costello's cheek!" He doused his own tea with enough brandy to cause a blaze if he sat too close to the fire.

She took the tea and nodded at him, triumphant to have the upper hand again. "It doesn't surprise me that you should mention pork when you think of your light-skirt."

He glared at her in exasperation, wondering why he could not ever win an argument with this feeble old woman. "Fae is a fine-looking woman," he said, trying to inject the proper amount of injury into his voice and avoid any suggestion that he was getting a little tired of her. "I *prefer* women with a little *avoir du pois*," he stated. That was true enough. However, the Irish woman did have a pleasant shape, even if she was a trifle thin.

But this was no time to allow the mind to wander, and his cause was not being served by the fumes that rose from his teacup. "If you will not help me, m'dear," he said after a long, thoughtful sip, "give me some suggestions. Mama has already arranged to have a lady's maid waiting for Sally when we return. You know, someone who knows the ins and outs of life here better than Emma would. And I assure you I will not leave Emma within ten miles of Robert Claridge, no matter how she irritates me."

"You could put her in the kitchen, John," Grandmama said, taking another sip of her brandied tea, and held out the cup for more. "That's a good place for the Irish." She giggled.

"Not Emma," he said, wondering how she would fare belowstairs with the servants he employed. Besides that, as much as he disliked her, he couldn't ignore Emma's obvious intelligence anymore than he could overlook her trim shape. The kitchen was no place for Emma, no matter how much she richly deserved to be sentenced there.

"This becomes difficult," he told his grandmother as he laced their tea with a little more brandy. "I don't need her,

Mama and Sally don't need her, the kitchen would be better off without her . . ." He went to the window and grasped the frame as the room wobbled. "Maybe she can clust and dean. I mean, dust and clean."

Grandmama made no reply. He looked over his shoulder and smiled. Her head drooped on her chest, and she was beginning to snore. He sighed and rested his head against the window frame. What was he going to do with Emma?

~

To Lord Ragsdale's infinite relief, Robert Claridge allowed himself to be taken quietly to Brasenose College in the morning. The two of them rode in silence through the narrow streets of Oxford, which already bustled with scholastic purpose. Lord Ragsdale introduced his sullen cousin to the warden and gave him his back without a qualm. After Robert had been ushered away, he spent more time with the warden, urging that worthy to let him know of any infractions.

"He's a worthless young man, sir," Lord Ragsdale concluded. "Had I known the extent of his worthlessness, I would never have moved heaven and earth to foist him upon you at this juncture of the term. But here he is, sir."

The warden regarded him with some amusement. "Do you have any sons of your own yet, Lord Ragsdale?"

"I do not, sir."

The warden smiled at him. "You cannot imagine, then, how many variations of your conversation I have heard before."

He paused and Lord Ragsdale understood. "My own father, eh?" he asked, with just a ghost of a smile playing around his lips.

"Yes, my lord. Somehow we managed to turn you into someone acceptable to the world at large. I suspect we will succeed with this American too."

Lord Ragsdale managed a reluctant smile. "The Brasenose touch, sir?"

"Exactly, my lord. I think we can render him sufficiently busy to keep him from the gaming table." The warden rose and held out his hand. "I will attempt to warn him with the perils of serving in the ranks, should he choose to indulge in a gaming career within our walls. Good day, my lord."

Grandmama Whiteacre kindly loaned him a horse and saddle for the return to London so it was not necessary to stifle himself inside the family carriage this time. The day was no warmer than before, but at least it did not snow. His horse, serviceable if somewhat elderly, plodded sedately alongside the carriage where Mama read, Sally slept, and Emma continued her everlasting stare out the window. He watched her and resolved to turn her over to his butler. Emma Costello could polish silver or clean out drains, for all he cared.

London was already foggy with the light of many street lamps when the carriage turned onto Curzon Street and released its grateful occupants. Lord Ragsdale remained on his horse. "Mama, I am off to White's," he told her. Lady Ragsdale, shaky and pale from a day's travel, nodded to him as Emma helped her from the carriage. The front door opened, and Lasker stood there with the footman and Mama's dresser behind him.

He left them without another qualm, praying that traffic would not be so terrible on St. James that he would be kept long from the brandy he had been thinking about all day. He would sink into his favorite leather chair, a full bottle near his hand, and pronounce himself liberated from all further exertions. Fae would be glad enough to see him later, he was sure. In her own practiced fashion, she would remove any rough edges that remained from the day. That was what he paid her for.

As he was dismounting in front of White's, he was struck by the thought that this was what he had done the day before yesterday, and the day before that. Barring any unforeseen eventualities, he would do it all again tomorrow, and the day after, and the day after that. The thought dug him in the stomach, and he clutched the reins tighter, ignoring the porter who stood by to receive them.

Something of his unexpected agony must have crossed his face. In a moment, he heard the porter ask, "My lord, my lord, are you all right?"

He looked down at the little man, and after another long moment, handed him the reins. "I am fine," he said, fully aware for the first time that he was lying. He had never been worse. As he went slowly up the steps and into the main hall, he realized that he would probably never be better, either. This was his life. *Mercy*, he thought to himself. *Mercy*.

The milkmen were already making their rounds when he returned to Curzon Street. His head was large as usual. He had drunk too much brandy at White's and then compounded the felony at Fae's by falling asleep, which irritated Fae. She muttered something she refused to repeat.

The house was dark and silent. In another hour or so, the kitchen staff, with yawns and eye rubs, would gird itself for another day of cooking, and the upstairs maids would answer tugs on the bell pulls with tea and hot water. Lord Ragsdale listed slowly down the hall toward the stairs, which loomed insurmountable before him. *I think I will sit down here until they shrink*, he thought as he grasped the banister to keep it from leaping about, and started to lower himself to the second tread. To his relief, it did not disappear. He sank down gratefully, leaned against the railing, and closed his eyes.

He opened them a moment later. He was not alone on the stairs. Someone else sat nearby. He turned his head slowly, wondering what he would do if it was a sneak thief or cutpurse come to rob and murder them all. Lord Ragsdale sighed philosophically and sat back to wait for the knife between his ribs. At least when they found his sprawled corpse at the foot of the stairs, the constable would think that he had died there defending his family. *It would be rather like Thermopylae*, he thought, and giggled.

"All right, do your worst," he managed finally, looking around.

In another moment, his eyes adjusted to the gloom. A woman sat near the top of the stairs, asleep and leaning against the railing. He looked closer and sighed again. *Heavens, it's Emma Costello,* he thought, *the plague of my life.* As he watched her, his mind began to clear and he wondered what she was doing there. Surely she was not waiting up for him.

Suddenly it occurred to him that she had no place to sleep. He remembered his mother mentioning something about hiring a proper lady's maid for Sally. The woman must have arrived and usurped Emma's place in the dressing room. He stared at Emma and wondered why his mother had not done anything about the situation, until he remembered her exhausted face as her own maid helped her from the carriage. Mama must have gone directly to bed, too tired for a thought about Emma.

And here she was now, at the mercy of his staff, and asleep on the stairs. He felt an unexpected twinge of remorse, remembering his own disparaging words about her to his butler. The staff knew how he felt about the Irish.

"Emma," he called out softly, not wishing to startle her into a plunge down the stairs.

He called her name several times before she straightened up, moving her head slowly as though her neck hurt. She was silent a moment. "My lord?" she finally asked, not sure of her answer.

"The very same," he replied. "Emma, what are you doing sleeping on my stairs?"

She was silent a long moment, and he wondered if she still slept. "I am sorry, my lord," she said finally. "It seems that all I do is apologize to you. I don't have a place to sleep."

He didn't say anything. After another small silence, she rose and shook out her skirts. "I'll go find the back stairs, my lord," she mumbled. "I can sleep there."

Without quite knowing why, he put out his hand to stop her.

"Just a moment, Emma," he said. "Help me up, will you?"

She could have left him there, and by morning's light, he probably would have put the whole thing down to an imaginary alcoholic haze. Someone else would find him and help him to bed, and it wouldn't be the first time. Emma would sleep on the stairs for a few more nights until his mother got wind of the situation and straightened things out belowstairs. It didn't have to be his worry.

He was about to withdraw his hand when she clasped it firmly in her own and, with one swift movement, tugged him to his feet. He swayed on the stairs, and she quickly grasped him around the waist and commanded him to take up his bed and walk. It was a voice of command, resounding inside his head, crashing around from ear to ear until he wanted to whimper and crawl into a corner. Instead, he did as she ordered, putting one foot in front of the other until he was outside the door to his own room.

"I'll be all right now," he gasped. "You can let go."

Other servants had helped him to his room before. Practice told him that he could negotiate the distance from the door to his bed and throw himself down on it, not to rise until afternoon or the resurrection, whichever came first. He tried to turn her loose, but she would not budge. Suddenly he realized, in spite of his weakened state, that the rules had changed.

"I'll see you to your bed," she insisted, her voice low but carrying into his brain where her earlier words still careened off his skull. "I'll not give you the satisfaction of telling someone tomorrow that your shanty Irish servant did you an injury, no matter how richly you deserve one," she assured him.

She lowered him to his bed, and he flopped there. In another moment his shoes were off, and she was covering him with a blanket.

"That should hold you until morning," she said.

His head throbbing beyond belief, he waited like a

wounded animal for her to hurry up and leave. To his cha-grin, she stared around his room until her vision rested on his untidy desk. He watched stupidly as she shook her head in amazement at the ruin of his life.

Then the whole thing made him giggle. He tried to raise up on one elbow, but he seemed to have misplaced his arm. He remained where he was, content to watch the two of her. "Reform me, Emma," he said, and then hiccupped.

"You are disgusting, Lord Ragsdale," she said at last, each word as distinct and penetrating as a bell. She shook her head. "I never saw a more worthless man, much less served one." Her words boomed about in his skull some more. She went to his desk and rummaged about for a moment. He raised up his head to watch her sit down at his desk, clear off a spot, and put ink to paper.

She sat there quite awhile, crumpling two sheets of paper and then resting her elbows on the desk as she contem-plated him lying helpless and drunk on his bed. In another moment, she dipped the quill in the inkwell again and wrote swiftly, pausing at last to read over what she had written in the dim light. She nodded, picked up the paper and the ink, and came back to the bed.

"Emma, would you get out of my room?" he insisted, wishing he did not sound so feeble.

"Not until you sign this," she replied, sitting down next to him.

"Here." She thrust the paper under his nose.

He tried to wave away the paper, but she would not relent. "What is it?" he asked finally. "At least tell me that."

"It has to do with what you just said, my lord," she said. "You have given me such an idea. Now sign, and then I will leave you."

Said? Said? What did I say? he thought wildly. *I really must stop drinking so much.* He closed his eyes, but she rattled the paper at his ear.

As drunk as he was, Lord Ragsdale knew that he could

leave the paper alone, roll over, and go to sleep. She would go away eventually, and he would be in peace. Nothing would change. By evening he would be at White's again and drunk, or at Fae's and miserable. He was on the verge of sleep when Emma Costello touched his hair. She smoothed it back from his sweaty face and rested her hand for a moment on his head. "Sign, my lord," she ordered, her voice softer now, and held out the quill to him.

He grasped the pen and managed to scrawl out his name. He closed his eyes then and relaxed as she stood up. He reached for her hand. "Emma, please tell me that I have just released you from that unpleasant indenture. Then you can go away and I will be happy," he said. It was his longest speech of the evening, and his head lolled to one side.

I should worry, he thought when she started to laugh. *Have I signed away my fortune to this Irish harpy?* But she was speaking now, and he strained to listen.

"Lord Ragsdale, I owe you two thousand pounds, and I will pay this debt," she was saying.

"How?" he managed at last, wondering at the effort it took to form the word.

"By reforming you, my lord, now that I have your written consent. It was your idea. Good night."

Chapter 6

EMMA'S NECK WAS ACHING IN GOOD EAR-
nest by the time the scullery maid nearly tripped over
her on the way down the back stairs to begin another long
day in the kitchen. She grabbed onto the banister, scowled at
Emma, and then snickered.

"Can't find a place to sleep, can we?" she mocked. "Find
a peat bog." The maid hurried on down the stairs, tying her
apron as she went and laughing at her own cleverness.

Emma drew her knees up to her chin and watched the
maid's progress. "No, but I will find a place someday," she
said, too quiet for anyone to hear.

Not that anyone was listening to her. As Emma sat on
the back stairs, she heard the butler giving his orders. Soon
the upstairs maids would be coming up the stairs, stagger-
ing under the weight of cans of hot water and then teapots.
Another day has come to the Ragsdale household, she thought
as she looked down at the paper still clutched in her hand.
She spread it out on the landing and wondered for a moment
at her audacity. She shook her head over the document containing Lord Ragsdale's shaky signature. *I must be crazy*, she
thought.

She made herself small in the corner—something she was
good at—as the first maid hurried upstairs with hot water.
Five years ago—or was it six now?—she never would have

done something that outrageous. *There was a time when I cared what happened to me*, she thought as she carefully folded the paper. *I wonder which room is Lady Ragsdale's?*

The problem was solved for her as she quietly moved up the stairs in the wake of the upstairs maids. The first closed door she identified from last night. No one went in there, and she knew it would be hours before anyone stumbled out. Two doors down was Sally Claridge's room, if she remembered right. Ah, yes. The woman who opened the door was the dresser who had made herself quite at home in the little space Emma had carved out of the dressing room before the trip to Oxford. Robert had slept in the room next, but now the maid was tapping softly on the door beyond. The tall, thin woman with the sneer who opened the door was Lady Ragsdale's dresser.

Emma thought at first that she would wait until the maid left and then knock, but hurriedly discarded that idea. The dresser probably would not let her in. She took a deep breath and followed in after the maid, who looked around in surprise and glared at her.

"I am sure you do not belong in here," the dresser said. The cold glint in her eyes told Emma that if Lady Ragsdale's servant had not been occupied with the tea tray, she would have thrown her out. As it was, the dresser could only sputter and protest as Emma hurried to the bed where Lady Ragsdale sat awaiting her first cup of the day.

"Emma, whatever are you doing in here? And for heaven's sake, why are you so rumpled?" Lady Ragsdale asked, staring at her unexpected morning visitor.

"I slept on the stairs because no one provided a room for me," she explained. She spread out her hands in front of her. "I know that you would have, my lady, but you were so tired from yesterday's journey." She flashed her most brilliant smile at the lady in the bed and was rewarded with a smile in return.

"Thank you, Acton," Lady Ragsdale said to her dresser,

who handed her a cup of tea and stood glowering at Emma. "That will be all for the moment. Sit down, Emma. And do excuse this ramshackle household. I will instruct Lasker to find you a place to sleep tonight."

Emma perched herself on the edge of a chair close to Lady Ragsdale's bed. She sat in silence for a brief moment, willing her heart to stop jumping about in her chest, then held out the paper to Lady Ragsdale.

The other woman took it and read the few words on the page as Emma held her breath. To her vast relief, Lady Ragsdale began to laugh. She set down the teacup on her lap tray and leaned back against the pillows, indulging herself until she had to wipe her eyes with the corner of the sheet. "Emma, you are a shrewd one! Why on earth do you want to attempt this Promethean task?" she asked as she handed back the document.

Emma chose her words carefully. "I owe your son a hefty debt and mean to pay him back. It was his idea, by the way."

To her chagrin, Lady Ragsdale regarded her in silence. Emma returned her stare, pleading in silence for the woman before her to understand. *I must have an ally, or this will not work*, she thought. *Oh, please, Lady Ragsdale.*

She leaned forward, testing the waters. "Lady Ragsdale, doesn't it bother you that he is frittering away his life?"

"It bothers me," the widow replied quietly after another substantial pause. She took a sip of tea. "John is a stubborn man. I cannot control him alone. Since his father's death . . ." She paused again, then visibly gathered herself together. "I'm afraid my guidance is not to his liking." She sighed. "He's bitter about the loss of his eye, and he can't seem to settle down. What he needs is a good wife, and so I have told him." She took another sip. "Naturally, he does not listen to his mother."

Emma settled back a little in the chair. "What I propose is this, Lady Ragsdale. Since he told me last night to reform him, I intend to do just that. When he is organized, dried out, and—hopefully—married, I think he will agree to ending my indenture. I will feel the debt is paid."

"*If* he will go along with any of this," Lady Ragsdale warned. "John sober is different from John drunk. What will you do if he denies all knowledge of this pledge of his and refuses to listen to you?"

Emma looked Lady Ragsdale right in the eye. "Then I will plague his life until he does."

How, she did not know. She knew as well as John Staples's mother that there was nothing she could do if Lord Ragsdale decided to ignore her. But Lady Ragsdale was looking at her with something close to hope in her face, and she knew she had an ally. She took a deep breath.

"The first thing I want to do is lock up the liquor supply in this house."

Lady Ragsdale opened her eyes wide. "I do believe you are serious."

Emma stood up and went to the window. The rain thundered down. It was perfect weather for reformation, she decided. "I have never been more serious. I truly intend to tidy up your son and receive my release papers from him in exchange." She hesitated, and then plunged on. "I have business of my own in London, and now that I am here, I need the liberty to carry it out."

The two women regarded each other for a long moment, and then Lady Ragsdale held out her hand. After another slight pause, Emma extended her own, and they shook hands. Lady Ragsdale smiled and called for Acton, who came out of the dressing room so fast that Emma knew she had been listening at the door.

"Acton, I want Lasker up here right away. We have a matter of a lock and key to discuss."

When the dresser left the room, Emma returned to the chair. "It is perfectly obvious that for some reason Lord Ragsdale cannot stand the sight of me," she said. "Why? I never did anything to him."

Lady Ragsdale indicated that Emma remove the tea tray, and she did. The widow settled more comfortably in bed as the storm raged outside. "It is not you, my dear, but the Irish that he loathes."

"Why?"

It was a simple question, but it seemed to hang on the air.

Emma watched as Lady Ragsdale's face grew as bleak as the morning outside. *I have to know*, she thought as Lady Ragsdale touched the corner of the sheet to her eyes again. She folded her hands in her lap and looked at Emma again.

"My husband commanded a regiment of East Anglia Foot—our family seat is located near Medford. He was sent to Ireland in 1798, to serve under Lord Cornwallis." She paused and looked at Emma. "Do you remember the '98?" she asked.

It was Emma's turn to look away. *Oh, how I remember it*, she thought. "Yes, I remember," she said, her voice low.

Lady Ragsdale looked at her, a question in her eyes, and Emma was grateful for once to be a servant. The woman in the bed knew better than to bother with the affairs of a servant, so she did not ask.

"John had finished his second year at Oxford, or nearly so. His father purchased him a captaincy in the regiment, and they were posted together in County Wexford. They were very close, Emma."

Lady Ragsdale was silent then. Emma sat back in her chair.

And somehow I know what follows, she thought. "Did your husband die at Vinegar Hill, my lady?" she asked, her voice soft.

Lady Ragsdale nodded and then waited a long moment to collect herself. "He was captured by that rabble and piked to death. John watched."

Oh, mercy, this is worse than I thought, Emma told herself. "And John was injured," she said when Lady Ragsdale could not continue.

The widow nodded, her eyes staring into the paisley pattern of her bedcovers. "His men managed to drag him away before they killed him too, but he lost an eye. And my husband . . ." Her voice trailed away, and she began to weep. "Emma, they never found enough of him to bury."

Emma sat in silence as Lady Ragsdale sobbed into the sheet.

"My husband was dead, and John was so gravely injured," she managed to say at last. "I despaired of his living, and then when he finally recovered, I knew that my son was gone too, to some private horror I cannot reach."

"Lady Ragsdale, I am so sorry to have asked you," Emma said, her own eyes filling with tears.

To her surprise, the widow reached out again and grasped Emma by the arm, her grip strong. "You needed to know. John has never allowed an Irish servant into this house. He is moody and bitter and drinks too much for his own good. He engages in frivolous pursuits and cares for no one. He uses people." She released her grip on Emma. "He may say some terrible things to you."

I am sure it will be nothing I have not heard before from the English, Emma thought, *and I doubt he will resort to torture*. "Words, my lady, only words. Will you help me, then?"

"Most emphatically," Lady Ragsdale said as she dabbed at her eyes and looked up as the door opened. "Ah, Lasker. How good of you to come to me. We have some work to do. Tell me, can we lock up the wine cellar?"

～

Well, thought Emma as she stood outside Lord Ragsdale's door, *this certainly can't be any worse than other indignities I have suffered at the hands of the British*. She crossed herself, said a little prayer, and opened the door. She took a step back as the odor of stale liquor assaulted her nostrils. *Courage, Emma*, she thought as she entered the room and closed the door firmly behind her.

The room was still shaded into darkness, so she hurried to the windows and pulled back the draperies. To her relief, the rain had stopped. Letting out her breath, she threw open the windows, and the cold air blew in like a declaration. Emma looked back at the bed where Lord Ragsdale lay sprawled on top of the covers, in much the same pose as she had left him.

"Johnny boy, you are a disaster," she whispered as she tip-toed closer. She looked down at him, his face pale, his eyelid flickering now as the light streamed across the bed. His dead eye was half open, staring whitely at her. He groaned and then belched, and Emma stepped back again. His breath was foul with stale liquor. At some point during the night, he had been sick all over himself.

She shook her head. *By all the saints, I am going to earn this release from my indenture*, she thought grimly as she squeezed out a washcloth in the warm water she had brought with her. She sat gingerly on the edge of the bed and wiped his face, brushing the hair back from his forehead as he tried to pull away from her.

"Not so fast, my lord," she muttered, pinning him down until his face was wiped clean. "I wish you would open your eye. It's morning." She smiled, in spite of her extreme revulsion. "Morning is probably a phenomenon you have not experienced in some years, my lord."

She did not expect an answer, and she did not receive one. She refreshed the cloth and continued to wipe his face and neck until the evidence of his evening of excess was gone. Emma watched him, grateful right down to her shoes that none of the men in her family were drinkers beyond an evening sherry or an eggnog at Christmas. "It is a vile business, Lord Ragsdale."

To her amazement, he opened his eye. "Yes, ain't it?" he agreed. He lay there watching her, as if trying to rally those parts of his brain necessary for rational thought. The attempt was unsuccessful, because he burped and closed his eye again.

She should have been revolted; he was a disgusting sight. As she sat looking at him, he sighed and rested his head against her leg, and she found herself resting her hand on his shoulder. In another moment, she brushed at his hair again. "So you are an ogre who uses people?" she whispered. "Well, I am an ogre too, and I intend to use you, sir."

Her thoughts were interrupted by a scratch on the door. "Do come in," she said, and the door opened on the footman and several housemaids, who carried buckets of water. The footman went into the dressing room and pulled out a washtub, setting it in front of the fireplace. Emma nodded to the maids, who stood on the threshold, appalled at the messy room. "Pour it in there. Is it good and hot, Hanley?"

The footman nodded, then grinned in spite of himself. "I disremember when he ever got up before noon."

Emma smiled back, grateful there was one person in the household who didn't regard her with indifference or disdain. She looked at the maids. "We'll need more water."

They left and Emma looked down at Lord Ragsdale again. His eye was open and he was watching her. When she glared right back, he looked away, his disfavor pointed.

Emma took Hanley's measure, and saw a young man in service, starting out as a footman and probably full of ambition. She gestured with her head, and he followed her to the corner.

"Hanley, I need your help. Lord Ragsdale is going to become furious and hateful in about a minute."

"More than now?" the footman joked, his voice as low as hers.

Emma nodded. "He might threaten to sack you. Will you trust me?"

He considered the matter seriously then. "If he turns me off without a character?"

"He will try, but I'll make certain he doesn't," Emma told him, wondering how on earth she could make good that promise. *Nothing ventured, nothing gained,* she thought. "You have to trust me."

Hanley favored her with a smile. "Aye, miss. Emma, my relatives are all from County Down," he whispered.

"Never!" she declared, then lowered her voice again. "You have no accent. None whatever."

"A man can't make it in service in a great house with an Irish accent," he said simply.

They regarded each other in perfect understanding. "Take off your coat and roll up your sleeves, my friend," she whispered back, then turned to the task at hand.

Lord Ragsdale now eyed her with suspicion. "I don't recall inviting you into my room."

"You didn't. I am here to hold you to your word, my lord, and a certain signed document." She turned to the footman. "Hanley, unbutton his shirt."

Lord Ragsdale stared at her, and she nearly laughed out loud as she watched a variety of expressions cross his face. He finally settled on irritation. "Leave my shirt alone, Hanley," he ordered.

The footman took a deep breath, glanced at Emma, then started on his employer's buttons. Lord Ragsdale tried to brush his hands away, but he still suffered from the effects of last night's liquid debauch and missed the mark. "Don't touch me, Hanley," he threatened again.

Emma put on her most cheerful face, which she knew would drive her employer into the boughs. "As to that, if you wish to take a bath with your shirt on, you may, but it seems a little ramshackle, even for an Englishman."

He tried to glare at her, but the effort of squinting must have hurt his tender head. "Who said I was going to take a bath?" he asked, rubbing his forehead.

"I did, my lord," Emma stated firmly. "You are disgusting and we have things to do today. Take off your shirt."

"I won't."

"You will."

They stared at each other. Emma hoped she had won when he blinked, but she could be charitable to the vanquished. She turned around. "I will not watch, of course, but you will remove your shirt and everything else that doesn't belong in a tub of water."

Oh, please obey me, she thought, folding her arms and staring at the wall. She heard the maids returning with more water, which they poured into the tub. They shrieked, and Emma knew that Lord Ragsdale was stripping in front of them. She couldn't help her smile as the maids ran for the door.

She heard the man step into the water, but she didn't hear him sit down.

"I seem to recall something last night. I signed a paper."

"You did, my lord," she said, hoping her voice sounded firm now, something like the worst teacher she had ever endured. "You asked me to reform you, and even signed a statement to that effect."

To her dismay, she heard him step out of the tub. Irritating, stupid Englishman, she thought. Now what? She heard footsteps and a door opened.

"What's he doing, Hanley?" she asked in a low voice.

"Going into his dressing room. Uh-oh. He has a bottle."

"Take it from him."

"This is going to get me sacked."

"Trust me."

She heard a tussle, then language better not repeated, ending in, "You are sacked, you worthless footman!"

"Naughty, naughty," Emma said. "You signed a document giving me full power. You cannot sack the footman. Hand me that bottle, Hanley."

The footman did as she asked, his eyes merry. Emma took a deep breath and walked to the window. She looked down to make certain no one was passing below and then dropped the bottle, listening with satisfaction to the crash and tinkle on the pavement below.

Lord Ragsdale sucked in his breath, but he didn't give up, even though Emma knew the game was over. His voice turned silky and wheedling.

"Hanley, my good man, go to the cellar and get me more brandy."

"I cannot, my lord. The wine cellar has been sealed, according to your orders."

"What?" he shrieked.

"Just so, my lord," Emma chimed in. "You signed a paper last night. I am to reform you."

"Never!"

Emma put her hands on her hips. "You are the worst kind of whiner, my lord. Sit down in that water."

"Who is going to make me?" The menace was there, along with a little-boy threat that suddenly reminded Emma of her youngest brother.

She thought of everything she had been through. "No one except yourself, my lord. You signed an agreement and I will honor it. If you are a gentleman, you will too."

The silence almost hummed. Emma closed her eyes in relief when Lord Ragsdale sat down in the water.

"Scrub his back, please, Hanley," she said.

"You could at least close the window," Lord Ragsdale said, sounding like a half dozen sulky boys. "I have goose bumps all over."

"I am certain that will not prove fatal, my lord," she said, wishing she could rush into the hall and laugh herself into a coma.

She heard a monumental sigh, followed by the sound of a washcloth, and pressed her lips tight to keep from breaking into a guffaw so loud that passersby could hear it on Curzon Street.

"Emma, you are no lady," Lord Ragsdale said.

"And you are most certainly no gentleman," she snapped back. "I have not peeked, nor will I."

"The water is deep. If I drown, you're to blame," he said, his voice virtuous now.

"It won't come to that."

The sound of washing continued. She heard him stand up to finish the job, then sit down again. "I usually sing in the tub," he told her, his voice conversational now. "Do you have a favorite selection?"

She laughed, unable to help herself. "Not one, my lord."

"Well, then." He cleared his throat and sang a ditty so filthy that even Hanley gasped.

When he finished, Emma applauded. "You could probably perform that in an alley behind Covent Garden," she said. "That might be enough, though."

Lord Ragsdale cleared his throat and began another song, worse than the one before.

"Dunk him under the water, Hanley," Emma ordered.

"You wouldn't d—"

Evidently Hanley would, and did. When the footman allowed Lord Ragsdale to resurface, sputtering and swearing, Emma just shook her head. "Tsk, tsk."

"I'll see you in Newgate Prison!" Lord Ragsdale roared, quite sober now. His washcloth swished past her face and landed against the wall.

"That was childish, my lord," she said. "I'll happily go to Newgate. I was planning to do that this afternoon. Your mother tells me that your secretary is incarcerated there, and I mean to ask his advice."

"You can't be serious. Hand me that towel, Hanley, you wretched excuse for a footman."

Her back still to her employer, Emma edged toward the door. "I am quite serious, my lord. If I am to be your secretary too, I had better learn the business from a master."

She heard the rustle of material, and Lord Ragsdale stood before her in his robe, water streaming down his face, soap still in his hair. His dead eye didn't even make her flinch. She had seen so much worse in the last few years.

Well now, she thought. *I am one step closer to far away from this place.* She regarded the angry man before her and felt the tiniest bit of sympathy. She knew it would pass.

"I promise not to cheat you, but I will reform you. After luncheon then, Lord Ragsdale?"

"I wouldn't follow you across the street, you presumptuous parcel of Irish baggage."

"Oooh, sticks and stones, my lord," she replied. "Then I'll go by myself. If you want anything, once you have dried and dressed, I will be in your book room, sorting out your bills."

"You can't do this!" he shouted, shaking his finger at her.

"Watch me."

Chapter 7

$\mathcal{E}$MMA SPENT THE REST OF THE MORNING in the book room, sorting through the clutter of bills, many of them unopened, that resided in dusty piles on the desk. As she arranged them chronologically, oldest first, she found herself wondering how Lord Ragsdale had managed to keep *himself* out of Newgate. *Does this man ever pay a bill?* she thought as she frowned over requests for payment from liquor wholesalers, procurers of livestock feed, and mantua makers.

Mantua makers? She scrutinized the bill at arm's length and then remembered that Lady Whiteacre in Oxford had mentioned a mistress. *Well, at least she's stylish*, Emma thought as she created a separate pile for bills from modistes, milliners, cobblers, and sellers of silk stockings and perfumes. *I had a pair of silk stockings once*, she thought as she picked up the bill. *I will not think about that.*

But she did think about it, leaning back in the chair as she sniffed at the faintly scented paper. *I wonder who is living in our house now*, she thought. *I hope they have not made too many changes. Mama had such exquisite taste.*

"Now, Emma, you know you cannot think about her," she said out loud and put down the paper. She knew she had to think of something else, so she concentrated on the house again. The china was gone, of course. The last sound she remembered as they were dragged from the front door was the crash and tinkle of china as the soldiers rampaged through.

Ah, well, the view is still the same, she reminded herself. *Even British soldiers cannot move the Wicklow Mountains.* She closed her eyes, thinking of the green loveliness of it all and knowing that she would never see her home again. True, Virginia had been a reasonable substitute, and she knew that she could return there with some peace of mind when this onerous indenture was fulfilled. Emma rested her chin on her hand. Springs could be soft there, with redbud, flowering dogwood, and azalea, but she knew in her heart that there would never be the shades of green from home, no matter how hard Virginia tried.

And so I must forget, she thought and picked up another stack of bills. *There is an Englishman here who should keep me sufficiently occupied. He is utterly without merit and ought to occupy my mind to such a degree that I do not have time to remember.*

"Seriously, Hanley, how *does* Lord Ragsdale keep himself from debtor's prison?" she asked the footman, who stuck his head in the room an hour later to see how she did. She indicated the neat piles on the desk and in her lap. "He hasn't paid a bill in at least three months. I can't find any posting books with accounts. Do you know where they would be kept?"

The footman looked around at the order she was creating out of catastrophe, his eyes appreciative. "Gor, miss, there's wood on that desk after all!" he joked.

Emma smiled and indicated a chair beside the desk. "What is his secret, Hanley?"

"Simple, miss. He's richer than Croesus, and all these tradespeople know that he will pay eventually. If they get tired of waiting, they petition his banker."

"I call that a pretty ramshackle way to live," Emma grumbled.

The footman shrugged. "If you or I were to forget a bill, now that would not be a pretty sight."

Emma nodded in agreement. "Too true." She placed her hands down on the desk. "Hanley, how did you manage with Lord Ragsdale?"

"Oh, he cleaned up pretty well after you left, miss." The footman laughed. "I think he's not your best friend, though."

Emma shook her head. "And he never will be! I suppose that radical reformation must always exact its own price." She changed the subject. "Hanley, do you know how to get to Newgate Prison from here?"

"Gor, miss, you can't be thinking of going there on *purpose?*" the footman demanded. "I won't tell you!"

She was about to reply when she noticed he was staring at her left hand. She put her hand in her lap, coloring slightly. "I have to, Hanley," she explained, hoping he would not ask any questions. "David Breedlow—I believe that is his name—is imprisoned there awaiting transportation, and I need to know something about Lord Ragsdale's account books, if I am to acquit myself as his secretary."

Hanley's eyes opened wide at that piece of information.

"*You're* going to be the master's new secretary? I never heard of such a thing!"

Emma blushed again. "It's part of my indenture agreement, and you needn't frown about it. Do you know who Lord Ragsdale banks with, or the name and direction of his solicitor? I need to speak to someone about his accounts."

The footman stood up, tugging at his waistcoat. "I wouldn't know, miss."

Emma sighed and deposited the papers from her lap onto the desk. "Perhaps I had better ask Lord Ragsdale, though I would almost rather ingest ground glass than do that."

The footman laughed out loud. "I don't think he'll cooperate with you today." He went to the door and peered out, obviously on the alert. "He told me to tell you that pigs would fly before he lifted another finger on your behalf."

"Oh, he did?" she said as she looked about for a pencil and tablet. "Well, then, this mountain will obviously have to go to Muhammad."

"Miss?"

"If the Almighty upstairs is in a twit, I will just have to visit his former secretary, won't I? Please tell me how to get to Newgate," she asked again.

The footman stared at her and shook his head. "Miss, didn't you hear me? You can't go there!"

Silently, she agreed with him. *I have had my fill of prisons,* she thought. *I hope the walls are thicker at Newgate than they were at Prevot. I don't want to hear anything.* "Of course I have to go," she said out loud. "How else am I going to find out how to straighten out His Excellency's books?"

"I don't know, miss," said the footman, his voice doubtful.

She could have left it at that, admitted defeat, and returned to pushing around papers into neater piles. It was on the tip of her tongue to say so, but as she regarded the footman, she knew she had to go ahead. If Lord Ragsdale knew he had the upper hand by refusing to help her, she would never be able to reform him. *And I will not stay in this indenture one more moment than I have to,* she thought grimly.

"Well, then, Hanley, if you won't help me, I'll just start out walking and ask the first person I meet."

The footman blanched. "You can't do that, either. Oh, very well."

Armed with Hanley's directions, she left the house on Curzon Street before the noon hour. The footman had suggested that she ride the distance into the City, but she had no money. *I've walked farther,* she thought as she tugged her cloak tighter about her and set off at a brisk pace. *I've walked from County Wicklow to Dublin, most of the time carrying my little brother. This will be a stroll.*

The day was cold, and she kept her head down, wishing for the luxury of a warmer cloak and a muffler for her neck. Pedestrians all around her were dressed for the weather, with fur-trimmed cloaks, muffs, and stout shoes. She hurried along, knowing how out of place she must appear in that elegant neighborhood, and hoping that her shabbiness would not attract the attention of a constable. Well-groomed horses minced by on dainty hooves, pulling curricles and phaetons of the latest fashion. She wanted to admire the bonnets of the ladies who passed, but she kept her eyes before her on the pavement, looking up at each curb to make sure she was following the footman's directions.

The broad streets of Mayfair, with its stylish row houses, gave way to the business end of Picadilly. She paid closer attention to her surroundings, knowing she had to watch for the streets that would eventually lead to the Strand and then Fleet Street. The cold clamped down, bringing with it a whiff of sewage from the river. She wished she had not come.

"So help me, Emma Costello, if I have to call your name one more time, I'll leave you here to freeze your Irish bones."

Surprised, she looked over her shoulder and then back down at the sidewalk. *Calm, calm*, she told herself. *No one knows you in London. It must be a mistake.* She started walking faster.

"Emma!"

There was no mistaking that peremptory voice. She stopped and looked into the street this time.

Lord Ragsdale, wearing a heavy overcoat and sitting under a lap robe, walked his horse and curricle beside her on the street. A tiger, fashionably dressed in the family livery, shivered behind the seat. When his master reined in his horse, the little Negro leaped down and indicated that she should allow him to help her into the curricle.

Emma stared in amazement and then allowed herself to be seated.

The tiger smoothed the lap robe over her too and then resumed his chilly position behind the seat. Lord Ragsdale snapped his whip over the horse, and they entered the stream of traffic again.

They passed several blocks in silence before Emma worked up the courage to speak. "I am going to Newgate, my lord."

To her further surprise, Lord Ragsdale smiled. "If only they would keep you, Emma," he murmured, before his voice became firm again. "Hanley told me. Tell me, Emma, and don't be shy. Is your head filled with porridge instead of brains? Have you not a single clue that you were walking into a neighborhood that not even a gypsy is safe in?"

As she listened to his bracing scold, she realized the idiocy of her plan. When he finished, she raised her chin and looked him in the eye.

"I only want information that will help me straighten out your bills and receipts, my lord." It seemed foolish now, and she stared back down at her hands.

"Your energy continues to astound me, Emma," he said dryly. "But why on earth did you leave my house with no gloves, no bonnet, and no muffler? I call that silly."

"I don't have any of those things, my lord," she replied, trying to keep the embarrassment from her voice. It was his turn to be silent for several blocks.

"Well, you should have waited for warmer weather, then," he muttered finally. "Those bills have kept this long; they'll keep until warm weather." He was silent then, his eye on the traffic.

Emma glanced at him, hoping he was not too angry with her. *Somehow I must learn to get along with this man*, she thought as she watched his expert hands on the reins guide his horse through city traffic. She was impressed, despite her suspicion.

He spoke to his horse, pulled back slightly on the reins, and looked over his shoulder. "Are we going back?" she asked.

"Oh, no, Emma," he replied as he turned the corner onto Bailey. "Actually, I'm looking forward to the opportunity to give David Breedlow a piece of my mind."

Are you sure you can spare that much? she thought and smiled in spite of herself.

Lord Ragsdale glanced at her and then pulled his horse to a stop. "I don't know what you find so dashed amusing about a prison, Emma Costello," he snapped.

She sobered immediately and tugged her cloak over her cold fingers. "There is nothing funny about prison," she said, her words more distinct than she intended.

He snorted and nodded to the tiger to help her down. "You say that like an expert, Emma Costello."

She didn't mean to respond, but the words came out anyway.

"I am, Lord Ragsdale," she replied, then turned to the tiger and took his helping hand.

As Emma waited for Lord Ragsdale to join her on the sidewalk, she looked up at the gray pile before her. *So this is Newgate*, she thought. *I wonder if they are here.* The view blurred over then, and she found herself in tears. Quickly she dabbed at them, intensely aware that Lord Ragsdale was watching her, a quizzical expression on his face. She waited for a jibe or a scold, but instead, he took her arm and steered her toward the entrance.

"It's a sooty neighborhood, Emma," he said as he pulled out a handkerchief and gave it to her.

He nodded to the porter who stood lounging beside the low entrance. "Mind your head, Emma," he directed as he ducked his head under the gloomy stone portal.

She followed him in, holding her breath against that first whiff of prison air that she knew was coming. The oak door beyond was open and topped with a row of spikes and transverse bars. She hesitated a moment, fearing all over again the sound of such a door slamming.

Don't be silly, Emma, she told herself. Another porter stood there, glancing out of the corner of his eye at Lord Ragsdale's elegant clothing and then ogling her own shabbiness. He winked at her, and when she drew back, surprised, he made kissing noises that stopped when Lord Ragsdale turned around and fixed him with a stare that could have melted marble.

"Dreadful place," Lord Ragsdale said as he waited for her to stand beside him. "I don't know why you couldn't have just asked me to answer your questions, Emma."

She looked at him, her eyes wide. "Hanley told me that you had no intention of helping me."

Emma thought he smiled at that, but the antechamber was gloomy with the light of only one lamp, and she could not be sure.

"He is quite right, of course," Lord Ragsdale said as he motioned the porter forward. "But perhaps I would have given you the information you needed in a day or two."

She couldn't tell if he was quizzing her, so she made no reply.

The stench of the place was appalling, and she held Lord Ragsdale's handkerchief to her nose, thinking to herself as she did so that British prisons smelled much like Irish ones. *Spoiled food, unwashed bodies, filthy straw,* she thought, *disease rampant, and I wonder, does despair have an odor?* She concluded that it did as she stood next to Lord Ragsdale.

"Tell the governor of this fine old institution that John Staples, the Marquess of Ragsdale, wishes an audience with him," the marquess was telling the porter. He held his hand to his nose a moment.

The man nodded, backed through a doorway, and vanished. He was back promptly. "It'll be a moment, my lord," he explained. He looked at Emma. "Is she with you, my lord?" he asked.

"Regrettably, yes."

The porter smirked at Emma. "Then she'll have to be searched by the warden over there before she goes any farther."

Emma looked to the left where he pointed and saw a pale, thin woman leaning against a doorframe. The woman straightened up and started toward her. Despite herself, Emma found herself crowding closer to Lord Ragsdale.

"A search will hardly be necessary!" the marquess snapped, and he stepped slightly in front of Emma.

"My lord, you'd be amazed what females try to smuggle in here under them skirts," the porter assured him. "Go with her like a good girl, miss, or I'll have her lift your skirts right here."

Emma took a deep breath, regretted it instantly, and steeled herself to step forward. *It's not that bad*, she told herself. *You've done this before*, she thought as the female warden gestured to her impatiently.

"I hardly think this is necessary" came Lord Ragsdale's smooth voice. "Emma, be a good girl and open your reticule for the nice lady."

She did as he said, and he peered inside first. "Hmmm, nothing more dangerous than a tablet, pencil, and what appears to be a letter. Are you satisfied, madam?" he asked the matron.

The woman looked inside too, then stared up at the marquess.

"I'll still have to look under them skirts."

"I don't think so," Lord Ragsdale said. "Emma is irritating and three parts lunatic, but I would wager that there is nothing under her skirts beyond a pair of legs."

The porter tittered behind his hand, and the matron glared at him and cracked him so suddenly on the side of his head that he dropped to his knees. Emma flinched and leaped back against the marquess as the little man howled in pain. Lord Ragsdale put his hand on her shoulder and moved them both out of the reach of the matron.

The woman jerked her hand back to strike again when the door to the governor's office opened suddenly.

"Mrs. Malfrey, remember yourself!" growled the man who stood in the doorway, a napkin tucked under his chin. As he came closer to the marquess, Emma noticed his greasy shirtfront and wondered why he bothered with the nicety of a napkin.

The matron slunk back to her side of the hallway as the governor of Newgate wiped his hand on equally shiny breeches and bowed elaborately to the marquess, who merely nodded at him.

"What can I do for you, my lord?" he asked. "It's a little late for morning callers." He laughed at his own humor.

"We have a matter of business to discuss with David Breedlow," Lord Ragsdale said. "He embezzled from me and is awaiting transportation."

"Breedlow, Breedlow, Breedlow," said the governor as he motioned them into his office. The remains of a leg of mutton and various pastries were jumbled over his desk, mingling with various papers and what looked like an earlier meal. "Ye caught me at table, my lord," he apologized. "I always eats in my office, I do." He leaned forward confidentially. "Do ye know, I was cited by the Lord Mayor himself last year. He called me a model of efficiency, he did."

"I am sure you are," Lord Ragsdale murmured, shaking his head when the governor offered him a chair. "We won't disturb you much longer. Show us to David Breedlow, please."

The governor looked longingly at the mutton again and then laughed. "I'll have to find the bleeder first, won't I?"

"I'm sure he can't have gone far," Lord Ragsdale said, more to Emma than to the governor, who busied himself with a row of books that looked old enough to have been in William the Conqueror's library, if that notable had been literate. He opened the newest-looking ledger on the row and thumbed through it, muttering, "Breedlow, Breedlow."

In another moment he stuck his head out into the antechamber and called to the porter. They conversed a moment while Emma stayed close to Lord Ragsdale, who was looking about him in real distaste. Finally, the governor turned back to them, bowed to the marquess, and indicated the door again.

"Follow this bloke. He'll have Breedlow taken to an assembly room."

"Come, Emma," Lord Ragsdale said. "Let's see what delights this charming place has for us."

The governor laughed out loud and then winked at the marquess. "Come back anytime, my lord, anytime."

"Not if I can possibly help it," Lord Ragsdale replied as they followed the porter down a narrow hallway, lit, almost as an afterthought it seemed, by candles here and there. "Emma, what did I do to deserve this?"

She thought a moment and then smiled in spite of herself as she hurried to keep up. "Well, you will own, my lord, that you have probably not thought about a drink lately."

He laughed out loud, and the porter stopped and looked back, startled. The marquess only gazed at him serenely. "That was laughter—a natural eruption of good humor that occurs when people are amused. Do lead on, man. If we stand here much longer, we will use up all the air in this part of this fine old institution, I am sure."

They continued deeper into the building, winding around in narrow passages that made Emma pray that the porter would not abandon them. *We would never find our way out*, she thought. They passed several gang cells, filled to bursting with men and women jumbled in together. Somewhere she heard a child cry, and her heart sank. She must have sucked in her breath or said something, because the marquess reached behind him and took hold of her hand. She clung to it gratefully.

They stopped finally before another oak door bound with iron, one of many they had passed through. *For all I know, we are back at the entrance*, Emma thought, her sense of direction confused by the gloom and the halls. The porter selected a key from the many that dangled at his waist and opened the door.

"In here," he said as he swung the door wider. "Breedlow, you have visitors."

Emma squinted in the gloom as she looked around. There were several other women there, sitting on benches facing a row of prisoners who were chained to the wall by one hand. Most of the men sat on the straw-covered floor, their one chained arm raised over their head as though they had a question.

"That's Breedlow, my lord, standing there on the end."

"I know him," the marquess said.

Emma looked at Lord Ragsdale, surprised at the uncertainty in his voice. She glanced at Breedlow, rail thin and pale as parchment, who gradually sank to the floor as though he had not strength to remain upright. His eyes were on the marquess, and in another instant, he started to sob.

The suddenness of the sound stopped all the low-voiced conversations in the assembly room for a moment. When Breedlow continued to cry, the talking began again, like water washing around a boulder in a stream. *All this misery, and no one has any pity,* Emma thought to herself as she watched Lord Ragsdale's former secretary. *Yes, this is very much like Irish prisons. I shall feel right at home.* She moved toward the bench and then looked back at Lord Ragsdale, who had remained by the door.

"My lord? My business will take some time, so perhaps if you wish to give your secretary a piece of your mind, you might go first," she said.

There was no reply. "My lord?" she repeated. *It is different, is it not,* she thought as she watched Lord Ragsdale's face, *to turn someone over to justice in a fit of rage, and then to see the results of it.* "Really, my lord, you may go first. I don't mind."

"No, Emma," he said finally. "I will wait for you in the hall." The door closed behind him.

Emma seated herself in front of Breedlow and handed him the marquess's handkerchief. "It is only a little wet," she said.

He took it, wiped his eyes, and then stared at her.

"I am Lord Ragsdale's new secretary," she said. "I believe that you can help me. You see, I am reforming Lord Ragsdale."

Chapter 8

*T*HE HOUR PASSED QUICKLY. SHE TOOK notes rapidly and trusted her memory for the rest of Breedlow's information about how to manage Lord Ragsdale's affairs. "I am certain he will ask you to write his letters for him," Breedlow continued as the guard by the inner door blew a little brass whistle. "He's not that difficult to please." He paused and looked toward the guard. "I only wish he had not been so lazy. Perhaps then I would not have been tempted . . ." His voice trailed away as the women on the benches started to rise.

"How long before you are transported?" Emma asked, wishing there was something she could do for the man.

"Very soon, I fear," he replied. He took a last dab at his eyes and then started to hand back Lord Ragsdale's handkerchief. He hesitated. "May I keep this?"

Mystified, she nodded. "Why would you want to?"

Breedlow bowed his head, and she could tell that her question had humiliated him further. "I can sell it for food." He raised his eyes to hers. "You can't imagine how hungry I am."

"Oh, I can," she said softly as the guard blew the whistle again. "Keep it, by all means. I wish I had some money to give you."

He shook his head and managed a ragged smile. "Actually,

I have enjoyed your company. You are my first visitor. My sister lives too far away to visit." Again he stopped and looked away as the tears came to his eyes. "And now I will never see her again, and it was all for twenty pounds."

They were both silent. Emma leaned forward then and reached into her reticule. "Please, Mr. Breedlow, can you do me a favor?"

He stared at her blankly. "How could I possibly do you a favor?"

"I want to hand you a letter. Please take it to Australia. See if you can deliver it for me." She kept her voice low as the guards began to herd the women together at the other end of the narrow room.

He shook his head. "You daren't hand me anything. The guards will only tear it up and beat me later."

"It was just a thought," she said then and withdrew her hand from the reticule. "Mr. Breedlow, good luck."

He started to reply, when one of the women near the door screamed and fainted. As the other women clustered around, jabbering and gesturing, the guards hurried to that end of the room.

"Quickly now." It was Breedlow, holding his hand out to her. She grabbed the letter again and thrust it at him, grateful for the unexpected diversion. It disappeared as soon as she handed it over.

Order returned quickly, and a guard gestured her toward the door and thrust his key in the lock that chained Breedlow to the wall.

"Good luck, Mr. Breedlow," she called again as he was led away. "Please don't lose that letter," she said softly as the other women, more of them crying now, hurried from the room. She watched the former secretary until the door clanged behind him and then sighed and stepped into the hall again.

Lord Ragsdale waited for her. He snapped open his pocket watch. "I trust you learned all you need to know, and

I hope you don't have anyone else to visit at Newgate. As it is, I am certain I will never get the stench of this place out of my coat."

"No, my lord, I have no one else to visit," she replied as he started back down the hall. "But I do want you to stop in the governor's office for a moment."

"Not if my life depended on it," he assured her and hurried faster.

"I want you to give the governor some money to keep Mr. Breedlow from starving," she said and then held her breath and waited for the storm to break.

She was not disappointed. He stopped, took her by the arm, and gave her a shake. "Emma, he robbed me!" Lord Ragsdale shouted.

Why am I doing this? she thought as she nerved herself to look into his eye and stand her ground, even though he was taller than she by a foot at least, and seemed enormously large in that many-caped coat he wore.

"And Mr. Breedlow is going to a lifetime in a penal colony for stealing a paltry twenty pounds from you," she continued, surprised at her own temerity. *I am not afraid of you*, she thought, and to her amazement, she meant it.

"So he is," Lord Ragsdale said, calm again. He let go of her arm and hurried her along the endless passage, past cells crammed with wretched people, prisoners for whom all time was suspended into a continuous, dismal present that she understood very well.

Emma did not really expect Lord Ragsdale to stop at the governor's office again, but he did. The governor ushered them into the office that still smelled of elderly mutton.

"This is for David Breedlow's upkeep," the marquess said as he slapped a handful of coins down on the desk and then scowled at Emma.

"Thank you, my lord," she replied and edged closer to the row of ledgers as the governor searched around on his messy desk for a receipt book. In another moment she was looking through the newest ledger, running her finger down the row of names of prisoners incarcerated in the last five years. There were so many, and the governor's scribe had such poor handwriting. *This will take me an hour at least, and I do not have an hour,* she thought as the governor scratched out a receipt and handed it to her employer.

"Come, Emma," Lord Ragsdale said. He stood next to her, and she jumped at the sudden intrusion on her rapid scramble through the ledger. "We have come to the end of this day's philanthropy, I trust."

She closed the book reluctantly.

"Looking up relatives?" the marquess asked. "Close relatives, I would imagine."

He was teasing her, she could tell. "Of course, my lord," she responded promptly. He could think what he chose.

Blessedly outside the prison, Lord Ragsdale nodded to his tiger, who unblanketed his horse.

They started out in silence. It was almost dark now, and Newgate was only a hulking shadow. She shivered, hoping that she would not dream tonight.

"I trust we needn't repeat a visit to my late secretary."

"No, my lord," she said. "Tomorrow, though, we need to visit your banker and find out what bills remain to be paid. Breedlow tells me that your banker has his ledgers."

"It can wait, Emma," he grumbled.

"It cannot, my lord. The sooner your finances are organized, the less I will bother you."

"Thank heavens," he replied fervently. "In that case, I am yours this evening too."

Silence filled the space between them. They might have been miles from each other instead of touching shoulders. She knew she should be silent, but Breedlow's face was still so vivid in her mind.

"My lord, did you ever ask Mr. Breedlow why he stole the money?"

"No. I don't care why."

The marquess spoke with such finality that Emma knew she did not dare to continue. But she did, as though some demon pushed her onto an empty stage, daring her to perform for a hostile audience.

"His sister's husband died, and that twenty pounds was to cover funeral expenses and a year's rent for her."

She could tell he had turned to look at her, but it was dark and she could not see his face. "I told you I did not care. Thievery is thievery, Emma."

She looked straight ahead and plunged on, driven by some imp that she did not recognize. "When I straightened out your desk this morning, I noticed that you wagered seventy-five pounds that Lord Lander could not push a peanut with his nose down St. James Street during the evening rush of traffic."

His reply was quiet, and she knew she should not prod him any farther. "It's my money, Emma," he said.

"Yes, it is, isn't it?"

"Emma, you are aggravating!" he said, his voice low but intense. "When we get home, I am going to find that stupid paper I signed and tear it up, and you can spend the next five years cleaning out my kitchen! To perdition with my reformation."

Well, that is that, she thought to herself as she pulled as far away from him as she could and stared into the gathering dusk. *Oh, why can I not learn patience? I have ruined everything.*

When they arrived at the house, Lord Ragsdale flung himself out of the curricle, snapped his orders at the tiger, and took the front steps in two bounds. Emma followed more slowly, drawing her cloak about her again. She sniffed at the fabric. Lord Ragsdale was right; the odor of Newgate had permeated the material.

He slammed the door behind him, not quite in her face, but almost. She opened it and forced herself to go inside. *I wonder if Lady Ragsdale found me a place to sleep,* she thought. *I cannot bear another night on the stairs.*

Lady Ragsdale and Sally Claridge, dressed in evening wear, stood in the front hallway conversing with Lord Ragsdale. The older woman nodded to Emma and then made a face as Emma slowly removed her cloak.

"I was telling my son how much Sally and I were looking forward to his escort tonight and during this Season, and what does he tell me but you have commanded his appearance in the book room this evening?"

Surprised, Emma glanced at Lord Ragsdale, who stood slightly behind his mother. He stared at her and gave her a slow wink. She understood perfectly and resisted the urge to cheer as she sighed and then shook her head at Lady Ragsdale.

"That is how we must get on, my lady," she said, striving for that perfect blend of regret and determination. "Until your son's business affairs are regulated, I must claim his attention. I am sure that later in the Season he will be delighted to accompany the two of you."

To her relief, Lady Ragsdale nodded. "I am sure we understand, Emma. Come, Sally. I don't believe Lord and Lady Tennant were expecting my son anyway."

Lord Ragsdale kissed his mother's cheek and managed a look of rue so counterfeit to Emma that she had to turn away to maintain her countenance. *I never met a more complicated man*, she thought as Lord Ragsdale expressed his profound sorrow at missing an evening with London's finest and closed the door behind his mother and cousin. He turned back to her, and she held her breath.

"To the book room, Emma," he said, handing his coat to Lasker, who frowned and held it at arm's length. "Burn it, Lasker," he ordered as he started down the hall. "Come along, come along! I suppose that right now you are the lesser of two evils. I would rather suffer an hour or two in the book room with you than spend even fifteen minutes in the home of London's most prosing windbags. If some latter-day Guy Fawkes were to blow up Lord and Lady Tennant, he would have the thanks of a grateful nation."

"Thank you, I think," she replied dubiously.

"You have your uses, Emma," he murmured as he held open the book room door. "Now I suppose you want me to go to my room and gather up all the bills on that desk and bring them to you, as well."

"Precisely, my lord," she said as she seated herself behind the desk and reached for the inkwell. "We will sort them and tie them in bales and contract a carter to haul them to Fotherby and Sons tomorrow morning."

"Emma, you are trying me," he replied, his hand on the doorknob.

She returned his stare with one of her own. "Of course, if you hurry, I am sure you can still arrive at the Tennants' in time for a fulfilling evening, my lord."

"And deprive you of my company, Emma? Never that. By all that's holy, you are a cheeky bit of Irish baggage," Lord Ragsdale murmured as he closed the door quietly behind him. To her amazement, he was whistling as he headed for the stairs.

He is a lunatic, she thought as she put more coal on the fire. *If only I didn't owe him so much money*. She seated herself again and folded her hands on the desk, thinking of Mr. Breedlow. *If he survives the journey, perhaps he will remember the letter. And if he does, perhaps it will get to my father or my brother. And if they read it, perhaps they will be allowed to write to me*. She looked down at the distorted fingernails on her left hand. *But I will not hope*, she thought. *For all I know, they are buried in a lime pit in Dublin*.

But I will not think of that, she told herself a few minutes later as she rested her head on the desk and closed her eyes. She raised her head a moment later as the doorknob turned.

"Caught you, Emma," Lord Ragsdale murmured as he dumped an armful of bills on the desk. "Which reminds me. Lasker, in his condescension, has permitted you to sleep with the scullery maid. Top floor, second door on the right." He sat down next to her. "All right, Emma. I dare you to organize me."

⌣

The clock in the hall was chiming midnight when Lord Ragsdale stood up and stretched. He looked at the neat piles of bills festooning the room and wondered all over again how he ever found the time for such profligacy. Emma Costello still bent diligently over the tablet, recording each bill in her rather fine handwriting. Every now and then she rubbed her eyes and seemed to sag a bit, but she kept at the work with no complaints.

They had indulged in several lively arguments throughout the interminable evening, and rather than resenting it, he found himself enjoying the spirited exchanges. As much as he disliked the Irish, he had to admit that Emma's native wit kept him on his toes. He came away bruised from at least one sharp encounter but invigorated by the intensity. He realized how few witty people he knew. His mother was charm itself, but her conversation had developed a predictability that made him yawn. And Fae Moullé? He glanced at Emma, writing and trying to stay awake. Fae wouldn't recognize a clever turn of phrase if it bit her on the bottom.

Their worst argument of the evening had come about because of Fae. After having sorted out a sizable collection of bills from modistes, chocolatiers, and glove makers, Emma had finally stared at him and waved the invoices in his face.

"My lord, are you aware that Miss Moullé must have enough gloves to outfit a small army?" she burst out, as though each glove paraded across the desk. "And what can she possibly do with all this perfume?"

"I hardly think that my mistress is any of your business," he snapped, perching on the edge of the desk. He thought he had spoken in the tone that usually quelled servants, but what with the late hour, he must have been mistaken. Emma rode right over his comment as if he had remained silent.

"Actually, I believe she is my business, if reformation

is our topic, my lord," Emma replied. "What are you, sir? Twenty-nine? Thirty?"

"I am thirty," he replied, wondering down what path she was leading him. "Your age, at least," he added to goad her.

She only grinned at him as though he did not know how to argue. Since it was the first time she had smiled, he over-looked the familiarity of it.

"Good try, my lord," she said. "You are thirty, then?"

He nodded, making sure that he did not smile, even though he wanted to.

"Would you agree with your mother that it is high time you set up your nursery?"

He nodded again, less eager. "So she tells me."

Emma folded her hands in her lap. "You stand a better chance of attracting someone proper if you discard your mis-tress. Just personally speaking, I would never marry some-one with a mistress. It smacks of the grossest hypocrisy."

"My wife wouldn't have to know," he hedged, thinking about Fae and those charms that she had perfected to a fine art. Of late, he had started to find her boring, but there was no need for Emma to know that. "I would keep Fae a secret."

"Then you must be planning to marry someone really stupid, Lord Ragsdale," Emma murmured. "And who's to say your children will have any intelligence whatsoever if there aren't brains on at least one side of your family?"

"Your impertinence knows no bounds, Emma!" he shouted. "Does reformation mean I must give up *everything* that is fun?"

Emma was silent for a moment, contemplating him. He almost made the mistake of taking her silence for acquies-cence but decided that might be premature. *Now what, you baggage?* he thought.

"I am sure you will correct me if I am wrong, my lord, but I don't really think you are having any fun."

If his Irish servant had been a barrister in a wig and gown, she could not have trussed him up more neatly. He stared at her and then down at the bills in his hand. He was at a total loss for words. In a moment she returned her attention to the list in front of her and continued with the entries, unconscious of the fact that he was opening and closing his mouth like a fish.

He watched her, noting how her rich auburn hair was coming loose from the knot she wore it in, and how her eyes closed occasionally. *You slept on the stairs last night,* he thought, *and I was glad. That was a bit churlish of me, no matter how pointed my dislike. And yes, yes, you are quite right, although I will never tell you. I'm not having much fun these days.*

"You think I should give up Fae?" he asked, keeping his voice offhand.

Emma nodded and rubbed her eyes.

"I'll consider it," he said. "Go to bed, Emma. You're about nine-tenths worthless right now."

She left the room without another comment. He sat down in the chair she had vacated and looked at her neat list and the column of money owed. He totaled it up in his head, going from page to page, all the while thinking of David Breedlow, chained to the wall in Newgate. *I could have loaned him twenty pounds,* he thought. *I could have concerned myself with his family's trials. I could have behaved as my father would have behaved. Why didn't I?*

He yanked off his eye patch and threw it on the desk, rubbing his forehead. "Blast the Irish," he said, remembering his last view of his father before he stumbled, fell back, and disappeared in a clatter of pikes and swords. "And blast you, Emma Costello, you and all your murderous Irish relations."

Lord Ragsdale went to bed, longing for at least a glass of sherry, and determined to throw a boot at Emma if she tried to bother him before noon. To his dismay, he woke up at nine, alert, hungry, and ready to go another round with Emma Costello. Hanley, who seemed to have appointed himself valet, brought him tea and stayed to help him shave and dress. He smelled ham and bacon and followed his nose to the breakfast room, where his mother and cousin were just finishing.

Lady Ragsdale looked at him in amazement and then took out her little pocket watch and tapped it. "Are you just coming in, John?" she asked finally as he filled a plate from the sideboard.

Lord Ragsdale had the good grace to laugh. "Mama, you know I am not! I think everyone ought to eat breakfast occasionally." He peered at the scrambled eggs and found that they did not disgust him. "So chickens still lay eggs?"

Lady Ragsdale laughed. "How clever of them!" She glanced at Sally. "My dear, perhaps we can importune your cousin into escorting us to the modiste for a male opinion as we attempt a wardrobe for you."

Oh, please, not that, he thought as he took a bite of scrambled eggs. He wanted to chew awhile and give himself time to think up an excuse, but eggs did not require that sort of exertion. To his relief, Emma came to his rescue yet again. He swallowed and smiled at his mother.

"My dear, you will think me a dreadful put-off, but Emma and I must visit the bank today. You should see how neatly she has the bills organized."

To his relief, his mother did not press the matter. "Very well, son, we will excuse you again." She looked at her niece. "Come, Sally, let us see what damage we can do by ourselves. Our bills will be yours, John, so if you wish an opinion on how we spend your money, this is your last chance."

Lord Ragsdale finished his eggs and waved his hand in a generous gesture. "Just give the bills to Emma when they come in. I'm sure she will have a file for everything." He took a sip of tea as his mother rose from the table. "Mama, you can do something for me at the modiste's."

His mother turned wary eyes in his direction, and he thought again about Emma's advice that he discard his mistress. "Could you order a warm cloak for Emma? Make it dark brown and serviceable. No telling when spring will actually arrive this year."

"A fur collar? Silk frogs?" his mama teased.

Mama, if you had seen her shivering in Newgate, you wouldn't quiz me, he considered thoughtfully. "Oh, no. The key word is serviceable. Now that I think of it, perhaps a wool dress too. Something with a lace collar." He glanced at Sally, who was regarding him with astonishment. "She's about your size, isn't she, my dear?"

Sally nodded, too surprised at his unexpected generosity to speak.

"Well, there's your template, Mama. Cousin, if you don't mind the observation, she's a bit thinner in the waist and shorter by an inch or two. Make that two dresses, Mama. A secretary ought to have a change of clothing."

He was still smiling as his mother left the room. *I should have asked her to pick out a bonnet too,* he thought. *Careless of me. I wonder if Fae could be induced to part with some of those gloves I have been buying for her. I mean, a body only has two hands.* He got up for another cinnamon bun and stood eating it by the sideboard. *No, no. Too much at once might make Emma think I had declared a truce or something. She can do without gloves and bonnet.*

Feeling pleasantly full, Lord Ragsdale strolled to the book room, where Emma was gathering the bound bills into a satchel.

She looked up and smiled at him.

"Good morning, sir," she said and continued her business. "If we get these to the bank and straighten out your affairs, I promise not to bother you for the rest of the day."

He raised his eyebrows at her and helped pack the bills.

"Emma, why the magnanimity? Can it be that you have a heart?"

"Of course I do," she replied promptly. "I also intend to retrieve your balance books from the banker and spend the afternoon making entries." She closed the satchel.

"I have a better idea," he said, taking the satchel from her. "I want you to visit Fae Moullé and see how the wind blows."

"My lord!" she exclaimed, unable to hide her dismay.

Aha, he thought, *I surprised you*. He waited a moment until he was sure he would not smile and then continued. "I have been thinking about what you said. Perhaps it is time she and I ended our arrangement. I want you to see what terms would be agreeable. It is your duty as my secretary," he added, when that now-familiar obstinate expression settled on her face.

"Very well, my lord," Emma said, and the doubt in her voice made him want to shout, "Got you!" He did not. Just the knowledge that he had ruffled her equanimity was pleasure enough for the moment.

"I will probably spend this evening at Almack's with my mother and cousin," he said as they drove to Fotherby and Sons in his curricle. "I should be an occasional escort, and besides, I must contemplate this Season's beauties." He nudged her in the side. "Tell me, Emma, how can I pick out a smart one?"

To his delight, she laughed out loud. She had a hearty laugh, and it startled him at first, because it was something he was not used to. It was no drawing room titter, no giggle behind a fan, but a full, rich sound as genuine as it was infectious. He laughed too.

"I have it, Emma," he said. "I will begin reciting a Pythagorean theorem and see if she can complete it."

She laughed again. "Then a canto from *La Divina Commedia*, my lord."

He reined his horse to a stop in front of his banking establishment. "Emma, there's obviously more to you than meets the eye."

He wished he had not said that. He might have slapped her, for all the gaiety left her eyes and that invisible curtain dropped between them again. She looked again like a woman devoid of all hope, the Emma of the taproom, waiting for her future to be decided by the turn of a card. It was a transformation as curious as her good humor only moments ago.

She said nothing more but stared straight ahead between his horse's ears. As he watched her, she drew her cloak tighter around her, sighed, and then reached for the satchel at her feet. He took it from her.

You could talk to me, Emma, he thought as he followed her into the building and then led the way down the hall to Amos Fotherby's office. *While it is a well-documented fact that I have no love for the Irish, you interest me. And while it is also certain that there is less to me than meets the eye, that is not the truth, in your case.*

Fotherby quickly recovered from his initial surprise when Lord Ragsdale introduced Emma, and the banker realized that she knew her way around a double-entry ledger. The banker's reserve melted further when Emma pulled up her chair, pushed up her sleeves in businesslike fashion, and pulled out the bills and her list. Fotherby hardly glanced up as Lord Ragsdale backed out of the room.

"I'll be in the vault, Emma," he said. "Join me there when you're done. I need an opinion."

She nodded, as preoccupied as the banker. Lord Ragsdale smiled to himself, thanking a generous God that there were people on the earth who actually cared about assets, debits, and accountings. He watched her a moment more, wishing he had asked his mother to get Emma a deep green cloak instead of a brown one, and then sauntered down the hall to the vault.

Emma joined him there an hour later, her glorious auburn hair untidy. He noted that it was coming loose again, and he chuckled.

"Emma, do you realize that when you concentrate, you tug at your hair?"

She blushed and tucked the stray tendrils under the knot again. "Your accounts were such a mess, my lord. Some tradesmen have applied to Mr. Fotherby for payment, and we had to go through the whole lot, so as not to pay anyone twice."

"I trust you have me in order now?"

"Oh, yes. From now on, you give all the bills to me, and I forward them to Mr. Fotherby for payment. I cannot get power of attorney to pay your bills myself because I am a woman, Catholic, and Irish." She ticked off the items on her fingers.

"I call that downright prejudiced," he joked.

"Well, at least it is more misdemeanors than the law allows," she agreed. "I am not sure which of the three is the least palatable."

There was no regret in her voice but only that businesslike tone that gave him the distinct impression that he had cast himself into capable hands. She had a relaxed air about her, as though she had just come from a hot bath or an entertaining party. *I suppose it is given to some to bask in the toils of finance*, he thought. He indicated a chair.

"Be seated, Emma, and tell me which necklace I should give to Fae," he ordered. "I thought a peace offering would be in order when you visit her." He looked away and coughed. "A bauble might make her not suffer so much when I cut the connection."

He held out several necklaces and placed them in her lap. She scrutinized them with the same intensity she had tackled his bills, and then picked up a simple chain with an emerald. "This one, by all means," she said, her eyes shining with more animation than he had seen before.

As Emma held it up to catch the vault's fitful light, he was struck by how elegant it would look around her neck. The stone winked at him as he took it from her hand and replaced it in the velvet-lined box.

"No, Emma, that one will never do. Think in terms of greed and avarice, and then choose between these three," he said, struck by the knowledge that he was about to come to the end of five years of Fae Moullé's demands. *Greed and avarice? Now, why did I never see that before,* he asked himself as Emma frowned and picked up a particularly gaudy chain with diamonds and rubies alternating.

"Excellent!" He put the rest back in the box and returned them to the teller, who hovered at his elbow. He slid the necklace into a velvet pouch and handed it to Emma. "Take this to Fae with my compliments and see if you can figure out how the deuce to get her to let go of my purse strings." He sighed. "I know she is attached to me, but as you say, it is time to reform."

"Very well, my lord," Emma said. As the teller was replacing the jewels, she picked up a plain gold chain. "Is this valuable to you, Lord Ragsdale?" she asked.

"No. Do you want it, Emma?" he teased.

She shook her head, blushed, and took a deep breath. "If you were to send this to the governor at Newgate, he would make David Breedlow's life almost pleasant." She looked at him, as if gauging his mood. "Or you could send it to his sister. He told me her name is Mary Roney, and she lives in Market Quavers."

He snatched the necklace from her and replaced it in the box, wondering at her nerve. "No, and that is final! You have stretched my philanthropy far enough for one day. Now, just go home and reconcile my books," he ordered. "You can see Fae in the morning."

She left hurriedly, as though afraid he would turn her impulsive effort into a humiliation. When she was gone, he took out the necklace again, and another one, which he handed to the teller. "Make up two packages. Address this one to the governor of Newgate and this to Mary Roney," he said. "I will write a note for both in Fotherby's office."

So there, Emma, he thought. *I really am a fine fellow. I only hope Fae does not repine too long over the news you bring.*

Chapter 9

*J*F ANYTHING, IT WAS COLDER THE NEXT morning when Emma left the house on Curzon Street. *Where is spring?* she wondered as the wind whipped around her dress and exposed her ankles, much to the noisy appreciation of a road crew replacing some curbing. She tugged her cloak tighter, grateful at least that the stench of Newgate was fading from the fabric. Even the scullery maid, no stickler for cleanliness, had insisted that she leave it outside the room the two of them grudgingly shared.

Emma hurried along, convinced that her earlier visit to Newgate was a pleasant excursion compared to this task before her. "Lord Ragsdale, you should have been drowned at birth to have foisted this assignment on me," she muttered. It was one thing to go to prison for him; it was quite another to initiate his dirty work in sloughing off a mistress. *Duties of a secretary, indeed,* she thought. *What it really smacks of is the most monumental bit of laziness imaginable, and so I should tell you to your face, Lord Ragsdale.*

She felt in her reticule for the necklace, wondering at the bad taste of someone to wear such a bauble. Satisfied that no leprechaun had spirited away the necklace, she kept her head down and turned into the wind on Fortnam Street. *No, I shall not scold you, Lord Ragsdale, although you richly deserve it*, she thought. *Not now, at least, when we seem to have declared a truce of sorts.*

Last evening spent with Lord Ragsdale in the book room was more pleasant than she had any hope to expect. To begin, when he had requested that Lasker bring him dinner on a tray, the marquess did not eat in front of her but shared his meal. It had been so long since she had eaten food of that quality that she could hardly force it down at first. Not until Lord Ragsdale looked at her and remarked, "Really, Emma, if you're thinking about smuggling this rather remarkable loin of beef to my miserable former secretary in Newgate, I don't think you could get it past the matron."

I suppose I was thinking about Mr. Breedlow, she reflected as she blushed and took some food on her plate. She chewed the tenderloin thoughtfully, amazed that Lord Ragsdale cared even the slightest what she was thinking.

He had been silent then, his long legs propped up on the desk, the plate resting on his stomach, concentrating on his dinner. *Actually*, Emma considered as she watched him, *you should dress in a toga and recline.* His profile was strong, and while his nose was not Roman, there was something patrician about the whole effect that impressed her. She smiled to herself and looked away, thinking, *If I can be impressed by Lord Ragsdale, when I have seen him blasted by an evening's liquor, I suppose anything is possible.*

"Do I amuse you, Emma?" he had asked.

She looked up, startled at first and then relieved to notice something approaching a twinkle in his eye. *Only candor will do*, she thought as he waited for her reply.

"In a way, I suppose you do, my lord," she replied, crossing her fingers and hoping that her own assessment of his character was not misplaced. "Only think how far you have come from yesterday morning, my lord. Reformation agrees with you."

There, now, make something of that, she dared and took another bite.

"Perhaps it does," he agreed, setting his plate aside but not moving from his relaxed position at the desk. "I have, only this day, forsaken liquor and my club. I have advanced some coins to feed my worthless secretary and plan to discard my mistress tomorrow. Next you will tell me that I must go to church, stop gambling, give up the occasional cigar, and take in stray dogs."

Emma laughed. "All of the above, my lord."

He pulled out his watch and stared at it. "And this time next week, we will go to Hyde Park, and you can watch me walk on water! Come, Emma, to the books. I want to get to bed early so I can be fresh enough in the morning to find more ways to torment you."

And so you have, Emma thought as she hurried along the street. *I am to go to your mistress and find a way to diplomatically ease your useless carcass out of her life. Oh, dear, I hope there isn't a scene. How does one do this?*

She looked at the direction Lord Ragsdale had written down for her, and to her dismay, the narrow house—one of a row of elegant houses—was precisely where he said it would be. *Did you think it would blow away?* she scolded herself as she took one last look at the address, then raised her hand to the knocker.

The woman who opened the door was obviously the maid. She started to curtsy to Emma, then stopped when she took a good look at her shabby cloak and broken shoes.

"Servant's entrance is through the alley behind," she said and started to close the door.

Emma stuck her foot in the door. "I come from Lord Ragsdale," she said, leaning into the crack that still remained open. "I have something for Fae Moullé."

"Miss Moullé to you," snapped the maid. She left the door and returned in a moment. Standing behind her was an overblown woman with hair of a shade not precisely found in nature. She had large blue eyes and lips of a color that the homely word "red" would not do justice to.

Emma moved her foot from the door and suppressed the urge to laugh. *Goodness, Lord Ragsdale*, she thought, *you really are in need of reformation if this is your idea of beauty.* She touched the necklace in her reticule again, thinking how well it would suit.

"I am Lord Ragsdale's secretary, and I have something for you from him," she repeated.

"You cannot possibly be his secretary," said the woman who must be Fae. "My lord's secretary is languishing in Newgate, I believe."

She smiled and stuck her hand through the narrowing crack in the door. "Miss Moullé, he won my indenture in a card game, and we have resolved that I am to straighten out his affairs."

Her choice of words almost sent her into whoops, so she turned away and coughed, hoping the hilarity that threatened to consume her would pass. *Now what will appeal to you, Miss Moullé,* she thought as she turned back. She reached into her bag and pulled out the necklace.

"He has commissioned me to bring this to your notice," she said, dangling the gaudy bauble just out of reach.

The door swung open, and Emma felt herself practically sucked inside. The necklace was snatched from her hand at the same moment the maid relieved her of her cloak. In another moment, she found herself arm in arm with Fae Moullé, being propelled into the sitting room as Lord Ragsdale's mistress issued orders for tea, cakes, and more coal for the grate.

As she glanced around the sitting room, it occurred to Emma that Lord Ragsdale did not stint on his mistress. The expensive draperies complemented the costly furniture, which sumptuously set off the deep carpet. She had to consciously force herself not to kick off her shoes and run her bare feet across its softness. Emma suppressed another smile; the only thing that didn't seem to fit in the room was the young man sitting on the sofa.

Fae's shrewd eyes turned a shade anxious as she followed the direction of Emma's gaze.

"Miss . . ."

"Costello," Emma offered.

Fae gestured toward the sofa and its occupant, who appeared poised to bolt the room. "This is my . . . brother," she said.

If this is your brother, then I am the Lord Mayor of London, Emma thought as she nodded to the young man. "Delighted," she said. "How fortunate for Miss Moullé to have relatives in the city."

A small silence followed that no one seemed to know how to fill. His cheeks flaming the shade of Fae's lip color, the young man leaped to his feet, babbled something about work to do or people to see, and fled the room. Fae watched him go, her face filled with a longing that disappeared as soon as she fingered the necklace.

"How kind of Lord Ragsdale to take such good care of me," she said, her French accent more pronounced. "Do sit down, Miss Costello, and here is the tea."

Emma sat in the chair closest to the fire, accepted the tea, and leaned back to bask for a moment in the wages of a sinful life. *Mama would be shocked if she could see me in the love nest of a debaucher,* she thought. *I wonder where Fae keeps all those gloves,* she considered next as she watched the woman scrutinize the necklace with the practiced air of a gem merchant. *I wonder she does not put a jeweler's loupe to her eye,* Emma considered. She sighed and reached for a macaroon, and then another. *It will not be easy to pry Fae Moullé away from these particular fleshpots. I know I would not give up such luxury willingly.* She waited for Fae to speak, hoping to take some cue from her words.

"Miss Costello, you say he won your indenture in a card game?" Fae was asking. "I can't imagine Lord Ragsdale doing anything that smacked of exertion, and card games can be rigorous affairs."

"It is true," Emma replied, wondering at a female so lazy that she thought cards a challenge. *How fitting for Lord Ragsdale,* she concluded. "But really, I think he is not the idle man you believe him to be."

She stopped, macaroon in hand, and wondered why she was defending Lord Ragsdale. *How odd,* she thought as she popped it in her mouth.

"Oh, he is lazy," Fae countered, leaping to her feet and taking a quick turn about the room. "He usually comes here to sleep off the exertion of an evening at White's." She paused delicately, then plunged ahead. "At least, that is all he has come for lately. I mean, he won't even exert himself to . . ."

"I think I understand," Emma interrupted hastily, her cheeks red.

Fae Moullé only nodded and took another circuit of the room, looking out the window as though she expected to see the young man outside on the street. "Sometimes he is so neglectful that I have to invite my . . . brother to keep me company."

You know I do not believe you, Emma thought as she nodded.

"Brothers can be a wonderful diversion," she said, preserving the fiction. She thought of her own brothers then, both the quick and the dead, and pushed aside the remains of the macaroon plate. She took another sip of tea and looked Fae in the eye. "I have come to negotiate with you, Miss Moullé," she began. "Let us first clear up some questions."

⌒

She left Miss Moullé's establishment as it was growing dark, a smile on her face and her stomach too full of macaroons. *What a turn I have done you, Lord Ragsdale,* she thought as she hurried along, hoping to beat the rainstorm that threatened. *Indeed, it is a pity that I could never study for the diplomatic corps. With scarcely the smallest difficulty, I have rid "Your Mightiness" of a mistress and managed to cheat you soundly in the bargain. Who would have thought the day to have had such promise when it began? I know I did not.*

It wasn't the sort of deception that would see her to Newgate, irons, and a berth to Australia. She had merely hinted to Fae that Lord Ragsdale was beginning to suspect that his loving light-skirt was playing a deep game. Fae had squeezed out some noisy tears and just the threat of a spasm, until Emma assured her that Lord Ragsdale had nothing more substantial than suspicions.

She knew that she could have told Fae that it was all over, and Lord Ragsdale's mistress would gladly have packed her bags and let it go at that, relieved that he had not discovered her other male visitors and made an ugly scene. There wasn't any need for Lord Ragsdale to spend another penny. But since he had many such pennies, Emma smiled inwardly and plunged ahead, content to fulfill his request to the letter of the law.

"Miss Moullé, Lord Ragsdale has authorized me to suggest to you that he would not be too unhappy if you left his employ," she said. "In fact, he is willing to make you an offer . . ." She paused, and coughed slightly. ". . . an offer to make up for the sadness such a parting will cause you."

Fae was fanning herself vigorously, despite the slight chill in the room. Her blonde curls fluttered from the effort. "Oh, I am not sorry!" she burst out, then stopped and considered what Emma was saying. Her eyes took on a more melancholy expression, her shoulders drooped, and she assumed such an air of wounded pride that Emma wanted to applaud the performance. "Perhaps I am a *little* sorry," she amended. "After all, five years of my life . . . What, uh, kind of offer did he have in mind?"

Emma looked beyond Fae as though studying the wall. "He told me he felt honor-bound to provide for you in some way, Miss Moullé." She folded her hands in her lap. "I suppose that is your decision. He especially wanted me to ask you what would make you the happiest."

Fae leaned forward and rested her elbows on her knees in a most unladylike posture. She stared into the grating, where the flames leaped about. Fae was silent so long that Emma wondered if she had drifted off to sleep. Emma was about to nudge her, when Fae looked at her, her practiced melancholy replaced with glee.

"I have it!" she exclaimed. "Tell your master that I want to open my own millinery shop in Bath."

"My, that will be expensive," Emma exclaimed, unable to keep the admiration from her voice. "Think what the inventory will cost, and the expense of a shop and probably living quarters."

"Of course I will need living quarters," Fae agreed, getting up with a decisive motion to stand by the fireplace. "And nothing paltry. After all, I am used to Half Moon Street, am I not? And who can make a success of such an establishment unless it is in the most forward part of town?"

"Oh, indeed," Emma replied. "After all, Bath is not a town for nipfarthing ways, or so I am told." She shook her head, aiming for the right degree of doubt. "This is an expensive proposition, indeed."

Fae rose to the bait. "Do you think it is too much?" she asked anxiously.

"I am sure there is nothing Lord Ragsdale would not do, no lengths to which he would not go, to make sure that your leaving is a pleasant experience," Emma said. *Did I actually say that?* she asked herself, knowing that she was spreading around as much fiction as Fae herself. And Fae knew it too. Emma could tell by the unholy look that came into the woman's eyes.

They looked at each other for another moment, then both burst into laughter. The next few moments were taken up with the most delicious merriment. It seemed to swell from the soles of Emma's feet upward. She laughed until her sides ached and then lay back in the chair, exhausted with the pleasure of such tomfoolery. The maid even stuck her head in the room's entrance, but Fae waved her away, then surrendered to a fresh spasm of jollity, at Lord Ragsdale's expense.

Fae was the first to recover her voice. "Miss Costello, that was outrageous."

"Yes, wasn't it?" Emma replied, wiping her eyes with her sleeve. "But now you wish to . . . uh, change professions?" she prompted.

Fae relaxed again and looked up from the carpet, which she had been contemplating. "I don't see a future in this one, especially if other men are like John Staples," she said simply. "And I fear they are." She met Emma's eyes then. "And I know how to make hats! Let me show you what I can do."

Emma spent the next hour in Fae's chamber, admiring the woman's dash and flair with bonnet trimming. "I buy the best from the shops here."

"I've seen the bills," Emma interjected.

Fae chuckled. "Then I rearrange them to suit myself," she explained. "A ribbon here, a bit of trim there." She placed a high-brimmed chip-straw bonnet on Emma's head and tied the green satin bow under her ear. "There now. See what I mean?"

Emma looked in the mirror, delighted with Fae's efforts. "It makes my eyes so green," she marveled, turning this way and that for the full effect and trying to remember when she had last worn a hat. She took it off reluctantly. "I know that you will manage very well in Bath, and so, I will tell Lord Ragsdale."

Fae hugged her. "Bless you. If Lord Ragsdale had sent that sourpuss David Breedlow, I'm sure I would have gotten my walking papers and nothing more." She frowned at Emma's expression. "But I hear that he is soon to be transported, and one shouldn't speak ill of the dead."

Emma shuddered. "Just because he is going to Australia does not mean that he is numbered among the dead!" she burst out, freeing herself from Fae's embrace. She was immediately ashamed of the ferocity of her outburst. *What must you think?* she asked herself, embarrassed in turn by the look of surprise on Fae's well-fed face. *I must not cry*, she thought next. *What will Fae think?*

But Fae only looked at her and took her by the shoulders again.

"So that's how it is?" she asked softly. "Bah, these English! Sometimes I think the guillotine is more merciful. Oh, Miss Costello, do let us soak this Englishman for all we can. It is a revenge of sorts."

It was easy then to dry her tears on one of Fae's wonderful rose-scented handkerchiefs, eat a few more macaroons, and then put her head together with Lord Ragsdale's mistress to create a list of necessities for the proposed shop. When Emma finally left the house with a kiss and a wave of her hand, she was wearing one of Fae's many pairs of kidskin gloves and clutching a precise account of Fae's demands. *While it will not choke you, Lord Ragsdale*, she thought as she hurried along, *it will give some satisfaction to two powerless women. Fae will have a future, and I will have . . . what?*

The rain began before she reached Curzon Street, but she tucked the list down the front of her dress to keep it dry. She knew that Lord Ragsdale would swallow Fae's demands and count himself lucky to be so easily rid of her. He would buy his horses, spend his money, and probably take another mistress later, after he was married. She stood stock-still in the rain, fully aware that John Staples represented everything that she hated about the English. *I cannot go back in that house*, she thought. *But I must. I owe him at least my services until this indenture is paid off.*

She went up the front steps slowly, dreading the people inside, the silence of the servants' hall when she appeared for dinner, the cold room she shared with a most reluctant scullery maid. She stood on the steps, unwilling to raise her hand to the knocker as she thought again for the thousandth time of the events of that last dreadful day in Wicklow. The weather had been like this, only she had been on the other side of the window glass, watching a solitary figure approaching her father's house. "And I let you in," she said, her hand on the knocker. "Oh, I wish I had not, for all that you were Robert Emmet." She spit out the name as though it was a bad taste. "Ireland's hero. Why, why did I do it? Why?"

The door swung open then, and she gasped out loud. Lord Ragsdale stood there in his shirtsleeves, staring back at her. When she did not move, he took her by the arm and pulled her inside.

"I saw you from the upstairs window, you silly nod," he scolded. "Don't you have door knockers in peat bogs? Really, Emma."

She wished her face did not look so bleak. She shook herself free of him, wishing she could just bolt the hallway and leave him standing there. She could only shiver and look him in the eye, daring him to say anything else.

"We had a door knocker," she said simply.

She didn't know what it was about her words, but he touched her arm again. "Emma, what's wrong?" he asked, bending closer to look into her face.

Startled, she looked at him. *Can you possibly care?* she thought first, wild to tell him, wild to tell anyone, wanting to talk out her misery until it didn't hurt anymore. Perhaps when it had all been said, he could help her. She opened her mouth to speak when Lady Ragsdale's voice came lightly from the sitting room.

"Johnny, are you ready yet? You promised."

Emma closed her mouth. *That was close,* she thought. *I almost wasted my breath telling my story to someone who would only shrug when I had finished. Thank you, Lady Ragsdale, for reminding me that this is my burden alone.* She took a deep breath and pulled Fae's list from the front of her dress.

"Miss Moullé offered these conditions, my lord."

Lord Ragsdale took them from her. "That's not what you were about to say," he commented, his voice mild as he scanned the list.

"No, but it will do," she replied candidly. "We had a rational conversation, and I presented your offer, and asked her what would make her the happiest."

She started down the hall toward the stairs that would take her belowstairs. The marquess sauntered along beside her. "And she decided that a hat shop would do. Women are strange, Emma."

"No stranger than men, my lord," she said without thinking.

He laughed. "I have it on good authority that men are simple."

"Whoever told you that has cotton wadding for brains."

"It was Fae, dear Fae, Fae with the round eyes and cotton stuffing for brains." He took her arm. "Well, tell me: what would make *you* happy?"

Locating my father and brother, she thought, *but I don't want you to know that.* She thought a moment, standing there with the rain dripping off her. "I would like a bed of my own and a chance to hear Mass." *There now. Make something of that.*

Lord Ragsdale nodded. "Too bad you were not my mistress, Emma. Think of the savings to me!"

"My lord!"

He laughed and held his hands to his face as though to ward off a blow. "Just kidding. I'd as lief kiss the devil as you, Emma."

So would I, she thought. "Now remember, sir, you are to become a model of deportment, if we are to proceed with your reformation," she said instead.

"Of course, Emma, how can I forget?" he murmured, and then grimaced. "And now I must gird up my loins—so to speak—and accompany my mother and cousin to Almack's." He sighed.

"... Where you will find any number of unexceptionable young ladies to choose among," she said. "One of them may even like you."

"Emma, I don't even know what I want in a wife," he protested.

"Johnny! You have progressed no farther than your shirt and breeches?" his mother said, coming from the sitting room and starting purposefully toward him down the hall.

"Emma distracted me," he hedged. "There she was, shivering on the front step, with no idea how to use a door knocker, bless her black Irish heart. What could I do but let her in?"

"Wretch," Emma whispered under her breath. To her amusement, he leaned toward her and cupped his hand around his ear.

"Hmm? Hmm?"

She continued toward the servants' stairs, and so did the marquess. "Emma, get me up by ten tomorrow morning," he ordered. "We need to discuss what I should be looking for in a wife, and I want to sign this list of Fae's over to you so my banker can deal with it."

She curtsied as Lady Ragsdale bore down on them and took her son by the arm. She shrieked when he flipped his eye patch up and grinned at her. "Mama, should I leave this off tonight or wear it? It's not fashionable."

Lady Ragsdale looked at Emma, who was struggling not to laugh. "Don't encourage him, Emma," she scolded. "Johnny, you would try a saint! Come along now, before I lose all patience."

Lord Ragsdale shuddered elaborately and grinned at Emma as his mother tugged him along the hall. "Tomorrow morning at ten, Emma. Find a tablet and pencil. And by the way, nice gloves."

"Yes, aren't they?" she agreed as she started down the stairs for another evening of cold stares and solitude.

Chapter 10

HE HAD NOT DANCED IN YEARS, SO IT did not greatly surprise Lord Ragsdale that he dreamed about Almack's. It was a pleasant enough dream, even though the sound was magnified and the events speeded up until he woke up dizzy with too much waltz and tepid conversation. He lay there, his hands behind his head, loitering somewhere between half-asleep and full-awake, reflecting that conversation with women was stupid.

"Do be charitable," he scolded himself as he settled more emphatically in the middle of his bed. He considered charity for a brief moment, then abandoned it. Most of the Season's beauties were uncomfortably young, undeniably lovely, and utterly bereft of idea. He did not require a great deal of conversation while dancing; indeed, country-dancing only permitted the occasional passing comment. The waltz was another matter. While he could not deny that he enjoyed gazing down upon the same beautiful bosom for the duration of one dance, dialogue of at least a semi-intelligent nature would have rendered the whole event more pleasant. As it was, he learned a great deal about the weather last night.

He stretched his charity a little farther. *It is entirely possible that I have forgotten the art of conversation. I will have to get Emma's opinion on the matter,* he thought as he yawned and rested his eye again.

He lay there, rubbing his forehead gently, remembering the brief disappointment last night of arriving home to find the book room dark. There was no Emma, sorting through his correspondence now, throwing away the rags and tatters of his disordered life. He had wanted to tell her about the scene in the card room, when Lady Theodosia Maxwell—she of the red-veined nose and towering turban—had accused her meek little husband of cheating at whist and thrashed him with his own walking cane. The young diamond of the first water he had been waltzing with merely tittered behind her gloved hand. Emma would have done such a scene justice with that full-bodied laugh of hers.

He reached for his watch on the night table, impatient for Emma to appear. The upstairs maid had already delivered the morning coal and the brass can of hot water. He had already convinced Hanley that he did not need help shaving and dressing. It remained for Emma to deliver his morning tea and furnish him with some good reason to rise.

Ah, there it was. She had a firm knock, which he preferred to the scratching of most servants.

"You're late, Emma," he said to the closed door.

"Your watch is fast," she countered and opened the door. "Besides that, the postman was late, and I had to sort your mail." She came closer to the bed and set the tea tray across his lap. "Look here, my lord. You are even getting invitations to places that Lady Ragsdale assures me are quite respectable."

He looked at her and grimaced. "Emma. I am already tired of orgeat and bad whist, and that was just my first visit to Almack's!"

She went to the window and flung open the draperies. "What you are is bored, my lord," she said, her tone firm. "I do not know what I can do about that. I would wish that you had an occupation, because you appear—somewhere under your lassitude—to have a great deal of energy."

He grinned and took a sip of tea. Ah. Just the way he liked it.

"Emma, you are the only person I know who can compliment and condemn in the same sentence. Is this an Irish characteristic?"

It was her turn to look thoughtful. "I suppose it is, my lord."

He wanted to tease her some more, because he liked the animation that came into her face when he challenged her with words. *I wish that I felt clever in the morning,* he thought, as her demeanor changed and she became all business again. In fact, she was clearing her throat and demanding his attention again.

"My lord, here are your bills outstanding. Please initial them, and I will see that your banker gets them." She pointed to a smaller pile. "Here are invitations. Your mother has already perused them and has indicated with a small check in the corner that these would further Sally's ambitions, and probably your own."

He picked up the one on top and sighed. "Emma, these people are boring, they have an indifferent cook, and their daughter is plain."

Emma was ruffling through the other pile of letters on his tray, ignoring him. Playfully, he slapped her on the wrist with the invitation he held, and she stopped and looked directly at him.

"Then you can study a little patience, not eat so much, and put your patch on your good eye." She handed his eye patch to him. "Put this on, by the way."

He set the patch on the tray. "Does my eye bother you?" he asked, trying to keep his voice casual, and at the same time, wondering why on earth he even cared what she thought. "It bothers my mother."

Emma was pulling out another letter. "Not particularly, my lord," she replied, her voice absentminded. "I've seen worse sights. See here, I really want you to pay attention to this letter, my lord."

He took it from her, filled with a strange new charity. *I*

honestly believe that my eye doesn't bother you, he thought. "I think you just paid me a compliment, Emma," he said.

Mystified, she held out the letter opener. "I cannot imagine what it was then." And there was her dimple finally, that visible expression of humor that gave her face even more character. "I'll make sure that it does not happen again, my lord. Do open that letter. Lady Ragsdale says it is from your bailiff on the Norfolk estate."

He did as he was told and spread out the letter on the tea tray as he took another sip of the cooling drink. It was Manwaring's usual reminder about the state of the crofters' cottages and the necessity for repairs that could not be put off, but which he had managed to avoid for some three years, mainly because it did not interest him.

"Something about new roofs for the crofters," he said, tossing the letter aside.

Emma picked up the letter. "Which are three years overdue, according to your bailiff," she added, glaring at him over the top of the letter. "And now he writes that some of the floors are rotting too, because of this neglect. He wants you to come to Norfolk immediately, my lord."

"Too much trouble," he snapped. "I do not know why the man cannot just attend to it without my presence."

"You landlords are all the same! I am certain Dante intended a special rung in the Inferno for you," Emma raged at him, folding the letter and shoving it in the pocket of her apron.

He stared at her in amazement, then glared back, wondering at her sudden vehemence, more curious than angry. "You think I should go there?" he asked. "To Norfolk, I mean, not Dante's Inferno."

"It is your land, my lord. You should attend to the needs of your people," she said, her voice quieter now, as though she regretted her outburst. She sat down in the chair next to the bed and pulled out the letter again. "You can visit your estate, approve the new roofs, and then at your next dinner party, impress the young lady seated next to you with your benevolence toward your tenants."

She said it so calmly, so factually, that it suddenly became quite clear that Emma Costello despised him. She did not have to express her loathing for his class in her voice or manners; it was amply evident in the matter-of-fact way she reduced any good intention—had he possessed any—to pure calculation.

"And you are disgusted that you must cajole me into doing what I should, eh, Emma?" he asked quietly, interpreting the wooden expression on her face. "I do not need a special rung in the Inferno, because you have already located me there."

He spoke quietly, biting off each word. He did not think she would reply, and she did not; she did not need to. In silence he picked up the eye patch and put it on, feeling strangely as though he was attempting to cover his naked-ness and failing utterly. He had been weighed in the balance and found wanting by a maid who, had she found him bleed-ing by the side of an Irish road, would probably have crossed on the other side. As it was, she must serve him, whether she liked to or not. The shame of it bored into his brain like an awl.

"Go away, Emma," he said quietly, rubbing his forehead. "I'll be ready in an hour, and we will see my banker."

She left without a word or backward glance.

He picked up the tea tray and pulled back to throw it across the room, then changed his mind. Such a stupid ges-ture would only confirm his unsavory character, he con-sidered as he set it on the end of the bed and got up. He shaved and dressed in fifteen minutes, then sat at his desk and read through his correspondence that Emma had sepa-rated for him.

Mama had decreed that he would accompany her and Sally to a boring dinner two blocks over, charades and parlor talk four blocks beyond, and then to a dance for four or five hundred of a distant relative's closest acquaintances. *By all that's holy, this is a paltry existence, and Emma is ever so right. I am lazy and bored and don't know what to do about it.*

Dressed and ready to go, he remained in his room and read over all his letters, penciling notes to Emma, instructing her to write his bailiff and tell him to proceed with repairs. He set aside two invitations that interested him, with directions that Emma respond. He worked his way through the stack, pausing on a letter with a peer's frank. It was from his father's old friend Sir Augustus Barney, whose land marched beside his in Norfolk. He would write a personal letter tonight and advise the old fellow to expect a visit soon. He spent a few minutes in conversation with Lasker, perused the correspondence in the book room, then made it to the breakfast room before the maid removed the ham and eggs.

He ate standing up, looking out the window, wondering if spring would ever put in an appearance this year.

"You'll ruin your digestion, son, if you take your meals standing up," said his mother from the doorway.

He smiled and turned around. "Mama, will you still be scolding me when I am forty or fifty?"

She stood in the doorway with a cloak draped over her arm and blew him a kiss. "If you do not marry, I am certain I will. As it is, I hope you will find a wife who can scold you instead of me."

He shook his head. "It's a heavy business, Mama. I don't think I made much of an impression on anyone last night at Almack's."

She nodded in agreement. "Thank goodness there is an entire Season stretching before you, with ample time for redemption."

He sighed inwardly, dreading the idea. "I am sure you are right, Mama. I am bound to develop a little polish." *Perhaps I can even get my secretary to tolerate me,* he reflected.

Lady Ragsdale came closer and held out the cloak to him. It was brown, quite plain, but heavy. "The first few items have arrived from the modiste. I believe you wanted this for Emma."

He took it from her, pleased with the weight of it. "This is almost warm enough for a London spring that refuses to come." He kissed her cheek. "Thanks, m'dear. Emma and I are off to the banker's again. She is determined to organize me."

Whether she will speak to me during the ride to the City, I cannot tell, he thought as he went to the book room and peered inside.

Emma sat at the desk now, her head bent over the ledger, copying entries. She looked up at his entrance and rose to stand beside the chair, as Breedlow always used to rise when he came into a room. He expected such deference from Breedlow, but coming from Emma, it seemed strangely out of place. *You do not wear servitude well,* he thought as he watched her. *Emma, what were you before you came here?*

He almost asked her outright but stopped himself before he committed that folly. One didn't inquire of servants' personal lives, for it was the one thing they were entitled to keep to themselves. He chose a less dangerous subject.

"I see you found this morning's correspondence," he said, indicating the pile in front of her. "Please be seated, Emma."

"Thank you, my lord," she replied. "I will have a letter to your bailiff ready for your signature this afternoon," she offered.

He came around the desk to look over her shoulder. She knew how to write a letter, he had to admit. Her writing displayed just the proper firmness and tone of command, exceeding even Breedlow's skills. "Sounds about right," he said. "Tell him I'll be there in a few days."

She looked up at him, surprised, then favored him with a slight smile. She made a notation about the letter, then finished her entries in the ledger as he sat on the edge of the desk and watched her. When she blotted the book and then closed it, he held out the cloak to her.

"Here. I can't have my secretary shivering every time the wind shifts."

He noted with a certain unholy glee that she was at a loss for words. *Feeling bad for ragging on me this morning?* he thought to himself as she took the cloak from him. *Blushing a tad from guilt, are we?* he considered as she stood up and draped the cloak over her shoulders.

"Thank you, my lord," she murmured.

"You're quite welcome. Now, please have Hanley burn that rag of yours," he ordered. "It still stinks of Newgate."

She nodded. "It will be burned at once, my lord." She ran her finger over the finely textured wool as though it were satin and smiled at him.

He searched her face for some sign of irritation with him, but there was none at the moment. She was a child with a new present, looking for all the world as though she wanted to hunt for a mirror and twirl herself around in its reflection. *How changeable women are,* he thought. *It's just a cloak, and not a very attractive one, at that, but if it gets me out of the dog-house, so much the better.*

"Are you ready to go to my banker's?" he asked. "I think one more trip ought to be enough to familiarize yourself with the business, and then you can do it alone."

She nodded and put the bills in her reticule, then pulled on the kidskin gloves that must have come from his mistress's collection. A bonnet would have been nice too, something to set off her green eyes and the attractive way her auburn hair curled around her face, but that was beyond his powers of both interest and philanthropy at the moment. Too much largess would only make her suspicious of his intentions, he reckoned.

~

There was a long silence in the carriage as the horses clopped along London's busy streets. He managed a glance at Emma out of the corner of his eye, and she looked as though she was on the edge of comment several times. He realized she was working up to an apology and chuckled inwardly.

She finally came out with it as the coachman slowed the horses in front of the bank. "I am sorry for the way I spoke to you this morning," she said, the words all tumbling out in a breathless rush. "I was inexcusably rude."

He nodded. "You were. It's a bit disconcerting for an Irish chit of no consequence to tell me my business with my tenants. And no one's wished me to blazes lately, except myself. That's not really your department."

She winced but was silent, looking straight ahead as the coachman let down the steps and opened the door. "I'm sorry," she repeated, her voice so low that he had to strain to hear it. "Mama always told me that I should think before I speak."

"Your mama was a wise woman," he agreed. He touched her arm as she leaned forward to take the coachman's hand. "But I should take better care of what is my own, Emma. Let us leave it at that," he finished when they were both on the sidewalk.

She nodded, too shy to speak, then followed him into the bank, staying several steps behind, as a good servant should. He thought he heard her sniff back tears as they passed single file down the long hall. An hour ago, he would have been glad to know that she was crying, but now he just wanted to clap his arm around her shoulders and tell her to forget it. *I can't do that,* he thought. *A little remorse won't hurt the chit.* Instead, he reached inside his overcoat, drew out his handkerchief, and handed it to her behind his back as the porter hurried them along. She blew her nose loudly, and he grinned; not for Emma a dainty dab at the nostrils.

In no time, the matter of Fae Moullé's demands was signed and sealed, with the banker's promise to deliver the draft that afternoon. "Unless you wish to do that in person, my lord," the banker suggested.

"Oh, no!" Lord Ragsdale stated, leaning back in his chair. "I'm through with that one. When Fae vacates the premises, you may tell my real estate agent to rent out the property."

"There, Emma, I am on my way to reformation," he told her when they stood outside the bank again. "I have finally done Fae Moullé a good turn. Soon I will be a pattern card of respectability. Women will swoon for my good report."

He looked sideways at Emma, wondering how to get a rise out of her. She almost said something but changed her mind. "Yes, my lord" was the response she settled on.

"Come, come, Emma," he chided. "You were about to say something much more interesting than 'yes, my lord.'"

The coachman held open the door for them, but Lord Ragsdale stood in front of it. "No ride for you unless you tell me what you were about to say," he ordered, a smile playing around his lips. "Come, come, Emma."

They stood there staring at each other, his arms folded across his chest. She pursed her lips into a straight line, then sighed.

"Oh, very well! I was merely going to suggest that you look rather too piratical ever to be mistaken for a pattern card of respectability." She smiled when she said it, and Lord Ragsdale sighed with relief. *Better and better,* he thought as he helped her into the carriage. *Emma, we have to get along.*

"John, take us to the gallery in Kensington," he said as he climbed inside.

He returned her questioning gaze with a smile. "Emma, you may redeem yourself for all misdemeanors this morning by accompanying me to the art gallery. I have it in my head to invite a young lady I met at Almack's to tour it with me and my cousin Sally, and I had better know where I am going if I do not wish to appear . . . well, overly piratical and uncouth."

She relaxed at his words and nodded. "You can probably purchase a guidebook at the entrance, my lord. If you commit it to memory, then no young lady will ever accuse you of being uncouth, lazy, and bereft of purpose."

He wagged his finger at her, and she blushed. "Emma, mind your own manners! If you ever wish to leave my indenture before you are gray-haired and toothless, you must learn to like me at least a little."

He leaned back in the carriage, satisfied with himself and pleased at the embarrassment on Emma's face. *Now I will deliver the ultimate blow,* he decided. "Emma, I almost forgot to tell you. I spoke with Lasker this morning, and he has arranged for you to move into a room of your own."

"What?" Emma exclaimed, her eyes wide.

He nearly laughed out loud at the look of chagrin on Emma's expressive face. "You'll still have to duck the rafters, but you did say your own bed would make you happy."

He absorbed himself in gazing out the window then, content to let Emma stew in her own juices. He heard her apply herself vigorously to his handkerchief, and his cup ran over with merriment. *Got you, Emma. I dare you to be rude now.*

Chapter 11

HERE IS NO LOGICAL EXPLANATION FOR my desire to visit the art gallery with Emma, Lord Ragsdale thought as the carriage began to move. *I am either a bigger bully than I thought, or I love art beyond my previous recollection.* The initial ride had begun with an ardent desire on his part to get the banking business done and then return Emma to the book room. He never considered himself a man susceptible to female tears, but there was something so oddly touching about Emma's obvious remorse at her mistreatment of him. He hoped she would not mind a visit to the gallery, but he was beginning to find her interesting.

And, he reasoned, there was at least some truth in what he had said to her about wanting to look over the place. He knew he needed to do as his mother and Emma had mandated and find himself a wife. A gallery would be a good place for a quiet tête-à-tête; he would test his theory on Emma. If it proved to be a good place to spark a lady (or at least, in Emma's case, discussion), he would store the knowledge for future reference.

Emma was still struggling with her emotions, so he did not overburden her with conversation. He was content to gaze out the window at the Inns of Court, where several wigged barristers were getting themselves into a carriage for the short ride to the courts of justice. *English law,* he thought, *a noble thing.* He glanced at Emma. She was watching the barristers too, but her expression was a set, hard one, as though she looked upon something distasteful.

"English law," he said out loud, and it sounded inane the moment he uttered it.

"Don't remind me, my lord," she murmured and directed her gaze out the opposite window.

How singular, he thought. *We see the same thing, and yet our estimations are completely different. I wonder if this is because she is a woman or because she is Irish. I suspect it is both,* he concluded.

～

So much silence, he thought as they rode along. He was not a man accustomed to silence. *I have spent too much time in drawing rooms, card rooms, and taverns, where conversation seems obliged.* It was different with Emma, he reasoned. Despite her remorse, she still did not wish to speak to him. *Or could it be that she is shy,* he wondered. *I see Emma as a budding good secretary, but perhaps ours is an odd association. After all, she is female. Indeed she is,* he thought for no good reason, and smiled to himself.

He wanted to ask a penny for her thoughts, and the realization gave him a start. He had never cared what any woman thought before. During his affair with Fae Moullé, never had it entered his head to inquire what was on her mind, because he suspected that nothing was. *My word, how strange this is,* he considered as he settled back in the carriage. *I want to know what this woman is thinking.*

He stared out the window, not seeing anything on the crowded road. *If she is thinking of me, it will not be charitable.* He glanced her way and rubbed his forehead, wondering why it mattered all of a sudden that she change her opinion of him. *She sees me as a dilettante, a drunkard, a rogue, and a wastrel,* he thought, *and she is right. And I am British.* He grinned at his reflection in the glass. *That I cannot change,* *and it may be the only thing that she cares about the most. I wish* *I understood Emma Costello.*

The gallery was bare of sightseers. There was only a cleaning woman, who wasn't dressed much better than Emma. The charwoman looked up from her brush and pail as they skirted around the area she was scrubbing. Lord Ragsdale could tell she was surprised to see someone so obviously a man of consequence with a woman in broken shoes and a plain cloak.

To his chagrin, Emma noticed the look too. "I really don't belong here, my lord," she whispered to him, her face red. "Oh, please . . . I can wait outside."

Serenity, John, serenity, he told himself as he touched her elbow lightly and steered her into his favorite room of the gallery. "Nonsense, Emma. This is a public place, and we are the public. Remember now: I want to bring a young lady here, and you are my trial effort."

That sounds pretty artificial, he thought as he sat her down on a bench; *I wonder if she will buy it.* He glanced at her then, gauging her response, and was relieved to see a brief look of approbation cross her expressive face.

"Oh, excellent, my lord! The sooner you are reformed and at least soundly engaged, the sooner you will be rid of me."

He laughed in spite of his own nervousness. "Emma! Am I that much of a trial? Come now, be fair."

To his relief, she smiled. *I wish you would laugh too,* he thought as he watched her. *Your laughter is almost a balm. Ah, well, not this time. Perhaps another day.* He put his hands behind his back and sauntered over to inspect a painting—it must be a Vermeer—he had not remembered from his last visit several years ago.

All was silence in the gallery; he found himself relaxing in the quiet. *This would be a good place to bring someone special,* he decided as he moved from picture to picture. *The devil of it is, I cannot imagine any eligible lady of my acquaintance remaining quiet long enough to absorb what is here.*

He glanced back at Emma, who remained where she was on the bench, as if afraid to move from where he had put her. He turned to watch her then, folding his arms across his chest and leaning against the wall.

As usual, she paid him no attention. She sat stiff at first, her feet in her poor shoes tucked up under her so they would not show. (*I must see to a cobbler, and when are those promised dresses coming?*) As she stared at the painting opposite her, her shoulders lost their tenseness and her face seemed to soften. She sighed once, and he could hear it across the gallery. Her eyes grew dreamy, and for the first time in their brief acquaintance, the wariness left her expression.

Emma was looking at one of Raphael's numerous madonnas, mellowed, as all his works, by a caressing brush and sweetness of expression on the face of Mary. She smiled at the painting of mother and child, and as he watched, she got up from the bench and stood directly in front of the work. There was no barrier in front of the painting, and she reached out her hand, outlining the child.

So you like children, Emma? he thought, wondering at the same time if he was going to have to spend the rest of their association guessing about her past. Presumably one didn't ask servants their business. *We have already established that you do not like me,* he thought. *I wonder if there is someone you do like. Or someone you love.*

He felt a moment's irrational jealousy, which made him laugh out loud and broke whatever spell Raphael was weaving on Emma Costello. She jumped away from the painting and put her hands behind her back, retreating to the bench, where she sat down again. *Serenity,* he told himself again as he nodded to her and continued his stately pace about the gallery, hoping she would relax enough again to explore the place herself.

She did not. After a half hour, in which he felt his own frustration growing, he returned to the bench and sat down beside her. She edged away from him slightly and moved forward on the bench, ready to bolt as soon as he said the word. He said nothing, wondering if she would speak first. Finally, she cleared her throat.

"You know, my lord, I could be finishing my perusal of your old correspondence right now and starting on that letter to Sir Augustus Barney in Norfolk," she reminded him.

"You could," he agreed. "But isn't it nice just to sit here?"

She did not answer, and he sighed and stood up. She was on her feet in an instant too, but he took her arm before she could move and held her firmly.

"Tell me, Emma. Is this really a good place to squire a young lady?"

He looked into her eyes, and her expression made him drop her arm and step back. He had never seen such terror before, terror that he was responsible for because he had taken her arm. He looked away and gave her time to collect herself, thinking, *So, Emma, you do not care to be grabbed, do you?*

His own mind in turmoil, he merely nodded to her and started to leave the gallery at a slow pace. In a moment, she was walking at his side and slightly behind him. "I didn't mean to startle you, Emma," he said. "Seriously, what do you think? Should I take a young lady here?"

"No, my lord," she replied, and her voice was smooth and in control. "She will want to chatter, and you will want to admire, and it will not speed any wooing you might attempt."

"How well you know your own sex," he murmured as he climbed into his carriage and made no move to help her. "But, Emma, you were silent as the grave in the gallery," he insisted. "How can it be that any young lady I would bring there would be a gabble box?"

She pulled her cloak tighter about her. "My lord, if it were someone who returned your regard, she would want to talk with you, wouldn't she? I mean, I would."

And so you were silent. Touché, Emma, he thought. He let it go at that, leaned back in the carriage, and closed his eyes.

He did not expect another word from her and was even dozing off when Emma spoke.

"Begging your pardon, my lord, but could I ask you something?" she was saying. "It is a favor, in fact."

"Only if you promise that it will not cause me any exertion," he teased.

"Oh, it will not," she assured him seriously, and again he was verbally flogged by her reply.

You think I am in earnest, he wondered. "Say on, Emma," he stated finally when she hesitated.

He thought for a moment she would not speak, after all.

"Well?" he prompted. "Come, come, Emma, you make me fear that it is an outrageous request."

"Oh, no, my lord," she assured him, her expression worried now. "Nothing of the sort. I was merely wondering if you would permit me a day off once a week."

Is that all? he asked himself, but he did not respond.

"I have some business in London," she said quickly when he did not speak. "Please, my lord. It is only once a week. I can see that everything is left in order before I leave." She was pleading now, and he wanted to know what it was she had to do in London.

He almost asked her.

"A half day then, sir? Oh, please," she was asking now, her eyes on his face.

He felt shame then. *I am a churl to make you grovel*, he thought as he sat up straight.

"A day, Emma," he said firmly. "Mr. Breedlow had a day, and it is only fair." He leaned forward. "And when would you like this day?"

"Tomorrow, my lord, if you please," she responded, a little breathless.

"You'll have that letter to Sir Augustus ready?" he temporized. "And another which I shall dictate tonight to my bailiff in Norfolk? I mean to leave in two days."

"Anything, my lord," she said.

"Tomorrow it is," he said, adding, "although I cannot imagine what it is that you would have to do in London."

It was only the tiniest opening, but she did not take it. *Of course she did not,* he told himself, feeling the fool, and a bully in the bargain. *John, you maggot, did you ever quiz David Breedlow about his day off? God knows you should have, in his case, but here is Emma Costello, and she is powerless, harmless, and poor. London is safe from whatever she could possibly be planning.*

"Thank you, my lord," she said, and her gratitude made him wince.

"You're welcome," he grumbled, "although I wonder what evil plans you have afoot." Ah, there. He was rewarded with a smile.

"If you're worried, Lord Ragsdale, you'd better lock up the silverware before I leave your house," she replied, with just the hint of a twinkle in her eye.

"Oh, I do not think it will come to that, Emma," he said as the carriage pulled up in front of the house. He sighed, considering the evening ahead. "Now I must gird my loins for an evening of fine dining and dancing." He helped her from the carriage, careful not to hold her elbow a moment longer than she needed. "I would almost rather stay in the book room with you and consider ledgers and double entries."

"And we all know what a fiction that is," Emma murmured as they walked up the front steps.

He smiled. "It's less of a stretch than you would suppose," he said as he nodded to Lasker, who must have been watching for them out of the peephole in the door. "Emma, it is somewhat daunting to converse with lovely young things on the right and on the left, and across the table, and try not to be too obvious staring at whatever charms they possess. Thank you, Lasker," he said as he relinquished his overcoat. "And then, in turn, I must suffer their sidelong glances as they try to discover if there is any substance beneath my shallow façade."

Emma laughed, and it was the glorious, heartfelt sound he realized he had been craving all day. "Are you saying, my lord, that there is rather less to you than meets the eye?"

He wanted to laugh out loud at the strangling sounds coming from his unflappable butler, who had turned away and with a shaking hand was rearranging a bouquet of flowers. "Well, as to that, I wonder, Emma. I think you are improving me already," he said as they continued down the hall toward the book room. "I have not been near my club, the wine cellar is locked, and Mama is looking on me with less chagrin than normal." He chuckled. "Now if only the young ladies will follow her lead . . ."

"They will, my lord," Emma assured him as she removed her cloak and sat down at the desk. "You need merely to decide what it is you are looking for in a wife, and follow through."

Follow through, is it? he thought as he watched her rummage for pencil and paper. *You are asking that of the man who could not save his own father from a rabble crowd? I wonder if I know how to see anything through to its completion. I was well on the way to my own ruin, but it seems I cannot accomplish even that.*

"My lord?" Emma was asking. "You wanted to dictate a letter to your bailiff in Norfolk?"

"Oh! Yes, yes, I did," he said as he clasped his hands behind his back and strolled to the window. "And you'll have the other one for Sir Augustus ready by the time I return this evening?"

"Of course, my lord."

It was on the tip of his tongue to ask her to call him John, but reason prevailed, and he did not. The letter was too soon dictated, then he had no more excuse to linger in the book room, and must face, instead, the prospect of shaving again, and dressing, and staring in the mirror and wondering what on earth he was doing. *It is not that I dislike women,* he considered as he suffered Hanley to arrange his neckcloth. *Quite the contrary. It's just that I begrudge the exertion I must expend to find a wife. Too bad they do not grow on trees, there for the plucking. Or something like that,* he concluded, grinning to himself.

Sally Claridge looked especially fetching in a pale blue muslin, her blonde hair swept up on her head in a style that earned a second look. He watched her descend the stairs, admired, from his viewpoint, her trim ankles, and idly considered the prospect of an alliance with his Virginia cousin. The quick glance of terror she turned his way before her more well-bred demeanor masked it convinced him that she would not be much fun to sport with. And even if she were, he thought as he helped his mother with her evening cape, sooner or later she would open her mouth and bore him into drunkenness or opium use, whichever came first.

His mother also watched with approval as Sally completed her descent of the stairs. "My dear, how lovely you look tonight!" she exclaimed, kissing her niece on the cheek. "John, only consider how well your guineas look upon Sally's back."

"Yes," he agreed. "Only think how well *we* are spending my money." That ill-advised remark earned him another look of terror from Sally and a cluck of his mother's tongue. "Glad to do it for relatives, glad to do it," he amended, hoping that his evening was not ruined before it started.

Mama was eager to be pleased (perhaps considering her own incursions into his fortune). "Quite right, John. Sally, do you have on your dancing shoes? I hear Lord Renwick has engaged a particularly fine orchestra for tonight."

Shoes. Shoes. That was it. "Excuse me, Mama, Sally. I forgot something in the book room," he said as he hurried down the hall.

Emma Costello looked up in surprise when he opened the book-room door without knocking. "Now, my lord, you are not getting cold feet . . . ," she began, putting down the quill pen.

"No, but you are, Emma," he said. "I need two pieces of paper and a pencil." He snapped his fingers and held out his hand for the items, which Emma brought to him. He put the papers on the floor in front of her. "Take off your shoes, Emma."

She hesitated. "Hurry up, now," he admonished, taking the pencil from her. "I don't want to miss a minute of what promises to be an evening of astonishing boredom."

"You are too negative, my lord," she grumbled as she removed her shoes—poor, cast-off things that should have been in an ash can years ago.

"Raise your skirt," he ordered as he knelt on the floor beside her and grasped her ankle.

She gave a noticeable start when he touched her stockinged ankle, then rested her hand lightly on his shoulder to steady herself while he outlined her foot with the pencil.

"Other foot."

She leaned the other way as he held that ankle. *Such a shapely foot*, he thought as he carefully traced it. Not small, he considered, half-enjoying the weight of her against his shoulder. He looked at the papers. "Well, what color do you want?"

"Black or brown; something sensible. And if you please, stockings to match, my lord," she said. She sounded embarrassed at the intimacy of their association, so he did not look at her while she stepped into her shoes again.

"I'm surprised your Virginia indenture holders didn't see that you were better shod," he said as he took the papers and stood up. He looked at her then, and her cheeks were still pink.

"My lord, I think you will understand the matter more completely when you consider that Robert Claridge's bills generally outran the family's entire quarterly allowance," was her quiet reply as she took her seat at the desk again.

He strolled over to sit on the desk, ignoring his mother's voice calling to him from the front entrance. "So you were the afterthought."

"I and the other servants, sir," she said, dipping the quill tip into the ink bottle again. She looked at him in that calculated way of hers, as though gauging his response. "And I have to tell you that I like going barefoot in the summer, so please don't feel sorry for me, Lord Ragsdale."

She turned again to the letter in front of her, effectively dismissing him from his own book room. He grinned at her impertinence and left the room.

Lasker hovered outside the door, obviously sent by Lady Ragsdale to tell him to hurry up but also obviously reluctant to tell him anything. "It's all right, Lasker, I'll go peacefully," he said, pleased with himself to earn one of the butler's rare smiles. "And you take these to wherever it is Lady Ragsdale gets her shoes made. I want one pair of sturdy brown shoes." He started down the hall, then turned back, grinning broadly. "And another pair of red Morocco dancing slippers. Good night, Lasker. You needn't wait up," he added, knowing that the butler would be sitting ramrod straight in one of the entryway chairs until the last titled member of the household was indoors and abed. It was their little fiction.

⌒

Truly enough, there was Lasker waiting for them when they returned in that late hour just before the dark yielded to the blandishments of another day, careering in from the east. He handed his mother and cousin their candles, wished them both good night, and went to the book room, hoping that Emma might still be up. He wanted to tell her about the diamond of the first water—a daughter of Sir Edmund Partridge—who had flirted with him mildly, and who appeared, when he worked up the nerve to converse with her, to have at least some wit. He wanted to tell Emma that he and Clarissa Partridge were destined to witness a balloon ascension—he whipped out his pocket watch—in eight hours.

But the book room was dark. He held his own candle over the desk, where Emma had arranged the letter she had composed for him to Sir Augustus Barney, and the other to his bailiff. He picked up the letter to his bailiff and read it, noting that she had changed some of his dictated wording and added other passages. He read it again and had to admit that her changes were salutary. "Really, Emma," he said out loud as he left the room, "you were supposed to be here so I could tell you about Clarissa Partridge. Do I have to do *everything* in this courting venture?"

Well, it would keep for the morning, he decided as he mounted the stairs. He stopped halfway up. Emma was taking her day off tomorrow, and he would not see her until the evening. *Perhaps I was a little hasty with this day off*, he thought. He continued up the stairs, putting Emma from his mind and wondering what one wore to a balloon ascension.

⁓

While the day could not have been deemed an unqualified success, at least Emma Costello ought to have the decency to hurry back from her day off so he could tell her about it, Lord Ragsdale decided the following evening as he paced back and forth in front of the sitting room window.

He had decided that he would begin by painting a word picture of Miss Partridge for Emma, describing her delicate features, her big brown eyes that reminded him of a favorite spaniel, long dead but still remembered, and her little trill of a laugh. Of course, by the time the balloonists had taken themselves up into the atmosphere, he did have the smallest headache, but he couldn't attribute that to Clarissa's endless stream of questions. He just wasn't accustomed to having someone so small and lovely who smelled of rosewater hanging on his every word and looking at him with those spaniel eyes.

"Emma, you are certainly taking your time with this day off," he muttered under his breath. He was beginning to feel that when Emma finally opened the door, a scold was in order. He would remind her that London was far from safe after dark and that nasty customers liked to prey on unescorted women, especially if they were pretty.

There wasn't anything else he could scold her about. When he had wakened in the morning, his correspondence was ready for his attention on the smaller table in his bedroom. He had signed the letters, initialed the morning's bills, and noted with approval a newspaper article about Norfolk that she had circled to catch his attention. A man never had a better secretary than Emma Costello.

But where the deuce was she now? He clapped his hands together in frustration, imagining her conked on the head and being delivered unconscious to a white slaving ship anchored at Deptford Hard, even as he wore a path from window to window. One would think she would have more consideration for his feelings. That was the trouble with the Irish.

And then he saw her coming up the street, moving slowly, as though she dreaded the house and its occupants. As he watched, she stopped several times, as though steeling herself for the ordeal of entering into one of London's finest establishments.

"The nerve of you," he grumbled from his view by the partially screening curtain. "When I think of the legions of servants who would love to have half so fine a household as this one . . ."

Perhaps I am being unfair, he thought as he kept his eyes on her slow progress. She trudged as though filled with a great exhaustion, discouragement evident in the way she held herself. He thought she dabbed at her eyes several times, but he could not be sure. He waited for her knock, which did not come. *You idiot,* he realized finally, *she has gone around to the alley and come in from the belowstairs entrance.* He rang for Lasker.

"Tell Emma Costello that I would like a word with her," he told the butler.

"I was not aware that a day off meant a night off too," he found himself telling Emma several minutes later when she knocked on the sitting-room door, and he opened it.

She mumbled something about being sorry, and it was a longer walk from the city than she realized.

She looked so discouraged from her day off that he felt like a heel for chiding her. Her eyes were filled with pain that shocked him. He wondered briefly if her feet in those dreadful shoes were hurting her, and then he understood that the look in her eyes was another matter. He stood in front of her, hand behind his back, rocking back and forth on his heels, feeling like a gouty old boyar chastising his serfs.

"I trust this won't happen on your next day off," he ventured, wishing suddenly with all his heart that she would tell him what was the matter.

If he was expecting a soft agreement from her, he was doomed to disappointment. At his sniping words, Emma seemed to visibly gather herself together, digging deep into some well of resource and strength that he knew he did not possess.

"It will probably happen again and again, my lord," she replied, each word distinct, her brogue more pronounced than usual. "Unlike some of us in this room, I do not succumb easily to misfortune."

"Emma Costello, you are impertinent!" he shouted, wondering even as his voice carried throughout the room why he was yelling at someone who did his work so well and who looked so defeated. Miserable and furious in turns, he waited for her to speak.

She took her time, and it occurred to him that she was as surprised as he was by his outburst. The wariness returned to her eyes, and he knew that he had erased whatever meager credit he had accrued in the last day or two. *I am British and you are Irish, and that is it*, he thought as he stared at her.

When she spoke, her voice was soft, and he felt even worse. "I am sorry for any inconvenience I have caused you, my lord."

He could think of none, other than the fact that she had not been there to hear his account of his day with Clarissa Partridge. Had he been a small boy, he would have squirmed.

"Is that all, my lord?" she asked.

Unable to think of anything, he nodded, and she went to the door. She stood there a moment, clutching the handle. "If I were not impertinent, Lord Ragsdale, I would have died five years ago. Good night, sir."

She was gone, the door closed quietly behind her. Filled with that familiar self-loathing that he had hoped was behind him, Lord Ragsdale resumed his pacing at the window. *I have heard this conversation before,* he thought, summoning up images of standing before his father when he returned late and endured the familiar scold that his mama assured him only meant that his father cared enough to worry about him.

He stopped walking and looked at the door again, wishing that Emma would walk back into the room so he could apologize. *Someday when I have sons and daughters, pray God I will remember how I feel right now,* he thought as he leaned against the window frame. Somehow he must make amends to his servant, even though he knew there was nothing he could do.

I would like to help you, Emma, he thought. *How can I convince you that I mean it?* He shook his head and smiled ruefully. *This whole thing begins to smack of profound exertion. I think I am going to be wonderfully ill-used during your tenure here, Emma Costello, drat your Irish hide. I had better find a wife quickly so I can release you from your indenture and be miserable in private.*

He went to the window again, wishing that spring would come. *I need a change right now,* he thought, *something that will sweeten my life.* He considered Clarissa again and smiled into his reflection in the windowpane. "Madam, you are a peach," he said out loud, rejoicing in the fact that he had only yawned a few times during their hours together at the balloon ascension. Tonight he was escorting his mother and cousin to Covent Garden Theatre. With scarcely any effort at all, he could train his glasses on the Partridge box and watch her from a distance.

He resolved to make the Norfolk stay a short one. The place only held ghosts and leaky crofters' cottages anyway. He would point his secretary toward his bailiff and let them do the wrangling. He would pay a brief visit to Sir Augustus Barney, then prop his feet up in front of a comfortable fire and think about Clarissa Partridge. *That ought to make everybody happy,* he thought. *Even Emma will approve,* he told himself, *provided she is speaking to me. I may even be forced to apologize. How unlike me.*

Chapter 12

I THINK I WILL MURDER LORD RAGSDALE, Emma thought to herself as she took off her dress and crawled into bed. She shivered in the cold, wishing for once to be still sharing a bed with the scullery maid. She may have snored, but she at least provided a warm spot. As it was, Emma could only lie there and warm herself with vast ill-usage.

She knew she should be tired. It had been a long, discouraging day, spent standing in the cold entry of the Office of Criminal Business, wondering when it would finally be her turn to speak to Mr. John Henry Capper, Senior Clerk. She sighed again and thumped her pillow soundly, trying to find a soft spot in the old thing. The first problem would be getting past that miserable worm of a porter. Thinking of that dreadful little excuse of a man, she thumped the pillow again.

She thought she had approached his desk with the proper amount of deference that the English seemed to require from the Irish. Her inquiry had been innocent enough; she just wanted a brief interview with Mr. Capper. One of her fellow servants in Virginia had told her that the illustrious John Henry was the man to see, and she had clung to that scrap of information through her own indenture, a dreary return sea voyage, and now incarceration in the household of Lord Ragsdale.

Something in the porter's eye should have warned her that he would stall and stall. Her inquiry had only earned her an elaborate stare, when the porter finally bothered to look up from shuffling the papers in front of him. When he gazed around and saw that no one else was with her, his stare turned into a smirk. "'Ave a seat," he said. "Ye'll 'ave to wait your turn, like everybody else."

And so she had waited all day in the cheerless anteroom, watching others go in before her to complete their business with Mr. John Henry Capper. She sat and fumed for the morning, and then in the afternoon, despair set in. As the shadows lengthened in the room and the cold deepened, she realized that there would be no audience with Mr. Capper that day. Her chances of ever getting past the porter shrank with every minute that passed and every man who secured an appointment before her.

She only left the building because the porter shooed her out and told her he was locking up. Swallowing her pride, Emma managed her broadest smile—the one Papa declared would melt marble—and asked when she might have an audience with Mr. Capper. The porter had looked at her in elaborate surprise, as though he were not aware that she had been the only inhabitant of the anteroom for the last two hours.

"Oh, miss, you're still here? What a pity Mr. Capper could not see you today."

She forced down the angry words that she wanted to shower on him and winked back the tears. "Do you think I could see him next week, sir?" she asked, knowing his answer even before he looked up from his desk many minutes later.

"I am sure you can try," he had replied and favored her with a mocking, superior smile.

By all the saints, she thought, in his better days, her own father would have had that porter whipped for insolence. *And in my better days?* she considered ruefully. *I would never be here alone and unprotected, without my brothers around me.*

I would be home with Mama, and there would be suitors, and I would marry one of them, and life would continue the pattern of centuries. She sat up in bed and hugged the pillow to her, thinking of change and turmoil and wishing with all her heart that she knew—really knew—where her brother and father were.

She lay down again, bunching herself into a little ball to defeat the cold. If all her searching led to a certain knowledge of their deaths, at least she would be sure. She could return to Virginia when this pesky indenture was up, and with Mr. Claridge's blessings probably find some kind of employment in Richmond. Experience had taught her that she could eventually wear down the sorrow until it was a manageable pain.

And if they were alive? She would spare no effort to join them, even if the cold trail, years old, led to a prison in Van Dieman's Land, or dismal servitude in Australia. "Perhaps Australia is not as bad as everyone says," she told herself, relaxing gradually as the moon peered through her window, then moved on. At least it would be warmer than here.

Warmer in many ways. Lord Ragsdale's scold this evening was almost a fitting culmination to a dreadful day, Emma allowed, wondering at the coldness of her reception. She prodded her tired brain, trying to make sense out of his surprising tirade but gave up as sleep finally overtook her.

Morning brought with it the guilty realization that she had overslept and a summons to Lady Ragsdale's chamber. Emma dressed hurriedly, hoping that Lord Ragsdale was still in bed and not looking about for his mail. She hurried, breathless, down the stairs, hoping to snatch up the mail from the table by the door and sort it upstairs after she endured whatever scold Lady Ragsdale had in mind. She scooped up the mail and was hurrying fast for the stairs again when Lord Ragsdale stepped from the breakfast room. He flattened himself in mock surprise against the wall as she hurried past.

"If there is a fire somewhere, Emma, perhaps you should let me in on the secret?" he commented.

She stopped, gritting her teeth and wondering if he was angry still. She looked at him, and to her amazement, he winked. Without even thinking, she smiled back and held out the mail to him.

He took it from her and stayed where he was, leaning against the wall. "I'm sorry I was so beastly yesterday evening, Emma," he said simply. "I was worried about you. The streets are dark, and London's full of ugly customers."

With that, he nodded to her as she stared at him in wonder, and started down the hall, opening a letter as he went. Before she could collect herself, he laughed out loud and turned back to her. "This is too good to keep to myself," he said. "It's from Fae Moullé. She expresses her—it's either gratitude or attitude, or possibly latitude—and declares that when I marry, she will trim a bonnet for the new Lady Ragsdale! I defy anyone to come up with a better offer from a mistress, Emma. What do you think?"

I think I am full of gratitude or attitude myself, she thought, dimpling at the idea of Fae Moullé presenting Lord Ragsdale's bride with a bonnet and sharing bedroom confidences.

"I think you will have to be extremely diplomatic, should this eventuality arise, my lord," she replied, feeling a slight twinge at her own deception with Fae. "Perhaps it would be best if Fae remained your little secret."

"My thought precisely." He paused then and a slight wariness crept into his eye. "Emma, you won't be needing me today, I trust."

"Well, we did need to look over your estate receipts before we leave for Norfolk tomorrow, my lord," she reminded him gently, not wishing to disturb the moment.

"Tonight, then, Emma. I am off to Tatt's to buy another horse," he told her. "When that arduous endeavor is completed, I will toddle over to Whitcomb Street and pay a morning call on Clarissa Partridge."

"Very good, my lord," she interrupted, raising her eyebrows.

"And then, with or without your permission, I will descend on White's for lunch, a brief snooze in the reading room, and then a gentlemanly glass of port. Only one, mind you," he assured her as he continued his progress to the book room. "I intend to become a pattern card of respectability."

She watched him go, shaking her head and wondering why men were so strange. *He must be in love,* she concluded as Lord Ragsdale took his correspondence into the book room and closed the door behind him. *This isn't the same tight-lipped man who greeted me with such a scold last night. Something wonderful must have happened at the theatre,* Emma decided as she climbed the stairs on light feet. *If this romance with Clarissa prospers, perhaps I will be sprung from this indenture faster than I had hoped.*

And why not love? she mused as she walked down the hall to Lady Ragsdale's room. He said he was thirty, high time for any man to be thinking seriously about marriage and a family. She knocked on the door, hugely pleased.

Lady Ragsdale was still in bed. She looked up over the newspaper and smiled at Emma. "Ah, my dear. Over there are the dresses John ordered for you. They came yesterday with Sally's things, and we didn't notice it until the afternoon."

"For me?" Emma asked as she approached the dresses draped over the chair.

"For you, Emma. And don't look so dumbfounded! John has a very kind streak, once someone calls his attention to a necessity," Lady Ragsdale stated.

"But I never said anything," Emma insisted, picking up the dress on top and admiring the softness of the deep green wool. There were lace collars and cuffs on the chair too, and a petticoat far better than the ragged thing she wore.

"No? Well, perhaps neither of us gives John credit for the good he does."

"I am certain you are right, my lady," Emma said. The other dress was black, and experience told her how good it would look as a background to her auburn hair and pale complexion. "Oh, please tell him thank you for me."

"Tell him yourself," Lady Ragsdale said with a smile. "And Emma, I have a paisley shawl inside my dressing room that I never wear. It's hanging on the closest peg to the door."

In a haze of pleasure, Emma went into the dressing room and was brought quickly back to earth by Lady Ragsdale's dresser, who obviously had been listening at the door. Acton thrust the shawl into her hands and hissed, "Don't think you'll get any more from my lady."

"I learned long ago not to expect anything," Emma whispered back. "I'm certain you'll be quick to tell me if I overstep my place here, Acton."

The shawl looked especially fine with the green dress. Emma remembered to drop a quick curtsy to Lady Ragsdale and another breathless "Thank you" before closing the door quietly behind her. She was down the stairs in a moment and knocking on the book room door.

"Emma, you needn't knock," came Lord Ragsdale's voice from within. "I'm not ingesting opium or chasing the chambermaid. At least not presently."

You are so outrageous, she thought with a grin. *It almost amounts to Irish wit.* She opened the door and came into the room, suddenly shy. "I just wanted to thank you for the dresses," she said.

He looked up from the desk where he was going over her neatly entered account books. "I hope they fit."

Some sense told her that they would be a perfect fit. "I am sure they will, my lord." When he continued looking at her, she hesitated. *Why do I dislike being under obligation to this man?* she considered as she watched him lean back and continue his perusal of the ledge. "Sir, you didn't need to go to such expense for me."

He closed the book and indicated the chair next to the desk.

"Emma, I may have many faults, but dressing poorly is not among them. I like the people whom I employ to look at least half as grand as I do."

She laughed out loud, and he joined in her laughter. "Well, I don't expect you to match my incomparable high looks, Emma, but you must agree that if we are to do business together, I have certain standards."

"Yes, my lord," she agreed, a twinkle in her eyes. "I have standards too. Does this mean that if I do not approve of your waistcoat or pantaloons, you will change them to oblige me?"

It was the closest she had ever come to a joke with an Englishman, and he seemed to know. He laughed again, reached out, and touched her arm. "By all means, by all means. I have it on unimpeachable authority that a good wardrobe covers a multitude of character flaws. You are welcome to correct me."

She watched him a moment more, struck by a sudden and wholly unexpected wave of pity. *You are so convinced of your own flaws,* she thought, *and how sad this is for you. And how strange that I am feeling sorry for an Englishman.*

"Emma, you must have something quite serious on your mind," Lord Ragsdale was saying when she paid attention to him again. "Can it be that my flaws cannot even be covered by a good tailor and boots from Hobie?"

I am going to be impertinent, she thought as she sat there. "You have far fewer flaws than you think, my lord," she said, her words coming out in a rush, as though she feared she would not be able to say them if she gave them thoughtful consideration. "And . . . and thank you for being concerned enough last night to give me the scold I deserved. I promise not to be out past dark in the future on my day off."

There, she told herself, *think what you will. I mean every word of it.* As she sat there in embarrassment, it was as though a great stone rolled off her heart. She could not have explained the feeling to anyone, because it was new to her. All she suspected was that it might not be such an onerous chore to serve this man until her indenture was up.

He regarded her as seriously as she knew she was looking at him. "Why, thank you, Emma," he said finally. "I believe you mean every word of that."

"I do," she said promptly as she stood up. "Now, tell me what you want me to do today while you are out, and I will get at it."

He considered her another moment, a half smile on his face, then set her some tasks that would keep her soundly busy until it was time to leave tomorrow for his Norfolk estate. "When I return this afternoon, I'll expect you to join me in the stables for a look at my new purchase," he finished, making room for her at the desk and going to the door. "I warn you it will be expensive, so if you want to prune up now, make faces, and act like a secretary and fiscal adviser, be at liberty."

She smiled. "I have no qualms about what you spend your money on, my lord," she assured him, "as long as it will lead to prompt double entries, your continuing reformation, and eventual marriage. You know the terms."

"Indeed, yes," he agreed, opening the door and leaning against it. "Do wear the green dress first, will you?"

She blushed and busied herself at the desk, murmuring something in reply.

"Don't mumble, Emma," he said. "It's a bad habit."

"Very well, my lord," she said distinctly. "By the way, I meant to ask: did you have an especially nice time at the theatre last night?"

"You mean, why am I so pleasant this morning?" he asked in turn, leaving her to wonder at his prescience. "Actually, I admired Clarissa's charms with my opera glasses from the safety of my own box and spent the rest of the time trying to figure out how to apologize to you. Good day, Emma."

She sat at the desk and stared at the door. He opened it again.

"And Emma," he continued, "if you should ever feel the urge to trust me enough with your own problems, I might even be able to surprise you with useful solutions."

I wonder if he truly means that, she thought several times that morning as she worked in the book room. This reflection was followed by the fact that no Englishman had ever kept his word to her or her family. She dismissed his offer but noted, to her annoyance, that his words kept popping into her mind as she answered his correspondence.

Such a plethora of invitations, she considered as she looked them over and sent regrets or acceptances, according to his instructions. *Now, I would prefer a picnic al fresco to a dinner at the home of some stuffy, gouty duke,* she thought. *Perhaps Lord Ragsdale prefers old cigar smoke to ants.* She wondered what would happen if she arrived at one of these events in his place, chuckling to herself at the imagined expressions on the face of her surprised host. Papa had always assured her—especially on those days when her brothers were more trying than usual—that she had the poise and ability to move in any social circle. *Of course, I would have to lose my accent and study the trivial so I could be sufficiently vacuous.*

Her thoughts drifted to Clarissa Partridge. "I hope you are intelligent enough to realize what you might have," she murmured. "Lord Ragsdale is certainly potter's clay for the molding, if you are suitably managing. He could even amount to something, with the proper guidance."

Emma was starting to rub her eyes and wonder where the day had gone when Lord Ragsdale reappeared in the book room, looking none the worse for wear for what must have been a strenuous day for one so indolent. *Do be charitable,* she thought as she looked up, wincing at the sharp pain between her shoulders.

"Yes, my lord?" she inquired, noting that in their brief

acquaintance, seldom had she seen him looking so pleased with himself.

His eye was lively with good humor, and he seemed to throw off that boyish, barely contained energy that she remembered—with a pang—about her own younger brother.

"Emma, you must see my horses!"

"Horses in the plural, my lord?" she inquired.

"Yes; singular, isn't it?" he quizzed. "I found myself in the middle of a wonderful sale, and who can resist a sale?"

"But two horses?" she asked. "I know sales are wonderful, but . . ." She stopped. "It is only two, isn't it?"

"Yes," he assured her, taking her by the arm and pulling her to her feet. "Sir Bertram Wynswich of Covenden Hall, Devon, periodically finds himself under the hatches, and he is obliged to lighten his stables. How lucky I am today. Emma, the letters can wait!"

She capped the ink bottle and let him lead her out of the house and into the stable yard, amused by his horseman's commentary on the finer points of his fortuitous acquisitions.

"Next you will be telling me they can fly," she grumbled as he hurried her along.

"Very nearly like, Emma," he agreed, and stopped before the largest loose box. "Well, what do you think? Is this not a sound investment?"

She could not disagree. The horse that came to the railing when Lord Ragsdale leaned his arms on it would have charmed the most discriminating gypsy. He was a tall chestnut, taller than she ever could have managed, with a noble Roman profile, deep chest, and legs that went on forever. He looked as well-mannered as a gentleman, with an intelligent face that seemed to broadcast equine good humor.

Emma stepped up on the railing and glided her hand over his nose. "Oh, you are a bonny lad," she whispered. "Lord Ragsdale, this must be your lucky day!"

He nodded. "Indeed. Didn't I say so? Do you know I even won at cards this afternoon? I have discovered that it is much easier to play when I am sober. Then I paid a call on Clarissa Partridge."

"And Miss Clarissa agreed over tea and macaroons to follow you to the ends of the earth?" she teased in turn.

Lord Ragsdale laughed. "Not precisely, you goose, but she did consent to let me escort her to Covent Garden when we return next week."

"Bravo, my lord!" Emma said, clapping her hands.

Lord Ragsdale bowed, then looked over Emma's shoulder. "And here is another beauty."

She turned around to look across the aisle at another horse, a gray mare, smaller, but just as interested in the people in the stables as they were in her. Her ears were cocked forward, almost as though she understood their conversation. Emma reached up to pat the second horse, admiring every inch of her elegant bearing. *Lord Ragsdale knows horses*, she thought as she found herself nose to nose with the little beauty. She thought of her father's stables then, remembering with a rush of pleasure completely independent of any regret or longing.

"Oh, Lord Ragsdale, I wish you could have seen my father's stable," she said, forgetting where she was. "He had a roan that would have given your hack a run for his . . ." She stopped, acutely aware of Lord Ragsdale's full attention. "But you couldn't be interested in that," she concluded. She stepped away from the mare, embarrassed.

Lord Ragsdale turned his attention back to his horse, sparing her further embarrassment. "Emma, you're no more shanty Irish than I am," he commented, not looking at her. "Something tells me that your father had a whopping good stable."

He cannot possibly be interested in anything I have to say about my family, she thought, suffering the familiar panic she always felt around Englishmen. "Yes, he did," she concluded, "but I needn't tax you with that." She glanced at the gray, desperate to change the subject. "This is a lady's horse, my lord. I hate to tell you, but if you bought this for Miss Claridge, you will be disappointed. She doesn't ride."

She waited as he continued his scrutiny of her, hoping he would ask no questions that would rip her wounds wide-open, leaving her to bleed inside again. *Oh, please, my lord,* she thought, *change the subject.*

He turned from his regard of her and fondled the gray's ears.

"If you must know, I was looking to the future," he explained, after a moment's hesitancy. "Perhaps Clarissa will enjoy this horse someday."

My, but you are in love, she thought, smiling at him and grateful he had taken another conversational tack. "Perhaps you are right, my lord. And now, if you'll excuse me, I have your work to finish."

He smiled at her and reached in his pocket, pulling out a sale's receipt. "Very well! Enter this and send it to the bank." He grinned at the astonishment on her face as she absorbed the amount. "I can afford it, so don't you dare scold, Emma!"

She shook her head, thinking that Lord Ragsdale's indulgence in two horses could feed small cities. She stared at the amount. Or build new cottages for all his crofters and the neighbors besides. *I hope he is so generous in another day, when he's inspecting thatching and rafters.*

And so it goes, she thought, as she took a last look at the beautiful horses and started from the stable. Lord Ragsdale fell in step beside her, shortening his stride to hers.

"Of course, I need to exercise both horses. Emma, could I convince you to ride with me tomorrow on our way to Norfolk? I am assuming that you are a rider."

A very good one, my lord, she told herself. *There was a time when I could match my brothers mile for mile across the whole of County Wicklow. You'd have thought we owned it, or at least, part of it. And so we did, but that seems like someone else's life, and not my own.*

"I would like that, my lord, but I don't have a riding habit," she temporized, grateful for an excuse and wondering why at the same time.

"That's no difficulty," he assured her. "I am certain my mother has a habit you can wear. She doesn't ride anymore, and it may be a trifle outmoded, but I fail to think that would bother you overmuch. Ride with me, Emma?" he asked again.

It wasn't a command. She knew she could say no. Emma hesitated.

"Of course, if you would prefer to ride in the carriage with Mama and Sally and Acton, I will understand," he continued smoothly.

Acton. The thought of riding for a day and a half in a carriage with that harpy glaring at her made her flinch. "No, no," she said hastily. "I'll ride with you, Lord Ragsdale."

~

Lady Ragsdale's habit was not a perfect fit, but her boots were, Emma decided, as Lord Ragsdale threw her into the sidesaddle the following morning. She settled herself comfortably and accepted a crop from him, enjoying the feel of the saddle and the particular pleasure of good boots. She tapped the leather with the riding crop, thoroughly satisfied, for all that she would have to think of something to say to Lord Ragsdale through a whole day of riding.

Leading out in front of the carriage, they negotiated London's early-morning traffic and soon left it behind, riding into the morning sun, which struggled to get away from the low clouds and fog that seemed part of London's perennial landscape. They rode steadily to the north and east, and soon the breeze blowing toward the Channel cleared the air of haze, presenting them with a blue sky of surpassing loveliness.

To Emma's relief, Lord Ragsdale chose not to converse. They rode side by side, but he was silent, and she wondered if he was already regretting his decision to go to Norfolk. Lady

Ragsdale had confided in her last night as Emma was help-ing with the packing that he had not been at Staples Hall since his father was laid to rest in the family cemetery there.

"And even then he was brought into the chapel on a stretcher," she said. "He has never been back since." She sighed and looked down at the petticoat in her hands. "And we do not talk about it."

Emma looked at Lord Ragsdale's profile. *At least you know where your father is buried,* she thought. *You don't lie awake at nights, wondering if he is alive or dead, as I do.*

"Yes, Emma?"

His question came out of the blue, and she glanced at him, startled. "I . . . I didn't say anything, my lord," she stammered.

"But you looked as though you wanted to," he offered.

She shook her head. "You must be mistaken, my lord."

"I must be," he agreed serenely and said no more.

As they rode along, mile after mile, she discovered it was not an uncomfortable silence. *I could almost like this,* she reflected, *even though I suspect I am boring company. This is a peer used to card rooms, and clubs, and teas, and drawing rooms, and levees, and balls. I hope he will not fall asleep because I am so dull, and dump himself off his horse.* She smiled at the thought.

"Yes?" Lord Ragsdale asked.

She laughed in surprise. "You must have eyes in the back of your head," she protested.

"Nope. Just one on the left, but it does yeoman's duty. What's so amusing?"

Obviously there was no point in holding back. "I was just picturing you ejected from your horse and supine on the ground, bored into sleep because I am a dull conversationalist."

He shook his head. "On the contrary, Emma, I was about to congratulate you on the pleasure of your silence. Do you know that just since the beginning of this interminable

Season, I have heard every stupid conversation that people such as myself utter? I am sure that the things we say over and over, thinking ourselves so witty, must be written somewhere on clay tablets." He looked her in the eye then. "You may reform me too completely, Emma. Suppose I become addicted to long silences and rational conversation that leads somewhere? Imagine the shock to my friends."

He joined in her laughter. "Seriously, Emma, we are half-way to luncheon, and you have not made one single remark about the weather, fashion, or the latest gossip."

"What would you like to talk about, my lord?" she asked finally. "Weather, fashion, or gossip?"

He reined in his horse, and she was compelled to stop too. "My father, Emma. Please."

Chapter 13

BUT . . . BUT . . . YOUR MOTHER TELLS me . . . I thought you did not wish to speak of him," she stammered. The mare sensed her sudden agitation and stepped in a dainty half circle. She patted the animal into control, searching for the right words. "I mean, your mother, your banker, David Breedlow even—they all warned me not to bring up the subject."

He spoke to his horse, and they continued. "They are wrong," he said finally when they were some distance in front of the carriage, and he could slow the pace slightly. "It may have been my choice at one time, but I find now that avoiding the topic breaks my heart."

His words were so simple and so full of feeling that they went straight to her own heart. As she rode beside Lord Ragsdale, Emma realized that she would never be able to look at him in the same way again. It was powerful knowledge and left her almost breathless. *What do I say to this man?* she wondered. He was looking at her, as though expecting something, and as she searched her mind for something to say, she thought of her mother, that woman of few words and much heart.

"Tell me, my lord," she said simply, remembering with an ache those calm words spoken to her so many times.

"I think he must have been the best man who ever lived,

Emma," Lord Ragsdale said, with a glance over his shoulder as though he feared his mother could hear him. The carriage was only a speck in the distance. He cleared his throat and smiled ruefully down at his saddle. "But I suppose that is part of the problem." He reached over and touched her arm. "Have you ever tried to measure up to an impossible ideal?"

She considered his question and understood him for the first time. She smiled at him and shook her head. "We were all so human in the Costello household, my lord. I . . . I was the only daughter, and my brothers either ignored me or were happy I was nothing like them."

He nodded. "I imagine it was a lively household, Emma. Perhaps you will tell me about it some time."

"Perhaps," she replied, trying to keep the doubt from her voice. "But we are speaking of you and your father, sir, are we not?"

"We are. He was all goodness, all manners, impeccable in character and possessing every virtue, I think. I was a younger son for much of my early years, thank goodness, so the onus of perfection rested on my brother. Claude was very much like Father."

He paused then, and she had the good sense not to rush into the silence. *Perhaps I am learning wisdom*, she thought as she watched Lord Ragsdale struggle within himself.

"Claude died when I was at Harrow, and then Father transferred his entire interest to me."

Again there was a long silence. *Quiet, Emma*, she told herself as they rode along, side by side.

"I don't mean to say he wasn't interested in me before, Emma, but this was different." He shook his head. "I am probably not making much sense, but that's how it was. Claude died of a sudden fever, and overnight, I was the family hope."

He looked at her. "There are some things that the heir learns that I never learned. I suppose it becomes a way of life. Too bad I was a poor student."

Two weeks ago—a week ago even—she would have agreed with him. *This is odd*, she thought as they rode along. *I want to defend him from himself, and he is someone I do not even like.* She looked at the sky; it was still overcast. She could not blame her strange thoughts on too much sun. Her next deliberation came unwillingly, but she considered it honestly as Lord Ragsdale rode beside her in silence. *Can it be that I have nourished myself so long on hatred that I do not recognize an attempt at friendship? I cannot even remember my last friend.*

It was a shocking thought, almost, but instead of dismissing it, as she would have done only recently, she allowed herself the luxury of considering it. *That is what I will do*, she thought. *I will leave myself open to a change of feeling.* She nodded. *It is a prudent measure, taking into allowance the plain fact that I must serve this man until he considers my debt paid.*

"Emma, what on earth are you thinking?"

It was a quiet question, coming almost from nowhere, so wrapped up in her own thoughts was she. Emma knew she did not have to answer it, but as she looked at Lord Ragsdale again, took in his seriousness where earlier there had only been a certain irritating vapidity, she felt that she owed him an answer. She reined in the mare and turned to face him.

"I am thinking, sir, that I would like to be your friend."

The impudence of her words caught her breath away, *Emma, you nincompoop*, she scolded herself as Lord Ragsdale stared at her. *You're hardly in a position to recommend yourself to a marquess. When will you ever learn to keep your mouth shut?*

"I . . . I'm sorry," she apologized when he continued to say nothing. "That was probably not good form, my lord. Forgive it."

I will die of embarrassment if he just stares at me, she thought, her mind in a panic now. *Suppose he turns his back and rides ahead? Or worse yet, makes me dismount and get in the carriage with the others and that witch Acton?* "I'm sorry," she mumbled again.

"Well, I'm not," Lord Ragsdale said. "Emma, let's shake on this. It's nice to have a friend."

She looked at him in amazement, well aware that her face was flaming red. He was holding out his hand to her and sidling his horse next to the mare. Instinctively, she held out her hand. They shook hands, Emma holding her breath and looking him in the eye. She took a deep breath then and plunged ahead. "Since we are resolved to be friends, my lord, you can rest assured that no matter what you tell me about you and your father, I will not judge."

He smiled, and some of the ravaged look left his face. "You will not dare, as my friend, will you?" he murmured. "Let us ride ahead a little." He put spurs to his hunter, and she followed just as nimbly.

When they were a good distance from the carriage, he slowed his horse, then rested his leg across the saddle as they sauntered along. "As a second son, I was supposed to embrace an army career. All that changed when Claude died. After Harrow, I found myself at Brasenose." He sighed. "I was not a good student. The warden remembers me well and probably is not suffering cousin Robert Claridge any better than he did me."

"Did your papa rake you down and rail on?" she asked. "I know mine would have."

He shook his head. "Papa was much too kind to do that," he replied.

I wonder if that was such a kindness, she thought. *Sometimes nothing says love like a really good brawl between fathers and sons,* Emma thought, thinking of some memorable rows. *I wonder if your father was as good a man as you think,* she considered, then tucked the thought away. Surely Lord Ragsdale knew his own father better than she, who had never met the man.

"He would come to Oxford and sigh over me and remind me that the family was depending on me," the marquess said. "He was right, of course."

"My lord, did you begin to drink and wench then?" she asked suddenly.

He was silent a moment, reflecting on her quietly spoken question. "I suppose I did," he said slowly. "Of course, it seems as though I have always engaged in too much gin and the petticoat line." He looked at her without a blush. "At least I do not gamble too."

She laughed. He joined in briefly, then put his leg back into the stirrup and cantered ahead. Again she followed.

"Papa commanded the East Anglia regiment, and they were called up during the '98," he continued. "I had always wanted an army career, and I badgered Papa to free me from Brasenose's environs. He did, finally, and I joined him in Cork. Oh, Emma."

She did not disturb the silence that followed, because she found herself forced back into the '98 herself. She was fifteen then, almost sixteen, and she remembered staying indoors when ragged mobs or uniformed soldiers passed the estate, the one slouching on the prowl, the other marching smartly. And Papa would bang on the dinner table and shake a finger at her brothers, warning them of the folly in getting involved in a quarrel that was not theirs. *And so we did not,* she thought, *and see where it got us. Mama and Tom are dead, and I do not know where the rest of you are.* She looked at the marquess and knew that sooner or later, he would ask the inevitable question.

"Was your family involved, Emma?"

She shook her head, relieved she did not have to lie yet. "We were not, for all that we lived not far from Ennisworthy and . . . and Vinegar Hill."

"Dreadful place," he commented. "How did you not get involved?"

She stared straight ahead. "My father was a Protestant landowner, my lord. It was not our fight."

"Truly, Emma?" he asked quietly.

"Truly, sir." It was right enough. If he did not know any

more about Ireland than Vinegar Hill, he would never come up with another connection, and she would not have to relive anything more, beyond that summer of 1798. She was afraid to look at him and chose instead to go on the attack. "But we were talking of you, my lord. Were you glad enough to be in the army at last?"

He shook his head, then motioned his horse off the road. She followed, wondering what he was doing. He dismounted then and helped her down. "Let's sit here, Emma," he said. "When the carriage arrives, we can wave them on."

She was glad enough to dismount and only hoped that she did not grimace as she walked with him to the tree.

"A little stiff, are we?" he asked, a touch of humor in his voice.

"I haven't ridden since 1803," she said, and then wished she had not.

"Now, why does that year ring a bell?" he asked, more to himself than to her.

Emma held her breath.

"Never mind, never mind," he said and sat under the tree, leaning back against the trunk. She threw the reins over her horse's head and sat down, when both animals were cropping grass by the road. "Where was I? Ah, yes, the army." He began to rub his forehead. "I discovered, to my chagrin, that I liked the army no more than I liked school." He made a face. "All those stupid rules. Papa had bought me a captaincy, and let me state here that you have seldom seen a more inept officer than I was."

"But I thought you wanted to join the army," she said. She sniffed at the pleasant, earthy aroma of autumn's leaves blending into the soil. *I could wish it were a sunnier day,* she thought, *and that our topic was a cheerful one. This could be a pleasant setting.*

"I thought I did want the army, but the fascination did not endure long." He turned to regard her. "Emma, has it ever occurred to you what a stupid system it is for a man to buy a commission? The most cloth-headed private in the king's East Anglia knew more than I did about soldiering." He sighed and picked up her hand absentmindedly. "And there we were among the saddest kind of poverty, and people who hated us. War is not all it is cracked up to be. Uniforms get dirty fast. Everyone starts to stink." He paused. "And people die. Oh, Emma, how they die."

He released her hand and sat in silence again, rubbing his forehead over his eye patch.

"My father died at Vinegar Hill because I did not have the wit to save him. My sorrows, Emma, for such a good man to die that way!"

The words burst out of him, and she jumped. He gripped her hand again, as if unable to go on without her physical presence. She squeezed his hand in return, and in another moment, he released her, mumbling some apology.

"I wish I could say it was a glorious battle, but it wasn't even anything important, Emma. Some of the mob had killed a cow not far from the picket line and butchered it for those enormous copper pots. You could tell they were hungry devils. I think I felt more sorry for them than anything else," he said. "I mean, we were just standing around watching and nothing more."

She could not wait through another silence. "And then what, my lord?"

"I don't know why, but one of my men leaped up from the picket line, stormed halfway up the hill, and grabbed a hunk of that wretched beef." Lord Ragsdale's voice had a wondering tone to it, as though the matter still puzzled him. "True, we had been on half rations for several days ourselves, but why that? It was such an irrational, impulsive gesture."

Emma leaned closer until their shoulders were touching. "I do not understand how this is your fault, my lord."

"Well, it was," he replied, his voice grim. "I was standing right next to the man, and all I could do as he sprinted up the hill was look around for my sergeant, to ask him what to do! By the time I found my sergeant, the mob had swarmed down the hill and dragged Father off his horse where he sat with his back to them. I'll never know if he was even aware what had happened, so fast did it occur." He slapped his fist in his hand. "I was so inadequate!"

Emma took his hand this time, but he shook her off and mounted his horse again. She hurried to join him, but he was far down the road before she was even in the saddle again. The carriage was close now, but she waved to the coachman and hurried at a gallop after Lord Ragsdale, thinking to herself how odd it was that sometimes the largest events hinged on the smallest actions. She felt the tears sting her eyelids. Sometimes innocently offering a traveler a bed for the night can lead to complete ruin. *But I cannot think about that,* she told herself as she dug her heel into the mare's side.

She caught up with Lord Ragsdale in another mile, but only because he had dismounted, his lathered horse following behind him now like a large dog. She walked her horse alongside him, and she wondered for a moment if he even realized she was there beside him, so deep was his concentration on the road in front of him.

"I started up the hill after Father, but there wasn't any point," he continued, his eyes on the road ahead, his voice dull. "From the time they grabbed him until I was wounded couldn't have been more than a minute, but it still seems to go on forever, when I think about it." He looked at her then. "And Emma, I think about it all the time. I don't suppose an hour goes by that I do not think about it."

Of course you think about it, she thought, her own heart full. *You are idle and have nothing to fill your time. Now, if you were serving out an indenture, you would discover that probably two hours would pass before you thought about it.* Emma longed to tell him that she understood what he was suffering, but she held her tongue. *For you would only demand to know why I think myself an authority on this kind of pain. I haven't your courage to tell yet.*

He stopped and raised his hands to her in an impotent gesture. "He disappeared into a crowd of men and women with pikes and clubs. Then I was struck in the eye by a pike, and I was blinded by my own blood. I don't remember anything else."

"Perhaps it's just as well."

"I suppose," he replied, but he did not sound convinced. "Others say that too. They took me by ambulance to Cork, and at least I was spared the sight of his head on a pike at the top of Vinegar Hill." He shuddered. "There wasn't enough left of his body to transport home for burial."

"Heaven help you!" she exclaimed and took him by the arm. He suddenly twined his fingers in hers then, and they strolled along hand in hand. After a few yards, he looked down at their hands.

"Someone would think we were having a pleasant outing," he commented as he released her. "I do not have many of those, Emma."

"You will, my lord," she said finally, not so much that she believed it herself, but that he needed to hear it. "You will return to London and drink tea in Clarissa Partridge's sitting room, and take her to the art gallery, and think of other things." She stopped and took his arm again. "It will help if you do not flog yourself on a regular basis, and if you find some suitable employment."

"Up you get, Emma," he said as he cupped his hands and helped her into the sidesaddle. He mounted the hunter again, and they set out to overtake the carriage. "There's the rub, Emma. I'm obviously not suited for the army, and I only squeaked by at Oxford. I would be a poor vicar, because I do not believe the Almighty is very nice. Mama assures me that I do not need to work ever, but you know, I will go crazy if I do not find something useful to do."

"Perhaps you will find sufficient occupation in managing your estates, my lord," she suggested.

He made a face. "Unlikely, my dear secretary. My land is

prodigiously well managed already and provides me with an obscene revenue."

She cast about for something to say to encourage him. "I suspect that soon enough you will be a husband and then eventually, a father. This can be time-consuming."

He smiled. "Ah, yes, the unexceptionable Clarissa. She is lovely, Emma, and I am eager for you to meet her. But seriously, one cannot breed all the time. Not even I," he added generously. "And Clarissa is probably not likely to . . ." He stopped, and grinned at her. "Yes, Emma, I need to find an occupation that will keep me too busy to think about what a wretched excuse for a man I am."

She could think of nothing else to say. Mama would have scolded him for being so centered on self as he was, but Lord Ragsdale's agonies struck too close to the bone for her to offer advice. *I am a fine one to suggest personal improvement, when I spend spare moments wishing I could reverse that awful day in 1803 and begin it again. It would end differently, if only I could take it back.*

There was no need for further conversation then or that night during their stay at the inn. After dinner, Lord Ragsdale announced his intention to take a stroll, and something in his tone told them all that he did not wish company. He was still gone when she crawled into bed and pinched out the candle. *Walk some miles for me, my lord*, she thought drowsily as her eyes closed.

They arrived at Staples Hall the next day around noon. Miracle of miracles, the sun shone on the East Anglia coast. The contrast of blue sky and low chalk cliffs was almost blinding, Emma thought as they rode along the seacoast route. The wind was bracing and reminded her of home more forcefully than anything she had yet experienced in England. *I like it here*, she thought all at once. There were no soft Wicklow Hills, and the shades of green were even now just struggling out from under winter, but the landscape was promising. She felt her heart rising like a lark.

Lord Ragsdale seemed to read her thoughts. "Most people think it too dramatic for comfort," he commented as he watched her face.

"I think it just right," she replied. "I suppose the wind can really roar through here."

He nodded, a smile of remembrance on his face. "The rain blows sideways so the glass doesn't even get wet."

The manor was much smaller than she expected, with gray stone and white-framed windows. The front lawn was sparse of shrubbery, and the few trees were stunted and permanently bent into the wind. She looked at Lord Ragsdale in some surprise.

"Where is the big house, you are thinking?" he questioned. "Grandfather resisted adding onto it, and Papa couldn't bear to change anything, either. I think it a little small myself, but Mama would probably be aghast if I changed anything."

The bailiff met them at the door with a short line of servants, who curtsied and bowed as they entered the hall. Emma looked about her in appreciation and allowed the housekeeper to take her cloak. Lord Ragsdale handed over his hat and overcoat and gestured to the balding man in well-worn leathers.

"Emma, this is Evan Manwaring, my bailiff. Evan, this is . . ."

The bailiff stepped forward and bowed, to Emma's dismay. "You didn't tell me you had married, my lord," he said, before Lord Ragsdale could finish his sentence. "May I say that your exertions have certainly borne fruit."

Emma gasped, and then laughed out loud. "Oh, sir, you do not understand."

"She is my secretary," the marquess said hastily, his face red. "Oh, don't look so startled! It's a long story, to be sure, but permit me to promise you that Emma Costello here has a right understanding of my correspondence and financial affairs. Emma, this is Mr. Manwaring."

They shook hands as the bailiff stammered out his

apologies, then had a chuckle on himself. He wiped his hand across his shining baldness and scrutinized Emma. "It's an honest mistake. You seemed so easy-like together." He stepped closer to the marquess and tried to whisper. "Your secretary?"

"My secretary," Lord Ragsdale replied firmly. "You will own that she is better to look at than David Breedlow, drat his carcass, and she does not cheat me."

Emma thought of Fae Moullé, and their inflated millinery shop figures, and had the good grace to blush. *What he doesn't suspect will certainly not hurt him,* she thought even as she owned to a guilty twinge. She shook hands with Mr. Manwaring and resolved not to worry about what he was thinking.

Lord Ragsdale clapped one hand on her shoulder and the other on his bailiff's. "In fact, I suggest that you two adjourn to the book room and you acquaint Emma with the sordid details of my estate neglect. She will truss up your figures and admonitions and present them to me in a more palatable form, I trust."

"We can do that," the bailiff replied dubiously.

"Excellent, then! Mr. Manwaring, I will watch for my mother and cousin, who should be arriving soon. I trust you will inform Mrs. Manwaring to provide luncheon for us."

"I already have, my lord," the bailiff said. "And do you know, Sir Augustus has invited himself over for dinner."

Lord Ragsdale smiled. "Well, if he hadn't, I would have talked my way into his house. Excellent, sir, excellent." He rubbed his hands together and started down the hall to the sitting room, as the bailiff gestured toward the book room.

Mr. Manwaring paused to watch his master go into the sitting room. "Looks better than he did ten years ago when I saw him last," he murmured, "all wan and white, and looking fit for fish bait. I wouldn't have given him one chance in five of surviving a strong wind."

"You mean he truly has not been here in all this time?" Emma asked.

The bailiff shook his head. "Not once, miss. Now, Lady Ragsdale comes every now and again to sit on a bench in the mausoleum, but Lord Ragsdale never has. Here, miss, have a seat, and let me get the books."

Whatever awkwardness there might have been wore off quickly, as Emma knew it would as soon as the bailiff realized that she understood what he was talking about. In the time before the carriage arrived, they sat with their heads together, poring over the estate records from the past ten years. From what a cursory glance told her, the estate was well run, the figures all in order. The bailiff finally sighed and pushed the books away.

"We look good on paper, miss, but the crofters' cottages are in serious need of repair."

"All of them?"

"Yes. We've been patching and making do, but it's beyond that now. Cottages wear out fast on this rough coast. It could be a prodigious expense," he warned, "and not one I was willing to undertake without his express knowledge and approval. In fact, I would advise new cottages from the foundations up. And what could I do, when he avoids the place?"

"He is here now, Mr. Manwaring," she said, "and he can be brought to do his duty."

Mr. Manwaring leaned back in his chair. "Then, it will be the first time since I can remember that a Marquess of Ragsdale has been inclined to exert himself for the benefit of others."

Emma stared at the bailiff. "But his father . . . he tells me . . . I mean, didn't the late marquess walk on water?"

"Oh my, no!" The bailiff laughed as he pulled the books toward him again. "I think our young lad has spent ten years putting together a mythology, Emma." He rubbed his chin, regarding her. "I'm wondering now if that is how he has managed to get through this pesky time. I mean, there were rumors everywhere about how the son had let down the father. I suppose if you hear something long enough, it almost becomes true."

"He would never believe anything ill of his father, even if you told him," Emma murmured.

Mr. Manwaring put on his spectacles and gazed at her over the top of them. "I know that. I'm thinking he might believe you, miss."

Chapter 14

*E*ASIER SAID THAN DONE, EMMA THOUGHT as she allowed Lord Ragsdale to help her into the saddle again following luncheon. It had been a quiet meal, what with Lady Ragsdale and Sally Claridge white-faced and exhausted from a day and a half of travel and capable of managing only a little soup. *Weaklings*, Emma thought as she watched them. *Exertion does not appear to be a strong suit among any of this family.*

She regarded Lord Ragsdale, sitting at the head of the table and tucking away a substantial meal. *Two weeks ago, I would have thought you would be the first to complain*, she reflected as she watched him down his meal with evident gusto. *Yet you have not complained about anything.*

"Well, Emma, are you up to a ride about the estate?" he asked, when his mother and cousin excused themselves and allowed Acton to help them to their rooms. "Let's see how bad the damage is that I have done."

It will be a thorny issue, Emma thought as they rode toward the first cluster of dwellings just beyond the back lawn of the manor. *How does one convince a lazy, care-for-nobody peer that he is not the beast he has painted himself to be? And if he discovers that he is a better man than he thought, will he be comfortable with the feeling? Heaven knows it is easier to live, when no one expects anything of you.* She resolved to try.

"My lord, I learned something of real interest from Mr. Manwaring," she began, feeling like a circus performer on a tight wire.

"I hope you did, Emma," he replied in a teasing tone of voice. "Heaven knows, that's what I am paying you for."

She laughed in spite of her discomfort, pleased to see a sense of humor surfacing through all the misery of the last day. "Do be serious, my lord," she began.

"Must I?" he interrupted.

"Mr. Manwaring showed me the estate records, my lord." She hesitated, took a deep breath, and plunged in. "No one has made any improvements to the crofters' cottages since before your grandfather's time."

He let her words sink in and then rejected them, as she feared he would. "You must be mistaken, Emma," he said, in a tone that wanted no argument. "My father was the best kind of landlord."

"I am certain that he had the best of intentions, my lord," she hedged, wishing she had not tackled the subject at all.

"You don't know what you're talking about," he said, staring straight ahead. "You never even knew the man. I'll thank you to keep your opinions to yourself about something you know so little."

She winced at his tone, wondering why she had ever involved herself in the matter. *I shall hold my tongue*, she told herself. *There is no reason why I need to make a career out of blundering into crises.* She glanced at his face, and it was set and hard again. She reined in the mare, and he stopped out of habit.

"John Staples, you have to tell me what is so attractive about thinking the worst of yourself," she declared. "Just because your father never got around to doing the work you're about to begin doesn't mean he is less of a man. It only means that he was human like the rest of us."

"Shut up, Emma," Lord Ragsdale said and put spurs to his horse. In another moment he was gone from sight, and she was left to kick herself in solitude and wonder why on earth she even cared what he thought about himself.

It was a new emotion, one she had not felt in years, this curious anger at the stubbornness of others. She rode slowly along, feeling the raw wind that began to blow in suddenly from the sea, but not regarding it beyond hunching down tighter inside her cloak. *I have not felt this kind of irritation since those days before 1803 with my family,* she finally forced herself to admit. *We fought, we brawled, but we loved each other. I had forgotten that special painful anger, and how it can sting. I want something better for this man, even though there is no real reason why I should.*

She looked down the road where Lord Ragsdale had ridden. *Oh, I would like to grab you by the shoulders and shake some sense into you,* she thought. *How dare you go through life thinking you are not a good man?*

"I have a few more things to say to you, Lord Ragsdale," she said out loud. "Now, where are you?"

She rode in the direction she had last seen Lord Ragsdale, but he was long out of sight. "You're not getting away from a piece of my mind that easily," she said grimly as the wind began to blow harder, twirling in odd circles as it seemed to blow both from the sea and toward it at the same time.

The rain came then, thundering down until she couldn't see the track in front of her. After a few minutes, she was soaked to the skin, and she determined to return to the manor house. But where was it? She looked behind her, but she could see nothing, in the pelting rain. *Oh, dear,* she thought as she reined in the mare and squinted into the storm. Somewhere not far were the cliffs overlooking the ocean. She leaned over and patted the mare.

"Well, it wouldn't be any loss to anyone on this miserable island if I rode off the edge of England," Emma told the horse, "except that I refuse to give Lord Ragsdale that pleasure."

"What pleasure, you baggage?"

A gloved hand grabbed her reins and then brushed her sodden hair back from her eyes. *Don't show too much relief, Emma,* she told herself when Lord Ragsdale, as soaked as she was, led her horse beside his.

"I just don't want you to think I'm not angry with you still," she concluded.

"Emma, you would try a saint," he said, his voice mild. "I wonder the Claridges in Virginia didn't just pay you to leave their indenture, and good riddance."

She laughed, despite her soggy discomfort. "You know they never had any money. Robert spent it all!"

He chuckled and gathered the reins in closer. "Well, unlike my cousin, I am rich as Croesus. Had I not signed an agreement with you—under duress, I might add—you would be a free woman now, and probably plaguing someone else. Let's find some shelter."

The rain was turning into sleet as Lord Ragsdale stopped before a crofter's cottage and dismounted. "When in Rome, Emma," he said as he helped her from the saddle, then knocked on the door.

The cottage was warm with the fragrance of both farming people and cows. "Good heavens," Lord Ragsdale said under his breath as the cows stared back at him, moving their jaws in rhythm. "I had no idea."

"Hush," Emma said out of the corner of her mouth as she observed the startled looks on the faces of the people within. "Oh, please, we are so wet," she began, and friendly hands pulled her inside.

Only minutes later she sat before the fire, a blanket clutched around her, a mug of warm milk in her hand, and her clothing draped demurely by the fireplace. She sipped at the milk, trying not to laugh at the sight of the marquess, similarly clad, but with more of him to cover. He tugged at the blanket, trying to cover both his shoulders and his legs at the same time.

"It's a mathematical problem, my lord, which is why

you probably cannot resolve it," she commented and took another sip.

"What are you talking about?" he snapped.

"There are only so many square inches of blanket, and more square inches of you, my lord," she explained, her eyes merry. "You might ask them which end they would prefer covered. It's their house, and we are guests. It's all the same to me."

He gave her a gallows smile and resolved the matter by cinching the blanket about his waist and moving closer to the fire to keep his bare shoulders warm.

"All the same to you, eh?" he asked finally as he accepted a cup of milk. "That cuts me to the quick. No preference, Emma?"

"My lord, I am not Fae Moullé," she retorted, swallowing her laughter when he blushed.

"No, you are not," he replied finally, when he could think of something to say. "And I say my prayers daily in gratitude for that tad of information." He looked up at the older man, obviously the head of the house, who stood beside him, as if wondering what he should do. "Do be seated, sir, and forgive this frightful intrusion. We thank you for your hospitality and promise to leave as soon as the rain lets up."

The man touched a work-worn hand to his forehead and sat down. "My lord, you and Lady Ragsdale may remain as long as it suits you." He looked about the crowded room and then at the cows behind the barrier. "After all, sir, it's your property."

Lord Ragsdale looked about him. "Why, so it is," he murmured. "Don't let us keep you from your tasks, uh, your name, please?"

"David Larch," said the man. "My father worked here before me, and his father before him, my lord." He stood up and looked toward the cow bier. "It's time for the milking, my lord, if you and your lady will excuse me."

Lord Ragsdale nodded, but Emma wondered why he did

not correct the man. She moved closer to the fire, careful to keep the blanket well-draped around her. "Why didn't you tell him we are not married, my lord?" she whispered to his back.

He set down the cup and grinned at her. "What? After teasing me like that? They wouldn't believe we weren't married, and I shan't confuse them."

It was her turn to blush. The marquess tugged her wet hair suddenly, then turned back to the fire. "It's so refreshing when you're speechless, Emmie dear," he said, loud enough for the family to hear him.

In another moment, to her relief, Lord Ragsdale gathered his blanket about his middle and padded on bare feet over to the cow bier, where he tucked in his blanket, leaned across the railing, and chatted in low tones with the crofter.

"Your lordship has a nice touch about him, my lady."

Emma looked around with a smile as the crofter's wife sat down beside her with her baby, opened her blouse, and began to nurse. Emma looked on in simple delight, reminded of her father's estate all over again, and the quiet people who inhabited it. *I wonder if they were driven out too*, she thought with a pang as she listened to the baby's soft grunt of satisfaction. She looked back at Lord Ragsdale. *He has a nice back*, she decided. *I hope Clarissa Partridge will appreciate the fact that I rescued him.*

"Yes, he does have a pleasant way with folk," she replied.

The wife leaned against the wall of the hut and admired her child, who was kneading at her breast now, his eyes closed. "Now, his father before him . . . there was a stiff man. I know he always meant well, but he just never could talk to people like us."

Emma touched the baby's hair, pleasuring in the fineness of it. "Tell me, Mrs. Larch. Did my . . . the late Lord Ragsdale ever make any repairs on your cottage?"

She shook her head and smiled, as if amused at such a naive question. "I disremember any repairs, but he did come by every now and again and promise them." She sighed. "I am certain sure he meant well, but promises don't butter any bread, now, do they?"

"They do not," Emma agreed, looking at the marquess and wishing he could have heard Mrs. Larch's artless declaration. They both watched the marquess then, and Mrs. Larch shifted her baby to the other breast.

"He looks a sight better now than he did ten years ago," she offered, her voice low. "We all went to the chapel for the memorial service for poor Lord Ragsdale, him all cut up in tiny pieces by the blamed Irish."

Emma gulped and wondered why the crofter's wife had made no mention of her brogue. "Dreadful affair," she agreed. "I did not know him then."

"I'm sure you didn't, my lady," the woman agreed. "You don't look much older than a baby yourself. Sometimes I wonder what men are thinking when they take a wife. Ah, well. The doings of the aristocracy are not my affair, so pay me no mind, Lady Ragsdale. All I remember was the sight of him on that stretcher, his eye covered in a bandage, and him so quiet." She shivered. "And then he began to wail. I can hear it yet, if I think about it." She shook her head as she burped her son and handed him to Emma. "He seems better now. Here, my lady. If you'll hold the little'un, I'll see to some supper. You must be fair famished."

Lord Ragsdale was quiet all through the simple meal of porridge and milk. Mrs. Larch had found a cloth to drape over his shoulders, "So ye'll set a good example for the elder'uns," she teased and glanced at her older children, who had come indoors, wet and shivering, from evening chores.

"Mind your tongue, mum," the crofter said, even as he smiled and nodded to the marquess. "Women do get uppity, my lord, as you may have noticed."

Lord Ragsdale dragged his attention to the crofter, whose shoulders were shaking in silent laughter over his own brazen wit. He smiled at Emma. "Yes, I have noticed.

Sometimes they even tell us things we don't want to hear."

The rain stopped while they were finishing the last of the porridge. Mrs. Larch cast an expert's eye at the variety of pots set by the smoking fire, filled with rain. "Storm's over, my lord and lady," she said. She winked at Emma. "I must say, my lady, what with all this ventilation, we always have rainwater for our hair and the little tyke's bath!"

"And that's why your daughter here has such a fine complexion," Emma said, entering into the spirit of the joke as she touched the cheek of the oldest daughter next to her.

"Almost as nice as yours," chimed in another daughter.

"Almost," Lord Ragsdale said as he touched Emma's cheek.

He winked at her and then looked at the host. "And now, sir, if our clothes are dry, I think it's time we gave you back your privacy."

"Dry enough?" he asked her after they had dressed and made their good-byes to the Larches. The family lined up outside the door and waved and curtsied them off.

"I think so, my lord," she replied, still embarrassed by the way he had buttoned up the back of her dress, as though it were something he did every day. "I think you are a thorough-going scoundrel, my lord, and I cannot fathom why I did not see this sooner. I thought you were merely a drunkard."

He thought about her words for a moment as they picked their way carefully along the road, guided by moonlight. "Maybe you just weren't looking deep enough, Emma," he teased. He touched her arm. "Or maybe I wasn't much fun, either." He cleared his throat then. "And, Emma, I owe you an apology."

"Let's see now, which of the myriad wrongs are you going to make amends for?" she teased, eager to lighten his tone.

"The one where I insisted that my father would never have neglected these people," he said, his voice so quiet that she had to lean closer to hear him. "You were so right, Emma, so right. David Larch told me all that over the milking."

"There's nothing to apologize for, my lord," she said softly. "You'd have discovered this same as I did, when your bailiff showed you the books. What matters is that you're going to do something about it."

"I certainly am, Emma," he replied. "Wouldn't you say it was time I spent some of my money on new homes *and* separate barns for these people who work my land?"

"I would," she agreed. "And I don't think it will reduce you to patching your shirts or blacking your own boots to economize."

He smiled at her and then tightened his grip on the reins. "What a relief! I don't know that my indolence could stand that much strain. Race you to the house, Emma."

⁓

Sir Augustus Barney was there when they arrived, pacing up and down in the sitting room, impatient for his dinner. Lord Ragsdale greeted him with a broad grin, striding across the room and grasping his hand and then clapping him on the back.

"I believe we are still a little damp, Gus," he said. "Emma, drop a curtsy to Sir Gus like a good girl. He was my father's best friend, and he can tell you any number of horror stories about my youth. I think he knows me better than I know myself—now there is a frightening thought."

Emma curtsied to Sir Augustus, wondering how soon she could excuse herself from the room. Lady Ragsdale and Sally Claridge were seated by the window, looking refreshed after a long afternoon nap. Emma wondered briefly what they would think if they knew about her afternoon with Lord Ragsdale, wrapped in blankets in a crofter's cottage. With any luck, she could retreat belowstairs to change clothes, and then to the book room to look over the estate figures.

"Emma, you'll join us at the table," Lord Ragsdale said as she made her curtsy and started to edge toward the door. "Mrs. Larch's bread and milk was good enough, but I'd like something more substantial." He winked at Emma. "Especially after a tough afternoon of stripping down and drying off by a crofter's fire. Got you, Emma."

Emma blushed and glared at him, carefully avoiding a glance in Lady Ragsdale's direction. "Very well, my lord," she said, "but then I must catch up on my work in the book room."

Sir Augustus stared at her and then at Lord Ragsdale. "'Pon my word, John, I thought your bailiff was quizzing me. She really is your secretary?"

"She really is," he agreed, taking the older man by the arm. "She knows my business better than I do, which, of course, has not been difficult." He steered his guest toward the door. "Emma, pay attention during dinner and let us both hang on such pearls of wisdom that Sir Gus chooses to drop about duties of landlords to tenants."

Emma escaped to the book room after the last course when Lord Ragsdale called for port and the ladies retired to the sitting room for cards. She sat down at the desk and ruffled through the pages of the estate ledgers, thinking to herself how fortunate Lord Ragsdale was to have such a useful bailiff. She thought again about what he had said yesterday. "But for all that, what a pity things are in such order, my lord," she murmured as she ran her finger down the neat columns of debits and assets. "You won't find employment here to occupy your mind and heart."

She thought suddenly of her brothers then, remembering their constant activity about the estate and their good-natured exhaustion at the end of each day. She thought of her own household duties and the work she was learning from her mother. *I always knew what I would do in life*, she considered, resting her chin on her palm. *I would marry someone like myself and take care of his estate and our children. It would have kept me busy all my life.*

"My dear, do you have a moment?"

She looked up in surprise, startled out of her daydream,

to see Sir Augustus standing in front of the desk. He smiled down at her.

"I knocked, but I don't think you heard me," he said. "May I sit?" he asked.

She stood up in confusion, and he waved her back to her chair.

"I want to talk to you a moment, my dear. That is all. John has gone to the sitting room to set up the whist table."

She sat down again, folding her hands in front of her on the desk. "Say on, sir," she said.

He seated himself across from her and regarded her in silence for so long that she began to get that uneasy feeling in her stomach. She swallowed, praying that her fear of Englishmen was not beginning to creep into her eyes as she sat and returned his gaze.

"I did not think to see John so improved, and something tells me that the credit is yours," he said finally.

She nearly sighed with relief at his calm statement. "I forced him into a silly agreement whereby I would improve his character and he would then release me from a rather expensive indenture."

He chuckled. "Yes, his mother told me about that while we waited for you to return this evening." He leaned forward then. "Good for you, my dear, good for you. John has some wonderful qualities to share with the world."

"I know," she agreed. "I am Irish, as you can plainly tell, and I was prepared to hate him forever. But I can't. I am determined to see him successfully married. Then remains the thorny problem of finding him some occupation to fill his time."

He nodded but said nothing, as though encouraging her to continue.

"He could easily take to the drink again, if he finds time hanging heavy," she went on, "and this I do not wish."

"Why not?" he interjected suddenly.

Why not indeed? she thought. She leaned forward too,

across the desk, drawn to this kind man, now that she knew he meant her no harm. "I like him, Sir Augustus. He's lazy and bears no resemblance to other people I used to admire, but I like him. I see . . . well . . . potential." She stopped in confusion. "I do not think I can explain it any better, sir."

Sir Augustus leaned back in his chair then and crossed his legs comfortably. "I think the finest quality about the Irish is their forthrightness, Emma. I like him too and would hate it right down to my socks if he continued to throw his life away." He shook his head. "One tragic death was enough."

"Exactly so, my lord," she agreed.

He sat there another moment, then rose to his feet, nodded to her, and went to the door. He paused there and looked back at her.

"My dear, have you ever considered pursuing him yourself? I think he would make you a first-rate husband."

Emma blinked and wondered if she had heard the old man correctly. When she realized she was staring at him with her mouth hanging open, she closed it.

"I wish you would consider it, Emma. Perhaps his friends would be surprised, but I don't recall that John ever cared much what people thought."

"You cannot be serious," she managed to say finally. "He's only now beginning to court an unexceptionable lady in London."

Sir Augustus considered her reply and nodded slowly. "Well, if you say so. I wonder that he did not mention her, but only spent the last few minutes over port, both extolling your abilities and saying how you drive him to the edge of patience on a daily basis."

She leaped on this opening. "See there, sir, you said it yourself. I drive him to distraction!"

"Yes, you do," he agreed. "If you maneuver this correctly, I don't think it would take more than a week or two to turn that into love, my dear, if it isn't already there. Think about it."

"Oh, I could never!" she burst out.

"Never?" he asked, his eyes bright. "That's a long time. Emma, perhaps you should consider how good *you* would be for John. Good night, my dear."

Emma made a point to dismiss thoroughly from her mind Sir Augustus Barney's closing remarks to her. "I think your eccentricity must come from living too long on a fog-bound, windy coast," she said grimly after the man smiled at her and bowed himself out of the room. She shook her head at the closed door, then picked up the outline of the letter she was to compose to Lord Ragsdale's banker.

She bent to the task in front of her, still at it two hours later, and wondering why. The floor around the wastebasket was littered with crumpled papers, evidence of her failure to compose a simple letter. *That's what comes from using old ink,* she thought, as she sharpened yet another quill. She looked down at the page before her, crossed out and agitated over. Of course, ancient ink would hardly account for her numerous misspellings.

This is a lost cause, she reflected as she put away the ink and paper finally. *I must admit that Sir Augustus's words have put me into a pelter.* She folded her hands in front of her and resolved to consider the matter.

"I don't love Lord Ragsdale," she said out loud and waited for something inside her to deny it. Nothing did; there were no whistles or bells or fireworks going off inside her, or even in the near vicinity, so it could not possibly be true. "Well, that's a relief," she said, and again, nothing contradicted that sentiment.

I suppose I am just tired, she thought as she surveyed the ruin around her. *This letter can wait until tomorrow.* She picked up the crumpled remains of her evening's effort and stowed them in the wastebasket, thoroughly irritated with herself. She stood at the window a moment and watched the rain thunder down, then sighed, blew out the lamp, and left the book room.

She closed the door behind her and noticed a paper tacked to the frame. It was in Lord Ragsdale's familiar scrawling handwriting that by now she could have picked out from a roomful of letters. "Emma, come riding with me in the morning. Be at the stables at seven. John."

She folded the note, amazed that Lord Ragsdale would rise so early. She could hear laughter from the sitting room, so he was still up. *I could go in there and remind him that I have his work to do in the book room,* she considered, then rejected the idea. Sir Augustus was probably in there too, and she didn't feel like facing him.

"Very well, sir, I suppose I will go riding," she said to the note as she hurried belowstairs.

She overslept the next morning, waking to the sound of someone rapping on her door with a riding whip. She sat up in bed, clutching the blankets around her when Lord Ragsdale came into the room. He clucked his tongue at her and shook his head.

"Really, Emma, weren't you the one who extolled the virtues of early rising?" He came closer, and her eyes widened. "Need any help pulling the bed off your back?"

She opened her mouth and closed it, bereft of conversation.

Lord Ragsdale laughed as he went back to the door. "Emma, you've been away from Ireland too long," he said over his shoulder. "This is the second time in as many days that I have found you speechless."

Impulsively, she grabbed a shoe on the floor by the bed and threw it at him, but it only slammed harmlessly into the closed door.

"And your aim is off," she heard from the other side of the panel. "Ten minutes, Emma, or I'm coming back in to help."

There is such a thing as too much improvement, she decided as she hurried into Lady Ragsdale's riding habit and pulled on her boots. She grinned to herself, reminded suddenly of Paddy Doyle, one of her father's tenants. After years of "the daemon dhrink," as he put it, Paddy reformed and spent the rest of his life driving his fellow tenants crazy as he extolled the virtues of abstinence.

"Lord Ragsdale, you could become tedious," she told him ten minutes later as she found him in the stables, giving a little more grain to his hunter. She yanked the brush she had carried with her across the stable yard through her sleep-tangled hair.

"I'll do that," he said, taking the brush from her and handing her the grain bucket. "Here, have some breakfast."

She laughed in spite of herself and looked in the half-filled bucket. "You wretch!" she exclaimed as he brushed her hair. "I mean, you wretch, my lord."

"Well, I would only say it to the least horse-faced woman I know," he replied, brushing her hair. "If you'll move with me over to the fence rail, you will see a biscuit I brought for you, and some ham. Really, Emma, you should practice what you preach about a good breakfast."

She turned around to say something, but he took her hair in a large handful and towed her toward the fence rail. "You are certifiable," she said as she reached for the ham. "I don't know why I didn't see it sooner. Thank you, Lord Ragsdale."

He chuckled as he finished brushing her hair. She handed him a ribbon, and he tied it in a tight bow while she started on the biscuit. He turned her around to admire his handiwork.

"You'll do," he said, setting down the brush. "You know, Emma, that's the trouble with reformation. Sometimes you get more than you bargained for."

She stood there, her mouth full of biscuit as he smiled at her. She noticed then he wasn't wearing his eye patch. *I wonder why I didn't notice that sooner,* she thought as she swallowed and wiped her hands on her dress. *Maybe because it doesn't matter to me.*

He did observe the direction of her gaze. "I'd rather leave it off, if you don't mind," he said. "I don't think we'll see anyone, and it's just you."

She smiled at him, reminded of her brothers and similar

offhand remarks. "It's fine with me, my lord," she said. "It doesn't matter one way or the other."

He took her by the shoulders. "You really mean that, don't you?" he asked.

She gently slid from his grasp. "I really do. If you're more comfortable without it, leave it off."

He thought that over and helped her saddle the mare. "I wonder how Clarissa would feel about that," he wondered out loud as he cinched the saddle.

"You could ask her," she said sensibly as she handed him the bridle.

"Emma, do you always reduce everything to black and white?" he asked, the humor evident in his voice as he put the bit in her horse's mouth.

I thought I used to know right and wrong when I saw it, she reflected. *But that was before that man, before Robert Emmet, came walking up the lane to our house, and I made the worst mistake of all. Since then, nothing has been black and white.* "Of course I do," she lied.

He was watching her face, and she turned away to busy herself with the stirrup.

"You're a liar, Emma," he replied, his voice mild. "I wonder when you will finally tell me something true about yourself."

Chapter 15

HER MIND FROZE AS HE HELPED HER INTO the saddle. She arranged her leg across the horse and spread her skirts around her, afraid to look at Lord Ragsdale. She said nothing as he watched her for a long moment, his face unreadable now. When she thought she would start to cry if he did not turn away, Lord Ragsdale whistled to his hunter and mounted him.

"I can wait, Emma," he said as she rode beside him, too shocked to look at him. "I am also led to wonder sometimes who we are redeeming here, me or you."

They rode in silence from the stable yard, until she managed to calm herself. "You could not possibly be interested in anything about me," she said finally, knowing it was her turn to speak, but not knowing what to say to this man beside her.

"And why not?" he asked.

She looked at him then for the first time since his quiet declaration. "Because I am just your servant."

He smiled then, reached over, and tugged her horse's mane.

"Emma, you've never been just a servant. I doubt the Claridges knew what to make of you, all skinny and ragged and covered with lice, from that voyage in the ship's hold. But I know your kind." He touched her arm this time, lightly, briefly. "When you want to talk to someone, I hope it is me."

What good could you do me? she reflected as they rode along. *You have to be flogged to do your duty, and you are busy now with wooing. If you are not lazy now, it is only a temporary thing. You will be indolent again, when you are bored.* To her relief, Lord Ragsdale changed the subject and began to talk of his plans for the crofters.

"I should think it would be best to build the cottages in a more central location, instead of sprawled here and there across the estate," he said as they rode along. "This area, for instance. It's far enough from the cliffs to cut some of the wind and close enough to their work for convenience."

They stopped in a pleasant clearing, a small valley tucked between the series of low, wooded hills that characterized the Norfolk coast. Lord Ragsdale dismounted and gestured with his riding whip. "See, Emma? Plenty of good water, and still some timber. We could erect barns close by for those who have their own livestock."

He held out his arms to help her down, but she shook her head and settled herself more firmly in the saddle. He leaned against her mare, absently fingering the horse's mane. "You don't like the idea," he said finally. He looked, to her mind, rather like a little boy in the throes of disappointment, too well mannered to show all his irritation, but not averse to a wry expression.

Diplomacy, Emma Costello, diplomacy, she told herself. *You have already ruined the morning for yourself; see what you can do to give these people what they really want.* "My lord, may I suggest that you ask your tenants what *they* want?"

She could tell by the look on his face that he had never before entertained the novelty of inquiry among those who worked his land. *Oh, dear,* she thought, *this is probably more democracy than an Englishman can stand.* She looked beyond his expression of slack surprise and smiled to herself, thinking of the Claridges and their Virginia neighbors, rich and poor alike, gathering to make decisions for their county. She remembered the noise, the hot words, the voices raised in clamorous agreement or disagreement, and then the rational calm that settled on the assembly when the majority spoke. True, not everyone went home satisfied, not even the major landowners, but there was harmony, because all had aired their opinion.

"It works in America, my lord," she said, warming to the idea, feeling animation rise in her own heart. "You can hear some fearful rows at Hundred meetings, but most come away satisfied, because they have had their say."

She watched him for signs of resistance but could see none. He rubbed his forehead thoughtfully and then mounted his hunter again. "It's a lovely spot, Emma," he said, drawing close to her. "Why would they object?"

She took a deep breath, at the same time wondering why she felt the inclination to fight for these people she hardly knew. *Am I fighting for them, or am I concerned that they understand that you take an interest?* she asked herself, and had no ready answer. "Sir, people do not like to be forced from their homes, no matter how shabby or inconvenient those cottages are."

"Like you, Emma?" he asked softly, a smile of understanding playing around his lips.

"You will not let me forget, will you?" she considered. "Yes, my lord, like me," she replied, her voice equally soft. "Present your argument for removal, but let them decide."

"Won't they think me a weak landlord if I succumb to their decision?" he persisted, and his interest sounded genuine to her.

"Of course not," she responded promptly. "They will think that you care about them, and they will follow you anywhere."

He mulled that one over, riding in silence for several minutes.

"I doubt even Sir Augustus has ever done anything that radical," he said. "My neighbors will think I am daft and count it a certainty that my father left a weak heir."

"Who cares what your neighbors think, John?" she said, blurting out his name before she even realized it. "They don't work for you, and you don't have to answer to them." She blushed then, aware of her social blunder. "Excuse me, my lord," she apologized. "I was forward."

He smiled at her. "Nonsense! Emma, you are a flaming radical, don't you know."

She nodded, relieved at his light tone. "Aye, my lord. But only think: there are so many ways to solve problems. Why limit yourself to what's been done over and over? Try something new."

She held her breath as he regarded her thoughtfully. "Very well, Emma," he said finally when she thought she would burst with waiting. "I'll do it your way. Let's return to the manor. I'll make it Manwaring's task to gather my estate workers tonight in the old barn by the threshing floor. You'll take notes of the proceedings, of course."

Emma grinned at him and clapped her hands, even as he wagged his finger at her. "See here, Emma, I'm going to the end of the plank for you on this one!"

"You won't be disappointed, sir," she replied happily.

"I wouldn't dare be," he said. He looked at her. "Well, speak, Emma. You obviously have something else on your mind. I am sure it is radical."

She nodded, wondering if this was going too far, but willing to chance it. "My lord, let the women come to the meeting too, and let them speak."

"Oh, that is radical," he agreed, half teasing, half serious. "Why ever would I want to do such a thing?"

"The women will know better than the men what they want in a new cottage," she said decisively. "Encourage them to speak, and they will defend you and serve you to their last breath."

They were in sight of the manor house again. "I'll do it," Lord Ragsdale said. They rode into the stables, ducking through the open doorway. He dismounted and held his arms out for her. She allowed him to help her down. He did not release her immediately but put his hands on her shoulders for a brief moment.

"What about you, Emma?" he asked, his voice quiet as Manwaring approached. "Will you ever speak your mind to me?"

She forced herself to meet his glance and felt an enormous urge to unburden herself completely, to tell him the whole miserable story and her dreadful part in it, until she was stripped right down to the bone. She hesitated, teetering on the edge, before she pulled herself back with a shake of her head. He released her and turned away.

"Maybe someday, Emma," was all he said as he left the stables with Manwaring.

Maybe never, she thought as she watched him go.

It was well after midnight before the last tenant left the barn, full of enthusiasms and new ideas. A smile on her face, Emma gathered together the sheaf of notes at the table where she had sat for four hours, carefully recording the evening's events, and watching with delight as Lord Ragsdale mingled so gracefully with his crofters. She looked through the open doors where the tenants still gathered together in little groups, reliving the give and take of the evening and then looking back at the barn with expressions of real respect.

Lord Ragsdale seemed unmindful of what was going on outside the barn. He yawned and stretched, then took off his coat, revealing a shirt and waistcoat drenched in sweat. He tossed his coat on the table and threw himself into the chair provided for him, which he had not sat in once throughout the night.

"Emma, this kind of exertion is difficult, indeed." He leaned back in his chair and propped his booted feet on the table, his hands behind his head. "I feel as though I have been pummeled, wrung out, and hung out to dry." He looked over at her and took off his eye patch, rubbing the rim of his eye socket gently. "Everything aches."

She merely smiled at him and continued sorting through the papers. "It's all here, my lord," she said, waving the papers at him. "You can look it over in the morning and decide what to do."

"It is morning," he corrected, "and I have already decided." He closed his eye and let out a pleased sigh. "We will build the cottages for the shepherds in that area I suggested this morning, and which they agreed to. The agricultural workers will remain there by the cliff road." He opened his eye and looked at her. "I thought David Larch was particularly eloquent in arguing the virtues of remaining by the main road, didn't you?"

She nodded. "And the women certainly knew what they wanted in cottage improvements, didn't they?"

"Most emphatically," he agreed and reached over to touch her hand. "A good idea of yours, by the way, Miss Secretary. Give that information to Manwaring in the morning. The construction will be his task." He sat up then, as if energized all over again. "How does this sound, Emma? I will appoint Larch to be Manwaring's assistant."

"Bravo, my lord!" she replied, genuinely impressed. "He'll never fail you."

Manwaring rejoined them in the barn after separating himself from one of the groups that had continued the discussion outside. Lord Ragsdale informed him of his idea for David Larch, and the bailiff nodded in agreement. "He'll do fine, sir," Manwaring replied, then smiled. "And if you don't mind me saying so, my lord, you'll do too." He leaned closer. "That's what your tenants are saying, my lord."

Emma looked at Lord Ragsdale in delight, and he winked at her. "And can I tell you something more, my lord?" Manwaring continued. "They're saying how nice it is to know that you care about their problems and do more than just nod and smile and clear your throat." He stood up and nodded to Emma. "Good night, my lord. We've a lot to busy us in the morning, now, haven't we?"

"Indeed we have," Lord Ragsdale agreed as he got to his feet and pulled Emma up after him. "My dear, I expect you in the book room at seven to begin making order out of this pile of notes. Organize it and have it ready for my perusal. I promised a brief visit to Sir Augustus, and then my nose will be to the grindstone too."

He draped his coat around his shoulders and waited for her to gather the papers, then nodded to the steward to douse the lamps. They started across the barnyard together, Lord Ragsdale walking slowly enough for her to keep up with him.

"It feels good, Emma," he said finally as they approached the manor house. "I can return to London with a clear conscience that I have done some good at last." He paused a moment. "There remains one hurdle."

She looked at him, a question in her eyes.

"My mother," he said as he continued to walk. "She will not be happy when I tell her tomorrow that I plan to add a wing onto the manor house." He sighed. "She would prefer that I left everything as Father had left it, but I want a better bedchamber, one that overlooks the ocean."

"More room, my lord?" she asked, her voice light.

"I think I will be spending more time here in the future, Emma, and I doubt I'll be alone. Mama will have to live with change, I suppose."

He put a hand on her shoulder, and she was again reminded of her brothers. "And now you will recommend that I devote my time to wooing the lovely Clarissa Partridge, especially if I am to add on bedrooms to this ungainly old pile."

"Most emphatically," she agreed, enjoying, despite her exhaustion, the comfort of his arm so casually about her shoulder. "Then when you are thoroughly redeemed, we will reconsider my indenture."

"Ah, yes. It always comes back to that," he commented, drawing her closer. "Those horses were expensive, Emma," he reminded her. "Suppose I insist on ten or twenty years more?"

She knew he was teasing, but she realized with a start that a decade in service to Lord Ragsdale would not be an onerous duty. *They were expensive horses*, she thought and smiled to herself. "You would never do that, Lord Ragsdale," she said out loud.

He merely shrugged. "How am I to get rational advice and sensible counsel if you leave me? I might revert to my foolish ways. Then how would you feel?"

How would I feel? she considered as they strolled slowly along. She stopped and looked at him. "I would consider it a terrible waste, my lord, a shocking waste, a tragic waste. Don't you dare throw your life away. I could not deal with it."

She was silent then, embarrassed that her voice was shaking.

He stood so close and had not released his grip on her shoulder, which tightened as she regarded him, sweaty and tired, but triumphant, there in the moonlight of the barnyard. She started walking again, faster now, and he released his grip.

Besides all that, my lord, I have enough death on my conscience, she thought. *Don't make me responsible for the loss of one more life.*

⁓

I must know more, but how? Lord Ragsdale asked himself several times a day during the next few days. *I could just come right out and demand that she tell me*, he thought as he watched her at work in the book room, her face a mask of calm again. She had gone from friend to servant again, assuming that unobtrusive manner he was familiar with in his other household servants. Her work was excellent as always, and innovative as usual, as she speeded up with the demands placed on her by the flurry of activity at the manor. She worked long hours with Manwaring, preparing drafts, itemizing invoices, even speaking with the contractors, masons, and sawyers, acquainting them with the task ahead. He knew that he could relax and visit his friends in the vicinity and pay some much-needed attention to Sally Claridge and his mother, because his affairs were in capable hands.

"I have to know, I just have to," he found himself telling Sir Augustus one night at the Barney estate. They sat together in front of a roaring fire, brandy in hand, watching the flames.

"I could ask why, John," Sir Augustus interjected as he reached for the bottle.

Ragsdale shook his head when the baronet offered him more. "I know that prison was involved. You should have seen her face when we made that trip to Newgate! The only thing that got her to put one foot in front of another in that dreadful place was her single-minded determination to do my business for me."

"A rare quality in a woman," Sir Augustus commented, filling his own glass and leaning back again to stare at the flames.

"I suspect you are right." Lord Ragsdale leaned forward. "I could make her tell me more, but I honestly think that she would begin to bleed before my eyes. There is something here so terrible . . ."

"Then why do you not just leave it alone?" the other man asked quietly. "You don't have a reputation as someone who takes much interest in others, John."

Lord Ragsdale leaned back, finished his brandy, and threw the glass into the fireplace, where it shattered and sparked. "I'm a fool, Gus. Why not just say so?" He touched his companion's arm. "But do you know something? I am changing."

Sir Augustus downed his own drink. "I think I see, John. She dragged you into reformation, and it seems to be taking."

Ragsdale nodded. "Yes. I expect I will be engaged and married before the Season is out, and living here again by summer."

"Bravo for Emma Costello, then," the baronet murmured. "Two words of advice, my friend, neither of which you have solicited, but which I offer because I loved your father and miss him too and want the best for you."

Lord Ragsdale swallowed and felt unfamiliar tears behind his eye. "Say on, sir."

"In your zeal at reformation, make sure you do not injure beyond repair what you seek to heal."

Ragsdale nodded. Sir Augustus stared into the flames and sighed. "There is another bit of advice?" Ragsdale asked finally when the baronet appeared to be on the verge of drifting off.

The older man smiled at the flames. "I don't know, John."

"Oh, now, you must tell me. I am a big boy now and can probably take it."

The baronet stood up and stretched. "Well then, chew on this for your ride home. Just make completely certain you marry the right woman. The wrong one will ruin you."

⁓

He chewed on that for the remainder of the week in Norfolk, chafing at first that he knew he was becoming remote again and then relaxing in the knowledge that Emma was relieved. *She does not want to talk about anything right now, and I am considering Clarissa and have nothing to say either,* he realized as they began the return trip to London. *She can have her mood and I can have mine, and we won't bother each other.*

It seemed a fair exchange, except that he found himself wondering, as they rode along, just how he might know if Clarissa returned his regard. He glanced at Emma, who was admiring the wildflowers by the side of the road. Spring had come while they were in Norfolk, creating a path of daffodils along the highway. True, the wind was cutting, but the flowers were there, with a ragged determination to stay, no matter what the North Sea threw at them.

"Emma, tell me something," he asked suddenly. "How will I know if I'm in love?"

She looked at him in surprise, disturbed out of her contemplation. "Well, I don't know," she said.

"Come on, Emma," he teased. "Surely you've been in love before. If I'm to redeem myself, and Clarissa seems a likely repository for my affections, I should have some idea, shouldn't I? What's it like? I cannot imagine that a pretty woman like you has never fallen in love."

She blushed becomingly, and he had to admire the way the color in her cheeks brought out the green in her eyes. *Emma, you're a rare one*, he thought. *Any other man would envy me right down to my socks, riding along with you.*

"Confess, Emma," he said.

She laughed then, and he felt a momentary relief. *So this is a safe topic*, he told himself and waited for her to speak.

"I suppose I fell in love two years ago in Richmond," she said finally.

"And?" he prompted.

"He was another of the Claridges' indentured servants," she said, her voice soft with remembrance. "A Scot, my lord, a cobbler by trade." She patted her horse, not looking at him.

"What made you think you were in love?" he persisted.

She flashed her eyes at him then, and it was a look that made his stomach tingle a little. *Emma, those eyes are a dangerous weapon*, he thought as he felt the sweat prickle his back. *Take a care on whom you use them.*

"If you must know—and I think you are nosy past all bearing—I felt comfortable around him, at peace, and not at all afraid that anything would ever hurt me." She returned her gaze to the flowers by the road's edge. "Things were always more fun when he was around."

He considered Clarissa Partridge and sighed. "I suppose

it must be a different feeling for men, then. Ah, well, I was curious."

"You don't feel that way around Miss Partridge?" she asked.

He shook his head. "Not yet."

"Well, it's still early days with you and her, isn't it?" Emma asked.

"I suppose." He looked behind him. They had been riding slower and slower, and the carriage would have to slow down. He picked up the pace of their travel, and they cantered ahead for a good distance.

"Well, what happened?" he asked finally when they slowed the pace again, and Emma still did not say anything. "I mean, between you and the Scot."

"Oh, well," she said, "it came to nothing. His indenture ended three years before mine would have."

"And?" he prompted. "Emma, you are so tight with information sometimes that I find you singularly exasperating!"

"It might not be your business," she responded tartly, then repented. "He was going beyond the mountains to take up some land in the Carolinas. He needed a wife then, so he married one of the other servants who was not under an indenture."

"The cad," Lord Ragsdale said with some feeling.

Emma laughed. "I was probably well out of that, my lord. If he could be so expedient, then he probably wouldn't have been too concerned about my welfare."

"I suppose not," Lord Ragsdale agreed. "I mean, he might have shot you if you had broken your leg or something."

And so they were on good terms again as they rode into London. *If I keep a light touch, and do not poke and prod about her family, we seem to rub along all right,* he considered as they entered the house on Curzon Street again. *But dash it, that gets me no closer to finding out anything, and I still don't know if I love Clarissa Partridge.*

He paid Clarissa a morning visit the next day, armed with

a pot of violets because Emma assured him that ladies loved violets, his eye patch on straight, and his clothes as orderly as Hanley could make them. He was not disappointed in his reception.

Clarissa cooed over the violets, just teetering, to his mind, on the edge of excess, then redeeming herself by sitting close to him on the sofa. Their knees touched once or twice, and he realized that it had been a long time since he had made love to a woman. Well, a long time for him. He dragged his mind along more appropriate lines then and thought he faked an impressive interest in her needlework. It was good, he had to admit, when she rose to put it away, affording him a particularly fine glimpse of her shapely hips and delicate walk.

I am being diddled, he thought and grinned to himself. *By all that's holy, it is fine.*

"Clarissa—may I call you Clarissa?"

Blush, blush. Titter. "Why certainly, my lord." She had a breathless voice, and he wondered if her corsets were too tight.

"You may call me John," he offered.

Another titter. Another blush. "Very well . . . John."

Take a deep breath, my dear, he thought, *or you may have to summon your dresser to loosen your stays. Of course, if you like to sit so close, I might want to do that myself.* "Clarissa, if I may be so bold, would you care to tour Hampton Court with me tomorrow?"

She cared to, and he left happily, wishing that Fae Moullé had not moved to Bath to set up her millinery establishment. *Emma would not approve*, he thought. *I will take a brisk walk home and behave myself.*

She was busy in the book room, catching up on his correspondence, when he returned and stood lounging in the doorway. "Yes, my lord?" she asked, her eyes still on the paper before her.

"Congratulate me, Miss Costello," he said as he came in

and flopped into a chair. "We are Clarissa and John now, and she will go riding to Hampton Court with me tomorrow."

Emma put down the pen and clasped her hands in front of her. "Bravo, my lord!" She smiled at him then, and his stomach did another tingle. "I think Manwaring will not be finished with that addition on your manor a moment too soon."

He nodded, not altogether satisfied with her reply and wondering why not. He also wished she would not waste those fine eyes on him. *You should get out more, Emma,* he wanted to tell her, *and meet some young men.* He regarded her a moment more, reminded himself that she couldn't because she was in his indenture, and felt vaguely silly.

She appeared not to notice but cleared her throat. "My lord, tomorrow is my day off . . . ," she began.

He made an expansive gesture, grateful to cover his stupid thoughts. "Of course, of course. Just don't come home so late this time, and I will not scold you."

"I won't." She was brief, to the point, withdrawn again, and looking at the correspondence in front of her. He eased himself out of the room, hoping that she would return in a better mood this time from her day off.

She was gone in the morning before he left, leaving neat piles of his correspondence in the book room, with directions on what to sign and what to tell Lasker to set out for the post. He initialed the little receipt for yesterday's violets, and on impulse added a note for another pot and directed it to the florist. *This one's for you, Emma,* he thought as he tucked that receipt with the others in the envelope for his banker and folded the note to the florist.

The weather was fine so he drove his curricle, leaving his tiger behind this time to fret. Since traffic was light, he turned toward the city first, thinking to drop off the note to the florist himself. Emma would probably enjoy a little surprise when she returned that evening.

He hurried through his errand and was moving into

traffic again when he noticed Emma, her eyes straight ahead, moving swiftly along the sidewalk not fifty feet in front of him. He almost hailed her, thinking to invite her to ride with him to her destination, then thought better of it. *I will follow her instead,* he considered.

It was an easy matter to travel behind her, moving slowly with the traffic, always keeping her in sight, but not dogging her heels, either. She had no notion she was being followed but hurried along with that purposeful, swinging gait of hers that he had admired on occasion. She walked like someone used to walking, someone who was going somewhere. It was a healthy walk, and one that stirred him somehow.

She led him deep into the City to a row of government buildings not far from the Admiralty. The traffic was thinning out now, so he drove to the curb and left his horse and curricle under the watchful eye of a street urchin and his little sister. "Mind that nothing happens, and you will have a crown," he admonished as he tied the reins and continued after Emma on foot.

He recognized the Home Office and waited on the sidewalk until she was inside. He sprinted across the road then, determined not to lose her in the building, and remembering it, from a visit years ago, as a regular rabbit warren of offices and cubbyholes.

There she was, walking slower now, almost reluctantly, as she had during their visit to Newgate. She appeared to hesitate before an open door. As he watched, she squared her shoulders, appeared to take a deep breath, and held her head up as she walked into the room. The gallant gesture went right to his heart.

He knew he dared not follow any farther, some instinct telling him that she would be unhappy to see him there. She appeared to be in a lobby or antechamber, and there were others standing and waiting. He turned to go and collided with a clerk, his sleeves rolled up, his expression harried, carrying stacks of papers that flew out of his hands and slid across the cold marble floor.

"I beg your pardon, sir," the clerk gasped, going down on all fours to retrieve his papers.

"Oh, my fault, my fault," Lord Ragsdale insisted and dropped to his knees to help. They gathered up papers in silence for a moment, then he sat back on his heels. "Tell me, what is that office?" he asked, gesturing toward the door where Emma had disappeared.

The clerk, his face red from exertion, took the documents from him. "It's the Office of Criminal Business," he said. "Mr. John Henry Capper is chief clerk, sir."

Lord Ragsdale thanked him, got to his feet, and brushed off his trousers. He strolled toward the entrance, his mind in a ferment. *Emma, what is your business with that band of thieves?*

He stood outside the building a moment, wondering what Emma would do if he joined her in the anteroom. *This is none of my business,* he argued with himself. *If she wanted to tell me, she would. I have given her plenty of openings.* He thought again of Sir Augustus's advice. *Do I dare poke at your wounds, Emma? You prodded mine, but then I agreed to it. I have no right to do the same to you.*

And Clarissa was waiting. "Blast it!" he said out loud, and started running toward his curricle. He looked back once at the building, then tried to put it out of his mind.

Chapter 16

LORD RAGSDALE HAD ALWAYS LIKED Hampton Court, even from his earliest days, when his mother and father took him walking there on one of their infrequent trips to London. He loved the sound that a pair of firm footsteps could make in the great hall, and never objected, no matter what the weather, to a perambulation about the whole building to gaze at the medallions on the walls and wonder about the arrogance of kings. As he grew older, he occasionally thought how nice it would be to bring a lady to Hampton Court. He couldn't imagine a better place for a little serious wooing.

But not today, not even with one of the Season's loveliest diamonds hanging on his arm and looking at him with those crystal blue eyes. On another day, perhaps he could have appreciated the way her bosom brushed his arm, and the way she had of running her tongue along her lips that had probably reduced other peers to blancmange. As it was, he entertained as best he could with tales of headless ghosts, thinking of Emma in that anteroom of the Office of Criminal Business.

Merciful heaven, criminal business. But Clarissa was tugging at his sleeve and pouting her prettiest pout, one that surely should have earned her a quick kiss at least. He swallowed, fighting down words of irritation that he knew he would regret, and resisted the urge to brush her off.

"You're not listening to a thing I am saying, John," she said.

She was right. He hadn't heard one word in ten of her babble.

What was she carrying on about? Could it be even half as important as what Emma was doing, even now as he dawdled through a musty old hall with England's prettiest woman on his arm? There were other tourists about, and he looked up occasionally from his contemplation of the parquet flooring to notice the envious glances other men were giving him. *I am a fool*, he thought, and the idea cheered him immensely. *But I was already a fool, so this is nothing to repine about.*

"I'm sorry, my dear Clarissa," he said, hoping he sounded contrite. He stopped and faced her, taking both her hands in his. "I do have a little business on my mind." He kissed her nose. "Let me resolve to forget it."

But he couldn't, no matter how hard he tried to devote his whole attention to the beauty he squired about. His head was beginning to ache. His scalp began to itch where the ties to his eye patch knotted at the back of his head. He found himself walking faster, as though trying to hurry up the afternoon so he could return to the Home Office. He could not fathom why he had ever considered Hampton Court such a favorite of his.

Clarissa, Clarissa, what am I going to do with you? he asked himself. *You are beautiful, and it could very well be that I love you, but right now, I wish we were anywhere but here.* He thought a moment, considering his options, and then decided that only the honorable thing would do; he would lie.

"Clarissa, I do have some pressing business in the City," he confessed. "It involves some . . . some charitable work I am doing at Newgate." *What a corker that is*, he thought. *The Lord may strike me dead. Why couldn't I have mentioned orphans at St. Paul's or the deserving poor under some bridge?*

"Newgate?" she echoed, her voice reaching a distinctly unpleasant pitch. "You?"

"Well, yes," he said, piqued that his reputation was so lackluster that she considered philanthropy out of the question and then ashamed of himself for the lie. "They are wretched creatures!"

That was no prevarication. He could testify to their wretchedness. He took her hand and strolled along, resisting the urge to whip out his pocket watch and begrudge each second that crawled by. "I have a transaction I must perform on their behalf at the Office of Criminal Business, and I really should not put it off." He placed his hand on his chest. "They need me."

He tried not to wince, waiting for an offended deity to smite him dead. Nothing happened, except that Clarissa clung to his hand even more tightly and gazed up into his face with an expression closely resembling adoration.

"What a wonderful man you are," she breathed, and again he wondered about the stress to her corset strings. "I am sure I never knew anyone as considerate as you."

Her statement was so ludicrous that only by force of will did he keep from laughter. He lowered his head and bit his lip and managed somehow to appear so modest that Clarissa rested her glorious blonde hair against his arm for a long moment.

"You must tell Papa all about your philanthropic work among the felons when we see him in Bath in three days."

Good heavens, what have I promised? he asked himself wildly. *When did I ever say I would go to Bath? Could that have been when I was admiring her bosom during the interval at the opera and nodded?* He quickened his pace toward the entrance.

"I don't precisely remember Bath," he began cautiously as he directed the porter to bring his curricle. He staved off the beginnings of a pout by a quick kiss on her forehead, wondering what else he had promised Clarissa Partridge. "Perhaps you could refresh my memory."

"Silly boy," she began, generous in her scold. "I'm sure you have so much more on your mind than little me."

You can't imagine, he thought and kissed her hand. "Oh, you are a dear one," he mumbled. It made no sense, but Clarissa would never know.

"Papa is in Bath because of his gout, and you promised Mama and me that you would accompany us there on Thursday," she reminded him.

Did I? He slapped his forehead. "Oh, of course, my love," he said. "Silly me."

She dimpled prettily and let him help her into the curricle. "You said you wanted to talk to Papa about something." She blushed and fluttered her eyelashes at him. "I can't imagine what . . ."

I am to be married, he thought wildly. It was a cool day, but he could feel sweat forming on his spinal column. He took his time going around to the other side of the curricle. *Calm, calm, John*, he told himself. *You know this is what you want.*

"I am certain Sir Cecil and I will think of something to say to one another," he teased, feeling as though someone else was speaking through his mouth and he was standing outside his skin, watching. "My dear, if it chances that my business should take another day, would Friday be amenable to your plans?"

"I am sure Mama and I would be only too happy to delay our departure and give you one more day to do good. John, you cannot imagine how I feel."

Nor I, he agreed, starting his horse off at a sedate pace, when he really longed to snap the whip and leap hedgerows. *I know this is what I want, and I will make Emma ever so proud. Why are my hands shaking?*

He was able to convince her to come to the Home Office with him, assuring her that he would only be a minute. He left her standing in the entrance and sprinted toward the Office of Criminal Business. He would go to the porter and ask for an appointment with Mr. Capper on the morrow; perhaps he could learn Emma's business that way.

He hurried to the anteroom door and stopped. Emma

stood there alone in the room, her back to the door. He looked around in surprise. No one else was there except the porter, who was busying himself with papers on his desk. *How strange,* he thought. *Surely Emma arrived early enough this morning for an audience.* He tiptoed quietly away from the office and met Clarissa at the main lobby.

"This is a dreadful place," she whispered to him as she grabbed his arm. "I have never seen so many sinister-looking fellows."

"And those are just the solicitors," he joked. She looked at him blankly, and he knew then that his future would involve explaining witticisms to his wife. "Well, never mind, my dear. Let me drive you home now."

He resisted her invitation to dinner, assuring her that he would not faint from hunger between Whitcomb and Curzon Streets, and promising her that he would take her driving tomorrow afternoon. "We will discuss this delightful expedition to Bath, my dear," he said as he blew a kiss in her general vicinity, leaped into his curricle as soon as the door closed, and sprang his horse back to the city.

Emma was not in the anteroom when he returned, out of breath from running through emptying corridors. The porter was gathering up his papers and climbing down from his stool by the inner door.

"We're closed now, sir," he said, nodding to Lord Ragsdale. "Come again in the morning."

"I am sure that won't be necessary now," he said as he approached the porter. "That pretty woman who was here a moment ago . . . did she finally get in to see Mr. Capper?"

The porter laughed and shook his head. "I love to diddle the Irish!" He winked at Lord Ragsdale. "She can keep coming back week after week until she wears out, and she'll never get through that door."

Lord Ragsdale stared at him. "What are you saying?"

The porter grinned back. "I'm saying that I have no use

for the Irish. I think they should all be transported, and not just a select few."

And so I thought too, he considered, pausing to catch his breath. *I hated them all, but now I just worry.* He tried again.

"Was she asking for information about someone transported to Australia?"

"Well, laddie, America's out now. Where else do we send them felons?"

"I'm Lord Ragsdale to you," he snapped, suddenly furious, and fighting down the strong inclination to grab the man by his neckcloth and do him damage. "Give me a straight answer, or it's your job tomorrow."

The porter obviously believed him. His eyes widened, and he hurried to straighten his coat and run a hand through his thinning hair. "I means no disrespect, my lord," he gasped. "She . . . she said something about wanting to know the whereabouts of some prisoners transported after the Castle Hill Revolt in 1803."

Lord Ragsdale nodded. Castle Hill. He remembered reading about it in the London papers over his morning brandy. There were hangings, which only pleased him at the time, and a man who declared that no one would write his epitaph until Ireland took her rightful place among the nations. He remembered laughing over that bit of high Irish drama.

"And you won't let her in to see Mr. Capper?" he asked quietly, turning his attention back to the porter. "What gives you that right? You are a scoundrel, and I don't mind telling you."

"Y-y-yes, my lord," the porter stuttered, retreating behind his desk again.

"How dare you humiliate that lady," he said, warming to the cause and coming around the desk.

The little man scrambled over the desk and darted for the door. "But she's Irish! She's fair game!" he shouted as he tripped over the doorsill, leaped to his feet, and ran down the hall, leaving Lord Ragsdale in possession of an empty anteroom.

It was dark out now. Lord Ragsdale shoved his hands in his pockets and walked slowly from the building, nodding to the night watchman. Outside, he leaned against the wall and collected himself. *How can we be so cruel?* he asked himself. *What gives us the arrogance to treat our own kind like the meanest vegetation? She has family somewhere, and no one will help her find them. I make her do my stupid business, when I should be doing everything in my power to help her find those she loves.*

He drove slowly back to Curzon Street, ignoring the curses of other drivers in more of a hurry. *I do not know that I could ever apologize enough*, he thought as he rode along, hunched down in the seat, the reins loose in his hands. *And if I were to try, I would probably be treading on her dignity yet again.*

He arrived in time for dinner, or so Lasker informed him as he came into the main hall, feeling as though he had just climbed one hundred steps instead of ten.

"I am certain Lady Ragsdale and Miss Claridge will understand if you do not dress, my lord," Lasker offered as he took Lord Ragsdale's overcoat.

He paused then and took a serious look at Lasker. "Did you ever think how silly that expression sounds?" he asked his surprised butler. "I mean, 'dressing for dinner.' I am already dressed. And who cares whether I address a roast of beef in proper attire?"

"My lord?" Lasker inquired.

"Nothing, Lasker," he said, waving his hand wearily. "I am just amazed at myself and people like me."

"Very well, then, my lord, but are you coming to dinner?" the butler asked, persistent to the end.

"I'm not hungry, Lasker, and I am not going to Almack's, or the opera, or any other blasted nonsense selected for me tonight." He wanted to say more, to remind his butler that there were people on the streets of London who were hungry, and cold, and who needed help, while people like him dressed for dinner and put their rumps in chairs at the opera. "I'm not going out tonight, Lasker," he said instead.

"Very well, my lord," Lasker replied, his face wooden.

Lord Ragsdale looked at his butler and took a deep breath. "I will be in the book room. I want you to send Emma Costello there immediately. We are not to be disturbed."

He turned on his heel and left his dumbfounded butler standing in the hall, holding his overcoat. He stood for a long moment in the book room doorway, acutely aware that this was no place to prod at someone's wounds until they bled again, but he could think of no other place. He closed the door behind him and lit a fire, noting with some surprise that his hands were shaking.

He was seated at the desk, looking at nothing, when Emma knocked on the door.

"Come in," he said, wishing that his voice did not sound so wintry. It was not her fault that he and his countrymen were weighed every day in the balance and found wanting. "Please," he added.

Emma came into the room and stood before him at the desk. He looked up at her, noting her red eyes and the defeat evident in the way she held herself. He pulled up a chair beside his at the desk. "Sit down, Emma."

She sat, leaning ever so slightly away from him, as though she feared the look on his face. He sighed and began to rub his forehead. He took off his eye patch and leaned forward, his hands clasped in front of him.

"Emma, I've just come from the Office of Criminal Business."

He heard her little gasp but spared her his scrutiny. "The porter there assured me that you would never get in to see Mr. Capper because you are Irish. I will have his job in the morning, my dear, and I promise you we will see Mr. Capper."

She began to cry then, a helpless sound more painful to his ears than any he could remember, including his own agony at the death of his father. She bowed her head and wept, and he could only sit there and watch her. In a moment, he handed her his handkerchief, and she hid her face in it, sobbing the deep, wracking tears of someone in the worst kind of misery. He let her cry in peace, wondering what to say. *I think I shall be wise and keep my mouth shut,* he decided finally.

Emma stopped crying and blew her nose vigorously. She dabbed at her eyes and glanced in his direction. "I am so sorry, my lord."

"No, it is I who am sorry. I want you to tell me everything. Don't leave out a detail. How can I help you if I do not know?"

She stared at him then, her face red, her eyes swollen. "You would help me?" she asked, her voice filled with disbelief.

"Oh, Emma," was all he could say.

She took a deep breath and leaned back in the chair. "My father was a landowner in County Wicklow. He was a Presbyterian, and his family had been in Ireland for generations. Mama was Catholic, but he loved her and married her anyway. There were four of us, two older brothers, me, and a younger brother."

She paused then, as though even that much was difficult. "I remember you told me once that your father went to Magdalen College," he said, trying to keep his tone conversational, hoping to relax her.

She nodded and gave him the ghost of a smile. It vanished almost before he was sure he had seen it. "Eamon was headed there in the fall." She shook her head and began to wail this time. The hair rose on the back of his neck as he remembered that keen from his days of trouble in Ireland. He wanted to leap from his chair, but he forced himself to stay where he was. He took her hand, and she squeezed it so tight that he almost winced.

"What happened, Emma?" he asked, feeling like a

brute in the face of her torment. "Why didn't Eamon go to Oxford?"

"Because he was dead by fall, or I think he was. Oh, John, I don't know! I have spent over five years not knowing, and it is killing me." Her words came out in a rush, as though they had been dammed up years ago.

She loosened her grip on his hand but did not let go. He put his other hand over hers too.

"Then tell me, Emma."

She nodded. "We never involved ourselves in Irish troubles, my lord," she said. "Da always said it was not our fight. After the '98, he severed any connections any of us had to the Society of the United Irish. Some of our neighbors belonged, but Da said to leave it alone, and we did."

"Are you Catholic, Emma?" he asked.

"Aye, me and two of my brothers. Eamon and Da were Presbyterian." She released his hand then and wiped her eyes again with the soaking handkerchief. He looked in his drawer for another and handed it to her. She accepted it with a brief smile.

"I suppose he thought we could rub along and not get involved," she continued, and her voice took on an edge. "And we would have, except that I blundered. What happened then is all my fault."

She bowed her head, as though the weight of her pain was too great. He moved closer and touched her hair, his hand going to the back of her neck and then her shoulder. She leaned her cheek against his hand for a moment, as if seeking strength. *Strength from me*, he thought in wonder. *Emma, this does reveal the measure of your desperation.*

"Tell me," he urged.

She straightened up then but would not look at him. He could sense the shame in her, the godly sorrow that went beyond bone deep, and it touched him as nothing ever had. "Emma," he said.

"Timothy—my younger brother—was ill with a cold.

Da, Eamon, and Sam were away on estate business. I was in charge because Mama was asleep from tending Tim all night. Oh, John, I can't," she said. "Don't make me."

"You have to, Emma," he insisted, feeling like a churl.

She rose and went to the window, looking out for the longest time. He turned to watch her profile, and he knew that the view she saw was not the one he was familiar with out that same window.

"He came walking to the house at dusk. I remember the time, because I had just lit the lamps and told the cook to wait dinner until Da and my brothers returned."

"Who, Emma?" he asked.

She turned to look at him then. "Robert Emmet, my lord."

Suddenly he remembered. "Castle Hill," he said.

Emma nodded. "He told me his carriage had broken down on the road from Cash and asked if he could stay the night. I . . . I let him in."

She turned back to the window and raised her fist as though to strike the glass. He leaped to his feet and grabbed her hand before she did herself an injury. She began to weep again, and he pulled her onto his lap, holding her so tight that he could almost feel her sobs before they came. He listened to her sorrow and began to understand. He kissed her hair and kept her close.

"Of course you did, Emma. I am sure your mother always taught you to help those in trouble. But you didn't have any idea who he was, did you?"

She shook her head. "No. It was just a name to me then. I told him he could stay and be welcome too. He said it would only be for the night."

He searched his mind, trying to recall the Castle Hill revolt just outside of Dublin and Robert Emmet's attempt to stage a rising. If he remembered right, it had fizzled and come to nothing.

"How old were you?" he asked, marking time and trying to help her calm down.

"I was nineteen, my lord. My little brother, Tim, was five." She was silent a moment more, and he could feel her relax slightly. He loosened his grip on her but kept his arm about her waist.

"When your father returned . . . ," he prompted.

"Oh, he and my brothers welcomed him too, and they sat a long time over port when dinner was done." She laughed bitterly. "Papa told me later they talked about hunting and fishing and Mr. Emmet's fiancée who lived close by. He said he was on his way there when his carriage broke down. Of course, Papa never saw a broken carriage on the Cash road, but he didn't think of it at the time."

She realized then that she was sitting on his lap and put her hands to her cheeks. "I am sorry, my lord. Please forgive me for being so forward!"

He smiled at her. "I put you there, Emma, and I believe I will keep you there."

He thought she would leap off his lap then, but she did not. She settled herself against him like a puppy seeking warmth. "He stayed the night, and then he was gone by morning light." She stared straight ahead then. "He was arrested by government troops at the entrance to our estate. I think they must have watched us all night." She shook her head and made an impotent gesture with her hand.

It was so clear to him what had happened then that his own mind recoiled from speech. *How could they?* he thought. *If the sins of nations must be atoned for at some distant judgment bar, England will pay for this one.*

"And they arrested your family for complicity," he whispered, when he could speak. "Oh, Emma."

She spoke then in a monotone voice, so low and chilling that he was reminded of tales of zombies his Caribbean nursemaid told in the nursery years and years ago. "They yanked Tim out of his sickbed and ordered me to carry him. Da, Eamon, and Sam were bound together. Mama and I carried Tim ten miles that day toward Dublin." She paused then, and her voice became wistful. "I remember that it was raining, and I lost a shoe in the mud."

"You walked all the way to Dublin?"

"Aye. Tim died on the way." She made another odd gesture with her hand, as though to wipe away the memory. "At least, I am sure he did. He was burning with fever, and the captain of the guard forced us to leave him in Diggtown with a family named Holladay." She burrowed closer to him. "His eyes were sinking back in his head, and there was a fearsome gurgle in his throat."

He chewed that over, letting her sit in silence until the coals settled in the fireplace, and she sat up, startled. He pulled her back against his chest again.

"The rest of you made it to Dublin?"

"Aye. Mama and I were taken to the Marlborough Street Riding School, where they were holding women involved in Castle Hill. The others went to Prevot Prison." She shuddered, and he understood why. He had been to Prevot himself in 1798, when he had escorted prisoners there from Cork before his own injury.

"Were they tortured?" he asked as gently as he could.

She nodded. "But they wouldn't say anything." She looked at him, her eyes huge. "What could they say? They knew nothing!" She pounded on his chest in her rage, then threw her arms around him and wept.

He held her close, murmuring softly to her, devastated at the depth of her sorrow and understanding her deep shame. *And you think you brought it on them all, my dear. This is too big a burden to bear alone.* "This is tragic, my dear, but hardly your fault."

"I am not through," she interrupted, her voice cold. "When they would not speak, the English took me from Marlborough to Prevot and tortured me in front of them."

"Oh, please no!" he exclaimed, feeling such a measure of horror and revulsion that his stomach writhed. "No, Emma!" he declared, as though his words could take it away.

She held up her left hand to him, holding it with her right to steady it. "You've noticed my fingers, my lord?" she asked, her eyes glittering with a fierce anger that burned into his body almost.

"Yes," he whispered. "They pulled out your fingernails, didn't they?"

"Aye." She looked at her hand, the fingernails grown back, but with bumpy ridges. "I tried not to scream, but I couldn't help myself. I even bit through my lip."

"Emma, don't," he pleaded.

"You wanted to know," she said calmly. "Well, now you will know. They told my father they were going to rape me right there. That was when Eamon confessed."

"But . . ."

"Confessed to crimes he never committed, to spare me." She stood up, and there was a dignity and majesty about her. "Now you begin to understand something of what drives me, my lord. It is not pretty, is it?"

Chapter 17

NO, IT IS NOT PRETTY, HE AGREED AFTER A night of twisting and turning in his bed until he was a prisoner of his sheets and weary with no sleep. As dawn was beginning to tinge the sky, he dragged himself to his armchair by the window and propped his bare feet on the ledge. *I wonder that she can endure. May the Lord smite me if I ever whine again.*

The rest of her story was told in fits and starts. How Eamon had been ripped from them and thrown into a cell for the condemned. They heard gallows under construction for some and learned from their triumphant jailers of Robert Emmet's death by beheading. They begged, they pleaded, but the authorities did not bother to tell them who else had died, as though Irish grief was as dismissible as a gnat before the face.

On his lap again, Emma spoke of her escape, her voice still wondering at the mystery of it all. They had kept her in Prevot for another week, and then suddenly all the prisoners were removed to Marlborough Street Riding School, hurried along through the streets of Dublin as night was falling.

"It was typhus, and they moved everyone," she explained into his soaked waistcoat. "Da and I were not chained together, and I know it must have been an oversight. When we passed a crowd and the guard wasn't looking, he pushed me into the mob and said, 'Indenture,' to the man who caught me."

Her voice lost some of its tightness as she told of being hustled that very night to the Dublin docks and put aboard a ship bound for America and the West Indies. "And so I came to the Claridges," she concluded. "I never thought I would have a chance to look for my family again, but when Mr. Claridge said he was sending Sally and Robert to England, I knew I had to come."

"And you have been treated shabbily," he concluded. "That will change tomorrow, Emma. We are returning to the Office of Criminal Business, and I assure you that Mr. Capper will see you."

"You would do that for me?" she asked in surprise, not realizing how her spontaneous question deepened his own shame.

"I will do that for you, Emma."

"I will do that for you," he repeated at dawn to the window. *And then what? Will there be tidy lists of prisoners bound for Australia, or am I only letting Emma in for more frustration and heartache? Put baldly, is this a kindness?*

He decided that it was as he watched, bleary-eyed an hour later, as the maid put more coal in the grate and started the fire. He knew he looked worse than usual because of her darting glances and the way she almost ran from his room. *Even if Emma continues to be disappointed at every turn, at least she will know that we tried everything we could,* he reasoned. *This is far better than going through life never knowing.*

Dressed and ready for the day, he came downstairs at six, surprising Lasker. "There is no breakfast yet, my lord," he apologized, even as he hurried to light the candles in the breakfast room.

Lord Ragsdale shrugged. "Tea then, Lasker," he said and sat down at the empty table with the newspaper. He looked up at his butler, whose face wore a quizzical expression. "Tell Emma to come here."

"Yes, my lord." The butler hesitated. "I do not believe she slept last night," he said. "The scullery maid heard her crying in the next room."

Emma, and I was not there to hold you? he thought. *I would have. I was sleepless only one floor below you.* He considered the paper a moment, then rejected it, struck by the fact that he was the best friend she had at the moment. "She'll be awake, won't she?" he asked and turned back to the paper. "Bring two cups."

She was there in a few minutes, pale and serious in the deep green wool dress he had commissioned for her. He gestured to a chair, but she did not sit. He looked up.

"My lord, it is not my place to sit here," she reminded him.

"It is if I say so. Sit."

She perched on the edge of the seat, as if ready for flight if another family member were to appear. He filled a teacup and pushed it toward her. She sipped it slowly, cradling her hands around the cup as though she were cold inside and out.

He read through the newspaper without comment, then folded it and looked at her. "I am remiss in something, Emma," he said.

She looked at him then, curious.

"Do you remember when I asked you what would make you happy?"

Emma nodded. "That seems so long ago, my lord."

"I think it was longer ago than either of us can really appreciate," he murmured. "You have your own bed and your own room, do you not?"

She nodded again, obviously mystified and wondering where he was leading.

He stood up and gestured for her to follow him. "I believe you also wanted to hear Mass. Let us go."

She took him by the arm. "You don't need to do this, my lord," she said.

He took her hand and pulled her after him into the hall.

"Of course I do, my dear. I will take you to St. Stephens, where you will have ample time for confession first and then Mass."

"You want me to tell this whole story to a priest," she asked, but it was more of a statement.

"I do indeed." He allowed Lasker to help him into his overcoat, and then he waited for Emma to retrieve her cloak. "Unless I have been misjudging the Almighty all these years—and I probably have—you are about to discover that you have nothing to be forgiven for."

She said nothing as they rode toward the city, only beginning to stir now with carters and other early risers. She stared straight ahead, but he knew it was not the angry, sullen mistrust of their earlier acquaintance. Again, he had the feeling that she was seeing things out of his vision. He looked down at her hands and noticed that they were balled into tight fists. He put his hand over hers.

"Don't worry, Emma. Have you ever considered the possibility that the Lord might be on your side?"

He could tell from her expression that she had not, and he wisely gave himself over to silence too.

There were only a few worshipers in St. Stephen's, a small Catholic church on the outskirts of the financial district that he knew about only from driving by on several occasions. The earlier Mass had just finished, and the smell of wax was strong in the low-ceilinged chapel. Emma took a deep breath of the mingled ecclesiastical odors and sighed.

"It has been so long, my lord," she murmured as she started toward a confessional. She looked back at him once, real fear in her eyes, and he longed to follow her, but he only smiled and seated himself in the back of the church, crossing his fingers and hoping that the Lord was the kind of fellow Lord Ragsdale thought He was.

She was a long time in the confessional, but he knew it was a long story and felt no impatience. He was content to breathe deep himself and allow the aura of the place to work its way into his spirits. When she came out, he made room for her on the bench.

He wanted to speak to her, but she dropped immediately to her knees and began to recite the rosary, murmuring softly. She had no beads, so she ticked off the litany on her fingers. He watched Emma and resolved to find a rosary from somewhere for her. *What a paltry gift for someone who has given me so much*, he thought.

When she finished, she sat beside him. "You were right," she whispered.

He leaned closer until their shoulders touched. "I thought so. Any penance?"

She smiled at him, and his heart flopped. There was nothing in her smile of reticence, calculation, or wariness this time, only a great relief probably visible to ships at sea or Indians in distant tepees. "He told me to recite one rosary," she whispered back.

"Small penance, my dear," he said, wishing she would turn her marvelous, incandescent gaze on some other man.

She grinned even wider. "Faith, my lord, he's an Irish priest."

He burst into laughter, forgetting where he was. Heads turned, parishioners glowered. He rested his long legs on the prayer bench and sank down lower in the pew, stifling the laughter that still threatened, and thinking suddenly of Clarissa, who wouldn't recognize a joke if it said hello.

The Mass began. He nudged her. "You know, Emma, we're very much alike," he commented.

She digested this, her attention divided between him and the priest at the altar. "Oh, we are?"

"I drowned myself in bitterness and alcohol, and you let yourself be captured by guilt. Such foolish damage we have done ourselves."

She nodded and sighed. "I probably would have taken to the bottle, my lord, but I had no money like you."

"Ah, my dear, the toils of the too wealthy . . ."

The parishioner in the pew in front of them turned around and put a finger to her lips. Lord Ragsdale winked at her, and she turned back swiftly.

"D'ye know, I think I will seek out the man I hate the most and give him the contents of my wine cellar," he whispered to Emma. "And my first choice is the porter at the Office of Criminal Business."

She laughed this time, and the priest paused momentarily, glaring at her. "Hush, my lord," she insisted. "You are a bad influence on me. In another moment, I really will have something to confess, and it will be your fault."

Lord Ragsdale behaved himself for the rest of the Mass, marveling at the prescience of the priest to deliver his homily on forgiveness. He watched, great peace in his heart, as Emma took the sacrament at the altar, then returned to kneel beside him. He knew she was crying, and he kept his hand on her shoulder for the remainder of the service.

"Well, my dear, can we face the porter now?" he asked her in front of the church as he helped her into another hackney.

"I can face anything," she assured him.

"It may be that we learn little or nothing," he warned her. "We may come away feeling worse."

"I know, my lord," she said quietly. "But at least we will know we are trying."

Her hand tight in his, they approached the porter in the Office of Criminal Business, who practically threw himself off his stool and asked in unctuous, kindly tones if they would like to see Mr. Capper.

"Indeed we would," Lord Ragsdale said. "You must want to keep your job." He looked the cowering man in the eye. "Do you know, it probably wouldn't be too hard to get *you* transported."

To his grim amusement, they found themselves hurried into a cluttered office. "Mr. John Henry Capper," the porter announced and then beat a hasty retreat.

Capper stood and motioned them into chairs in front

of the desk. He took a few swipes at the piles of paper surrounding him, gave up, then seated himself.

"I am Lord Ragsdale, and this is my servant, Emma Costello," he began, gesturing to Emma. "She has a story for you." He sat back then, and let Emma tell it all again, leaving nothing out. He watched the clerk's face, wondering if such a man in such a job would be moved by her words. *I wonder if it is possible to become hardened to such wretchedness,* he thought and then decided it was not. Capper listened intently, asking questions quietly but not disturbing the flow of her narrative. Several times he passed his hand across his eyes, but his attention never wavered.

When she finished and blew her nose on the handkerchief Lord Ragsdale kept handy, Capper looked from one to the other, his lips set in a tight line. He asked her the names of all her family members and scribbled them on the pad in front of him.

"Your mother, Miss Costello. Do you think she is yet alive?"

Emma shook her head and reached for Lord Ragsdale's hand again. "She was so sick when I was taken out for torture in Prevot."

Capper drew a line through her name, and Emma flinched.

Lord Ragsdale tightened his grip. "And here, your little brother, Timothy?" he asked, his pencil poised over the next name.

"Oh, no," she whispered. "He is the only one I am certain of." Lord Ragsdale felt his own nerves tingling at the pencil's brief scratch.

Capper quickly drew a line through Eamon's name. "I suspect he was hanged, as you fear. You say he was separated from you after his confession?"

Emma nodded, her face pale. Capper sighed and drew a circle around the two remaining names. He stared at them a moment, as though wishing the names would turn into information, then reached behind him to pull down a ledger. He searched through the pages, then opened it on his desk.

"Miss Costello, you must be aware of one thing that might render any search futile. A great number of those Irish insurrectionists were never tried but were sent directly to Australia or Van Diemen's Land. I am telling you this because there will likely be no record of them in any Home Office or judicial files."

"They just vanish then, as though they had never lived?" Lord Ragsdale asked in amazement.

Capper nodded. "It certainly makes for untidy records," he said.

"Blast your records," Lord Ragsdale said. "These are people we are talking about."

"I know, my lord, I know," Capper said. He directed his attention to Emma. "Miss Costello, I can think of only one way to learn anything, and that is to locate the ship's manifests for those convict voyages. They may or may not contain the information you seek on prisoner rosters."

He turned back to the ledger and ruffled through several more pages before pausing. He pounded on the ledger in triumph. "And here we have the ships, my dear." He leaned closer to the book, then began to write on his pad again. "There were six ships in the 1804 transport." He looked up at them. "And we are only assuming here that they were transported in 1804, and not 1805. It could not have been 1805?"

Emma shook her head. "I think it was almost October when I was taken to Prevot."

"Well, then, here we are. The *Minerva*, the *Lady Penthyn*, the *Friendship*, the *Marquess Cornwallis*, the *Britannia*, and the *Hercules*." He wrote down the names of the ships and handed it to Emma. He spoke to Lord Ragsdale. "I will send you with a porter to the Home Office archives. I do not know that they can offer you any assistance, but the records could be there."

Lord Ragsdale rose and shook hands with Capper. "We appreciate your efforts."

"It was paltry," he said, nodding to Emma. "And you must also realize, my dear, that even if you discover they were transported, that is far from being a guarantee that they are alive."

"I know that," Emma replied, looking at the names on the paper she held. "But I must try."

Capper nodded and walked them to the door. He handed a note to the porter, who led them quickly through the corridors to the Home Office, looking over his shoulder in fear at Lord Ragsdale several times. They followed him up a flight of narrow stairs and into a room filled with file boxes. "Criminal Business there in the corner," he said, gesturing to a row of boxes stuffed on shelves.

"You are all kindness," Lord Ragsdale murmured. He rubbed his forehead, feeling the beginnings of a headache. "Well, Emma," he began when the porter left. "Shall we start?"

Hours later, his head was pounding in dreadful earnest as he paused and looked at the pile of papers that surrounded them. His good eye was beginning to tear and blur, and he knew he was defeated. Emma watched him from the middle of her pile of papers, and he could see nothing but concern in her eyes.

"You have to stop, Lord Ragsdale," she said, her voice practical, as though she admonished him over tea and biscuits. "I am discovering how much I can bear, but I could not bear it if you lost the sight in your eye because of this."

"I'm sorry, Emma," he began, but she stopped him with a gesture.

"I'll stay here a little longer," she said. "Why don't you go home?"

"I feel like a quitter," he protested. "Perhaps if I just lie down for a while and close my eye . . ."

"I won't hear of it," she insisted as she got to her feet and pulled him to his. "You used to tease me about 'too much exertion,' but this is truly too much for you. Just leave me a little money for hackney fare."

He fished in his pocket for some change and handed it to her.

"We can return tomorrow . . . ," he began, then sighed in exasperation. "Oh, bother it! Emma, I am to go to Bath tomorrow with Clarissa Partridge!"

She smiled at him, "That is hardly lover-like, my lord. It is a good thing I do not intend to tattle to her. I will return here tomorrow, if I have your permission. And you will go to Bath and fix your fate."

He wished she would not put it like that and nearly told her so.

Before he could speak, she stood before him on tiptoe and dabbed at his eye. "Please go right home and have Lasker give you a cold cloth for that. I'll follow soon enough. I promise."

"Oh, very well," he grumbled.

He was still muttering to himself as he descended all those stairs and found himself on the street again. He hailed a hackney, gave his direction, and sank into it with some relief as the jarvey cracked his whip and they started off. He closed his eye, wondering if he would be dreaming of ships and lists all night, and praying that Mama and Sally had no evening plans that would affect him beyond a little polite conversation over dinner.

They had traveled several blocks toward Mayfair when he suddenly realized where they had gone wrong. He sat up and pounded on the side of the cab. "Stop this thing!" he roared.

The jarvey did as he was bid. "Sir?" he asked in frosty surprise.

"Turn around," Lord Ragsdale said decisively. "Take me to the docks."

He sank back into the cab two hours later, just as the sun

was going down. He could scarcely see out of his good eye, and he wondered how much of a peal Emma would ring over him. He held the lists tight in his hand and brought them close to his face. "Yes!" he said in triumph and closed his eye for the return trip.

His eye had stopped blurring by the time the jarvey let him off at Curzon Street, and he had no trouble negotiating the steps to his front door. He knew that Emma would be waiting for him as soon as he opened the door, and she was. He wanted to grab her and whirl her about, but the look on her face brought him back quickly to his own state.

"Where have you been?" she asked, and she helped him from his coat, ignoring Lasker, who hovered nearby. "I have been beside myself."

He knew she was telling the truth. Her own eyes were puffy from crying, and it touched him to the bone that she cared so much. He let her help him to the book room, where she pushed him down on the sofa and told Lasker to bring a cold cloth for his eye, scolding all the while.

"I am certain your doctors tell you not to strain your eye, my lord," she said as she took off his shoes and made him swing his legs onto the sofa. She covered him with a light blanket and gently put the cloth to his eye when Lasker returned. The darkness was soothing, and he almost allowed himself to sleep. The lists. He sat up, even as she tried to push him down again.

"Emma, don't be a carbuncle," he protested. "Hand me my overcoat. I have something for you."

She did as he asked. He kept the cloth to his eye as he groped in the inside lining. He held up the sheaf of papers to her. "I was starting home when it occurred to me that I should check some ships' offices at the docks. Emma, we were looking at this problem from the wrong end!" He handed her the papers and lay back down again.

"My lord, these are three rosters!" she said, her voice filled with wonder.

He grinned at her. "There they were, languishing on yet another dusty shelf. Mr. Capper didn't stop to consider that sometimes the prisoners were transported in vessels contracted by the Royal Navy and other times, by commercial carriers arranged by the Colonial Office. I can only conclude that 1804 was a year for the merchants, and not the navy." He paused then and took the cloth off his eye. "Much better, Emma." He rose up on his elbow. "I do have some bad news. The *Lady Penthyn* went down in a gale with all hands."

She considered that information, sitting beside him on the sofa.

"I intend to believe they were not on that ship," she said quietly. She looked at the papers in her hands. "Thank you, my lord."

"You're ever so welcome, Emma," he said. "You peruse them, and then I must see the lists are returned. I have promised half my kingdom and my firstborn son as ransom for those rosters."

She smiled and looked at the lists. "That leaves the *Hercules* and the *Minerva* unaccounted for now. No trace of them?"

"None," he agreed, "but they're out there somewhere. They have to belong to someone."

Emma nodded, then looked up as Lasker came into the room.

"Yes?" she asked. "Lord Ragsdale should not be disturbed, if you can help it, Lasker." She rested her hand on his shoulder, and his cup ran over with the pleasure of it all. "He's had such a day."

"Then I hate to add to the misery," came a vaguely familiar voice. "Lord Ragsdale, may I trouble you to take your miserable cousin off my hands before he causes the complete downfall of Oxford University?"

Chapter 18

*H*E SAT UP QUICKLY, DESPITE EMMA'S PRO-
tests, and slowly took the compress off his good eye,
hoping that when he did so, his sight would have returned to
normal, and it would not be Robert Claridge smiling down
at him.

But it was Robert, and there was his old warden from
Brasenose, even more grim-lipped than usual, standing
beside him. As he stared at his cousin, Robert's grin widened, as though he had never been so happy to see anyone.

"Merciful heaven," said Lord Ragsdale. He had long
believed the apocrypha that the warden never even left the
quadrangle of Brasenose, much less ventured to London.
And here he is, glaring at me, he thought. *Oh, the wonder of it
all*. He sank back down on the sofa again and put the compress over both eyes. "I think I am hallucinating, Emma.
Please wake me in an hour or two when both of these gentle-
men have disappeared."

It seemed a reasonable request, but in another moment,
the warden was leaning over the back of the sofa and staring
down at him. "Lord Ragsdale, remove that cloth at once and
listen to me!" he uttered in crisp tones when Lord Ragsdale
continued to cower behind his compress.

Lord Ragsdale did as he was told. Not for nothing had
he suffered through two interminable years at Oxford with

this warden. He would be compliant; he would grovel if, indeed, groveling were needed. And that appeared to be the case. There was nothing remotely pleasant in the gaze that the warden fixed upon him. He deftly tossed the compress into a wastebasket, stood up, and would have promptly sat down again if Emma hadn't been there to support him. He opened his mouth to apologize, but he had not reckoned on his little secretary.

"Sir, I wish you would leave," she said, addressing the warden in tones as stringent as his own. "Lord Ragsdale has had a rather trying day, and he does not need this kind of donnybrook."

I *have had a trying day?* he asked himself, as his estimation of Emma rose another level. *My dear, you must be full to bursting with anxieties, and you are worried about me?* He looked at the warden, determined not to whine or grovel, after all. *If Emma doesn't, I won't,* he decided. *I'd like to think I have learned something in these few months.*

"Please be seated, sir," he said, indicating a chair. He sat down again. "Tell me what my wretched cousin has been up to. I am eager to know whether we should flog him, place him in irons, hurl him into the ranks, or let some mythical bird or other peck out his liver while we chain him to a rock."

To his gratification, the warden blinked and sat down. "Well, I do not know as it is all that serious . . . ," he began, almost put off by Lord Ragsdale's plain speaking. Then the ill-used look came into his eyes again, and he leaned forward. "Your cousin has perpetrated the most fiendish deed ever to sully the golden stones of our fair university on the Isis." He sat back in triumph, daring Lord Ragsdale to respond.

"Oh, surely not," he replied easily, with a glance at his cousin. "Robert is not intelligent enough to bring down a . . . let me see now . . . six-hundred-year-old institution. I seem to remember a multitude of pranks, especially one involving a number of naked men and a traveling circus. Please be more specific, Warden."

"Was that you, sir?" Robert interrupted, his eyes wide. "That is still talked about in hushed tones."

"Oh, really?" Lord Ragsdale asked, pleased with himself and kindly overlooking the choking sounds coming from Emma as she went to the window and stood there with her back to the men.

"It was cards, Lord Ragsdale, cards!" said the warden, indignantly playing his own trump. "Exactly as you warned him."

Oh, drat and bother, thought Lord Ragsdale wearily. *Does this mean I will actually have to make good on my promise and send this useless fribble into the army? I feel sorry for our side already.* He twisted around to look at his American relative, who was still standing by the door. "Well, sit down, lad, sit down where I can see you, and tell me the whole sordid tale."

Robert sat next to him, which Lord Ragsdale thought a bold piece of impertinence, considering the cloud of ruin that hung over him. He continued to smile with an expression that Lord Ragsdale could only call cherubic. His eyes were even a little dreamy.

"John, it was the most magnificent opportunity, and I could not resist. I tried, though, I really did. Imagine, if you will, all those men in each hall and quad. It was, it was . . ." Robert raised his hands helplessly. "Words fail me," he concluded in a modest tone.

"They don't fail me!" said the warden, pointing his finger at Robert Claridge. "He organized what he called a floating poker game that traveled from college to college, until the entire university was involved. It was scandalous!"

"The whole university?" Lord Ragsdale asked, his voice an octave higher than usual. "Even those tight rumps at All Souls?"

"Oh, especially them," Robert said, warming to his subject. "I think they were dashed grateful to be asked to join in the fun." He cast a kindly glance at the warden, who was turning whiter by the second. "Really, I think they ought to get out more, sir."

The warden leaped to his feet, stabbed the air with his finger, then sank into his chair again, a much older man. Emma snatched up the ships' rosters and began to fan him, crooning little nonsensicals until he regained his color and waved her away.

"You should know there were vast sums involved," he concluded, enunciating carefully.

Lord Ragsdale sighed. "I was almost certain there were, sir." He fixed his blurry eye on his cousin. "What do you have to say?"

"Only that it will never happen again."

Lord Ragsdale and the warden sighed in unison and then indulged in a hearty bout of silence, which was broken at last by Robert.

"I suppose you do not wish me to continue at Brasenose," he said to the warden, his tone hopeful.

"Most emphatically not," the warden stated. "We will be lucky if anyone decides to study again before the end of term." He appealed to Lord Ragsdale. "And now, my lord, what are you going to do with this worthless bit of pond water?"

By the eternal, I wish you would stop grinning in that idiotic fashion, Lord Ragsdale thought, looking at his cousin. "I will think of something terrible," he told the warden. "It will probably be so bad that it will even eclipse the naked men and the circus."

The warden waited expectantly, but Lord Ragsdale only smiled and rose to his feet. "Thank you so much for bringing him here in person, sir," he said.

"I wouldn't have it any other way," the warden replied. "I would not for a minute wish this American on an unsuspecting population!"

Lord Ragsdale nodded. "I share your concern. I trust we will meet again in the future under more kindly conditions."

The warden bowed and moved purposefully to the door, which opened as if by magic. Lasker, his face utterly unreadable, stood there to usher him out. The warden looked back at Robert and shuddered, then delivered his parting shot.

"We will not meet again, my lord. Should you, by some grave mischance, ever find a consenting female, marry, and reproduce yourself, do not send your offspring within a mile or two of Oxford."

Lord Ragsdale took it all in and managed to avoid catching Emma's eye. *If I look at you, I am doomed,* he thought. "Very well, warden, very well," he said, his voice contrite and almost without a quaver. "The lady I am contemplating an alliance with comes from a Cambridge family, so we need not ever trouble you again." He looked at Lasker, who held the door for the warden. "Lasker, because the warden is still so upset with us, you have my permission to slam the door on your way out. Ah. Excellent."

How I wish I could laugh, he thought after the slam had finished reverberating throughout the main floor. He turned instead to Robert, then sat down.

"Now that I am seated, you can tell me the total of your losses." He glanced at Emma. "I cannot tell you how delighted I am to have a problem that I can solve merely by throwing money at it. This will be close to a pleasure, Robert."

It was Robert's turn to stare at him. "Cousin, you have changed," he exclaimed.

"I suppose I have," Lord Ragsdale agreed, pleasantly surprised that someone noticed. "Come on, tell me what I am to pay, and to whom."

Robert pursed his lips and perused the carpet for some time, as though seeking guidance. When he looked up, he still had that silly grin on his face. *It's entirely possible that I could throttle him yet,* Lord Ragsdale thought. *I wish he would not chortle over my upcoming losses.*

"Cousin, I think you do not perfectly understand the situation," Robert began, choosing his words carefully.

"Oh, no?" Lord Ragsdale asked.

"No, sir, you do not." Robert leaned forward and looked around as though the warden were within ten or twelve blocks. "I won this time." He looked at Emma. "Seven thousand pounds, Emma!"

Lord Ragsdale closed his eye. Emma gasped and sank down beside him on the sofa. He reached over and patted her. "Tell me I heard what I heard, Emma. My eyes are gone, my hearing is going. Who knows what will go next?"

"You heard me," Robert insisted. "I won fair and square." He opened his blue eyes wider. "Of course, I don't think that Brits are any great shakes at poker yet. It may take some time." He pulled up a chair closer to the sofa. "That's what I want to talk to you about."

Lord Ragsdale opened his eye. "You want to pay me back?" he asked.

"Possibly," Robert temporized. "I could pay you back, and then I could release Emma from her indenture." His voice became contrite, hesitant even. "It's the least I can do, Emma. I know that it has not been a pleasant situation for you."

"It's not that troublesome," she said simply, looking down at the unread ships' rosters she still held in her hands.

"You could do that," Lord Ragsdale said, wishing suddenly that Robert were still at Oxford and had never considered poker. *Couldn't you have waited a week or so, Robert?* he wanted to ask. *I'm busy here with something of substance for the first time in my life.*

But Robert was not through. He looked at Emma until she glanced up and met his eyes. "Emma, may I tell you what I would rather do with the money?"

She nodded and set aside the rosters. Lord Ragsdale could feel her tension, so he moved closer until their shoulders were touching.

"I would rather take all the money and go home, throw myself on my father's mercy, and start repaying him what I owe." He looked at Lord Ragsdale soberly. "I truly do not

wish to gamble again. What would you have me do, John?"
he asked.

I would have you take the money and run, Lord Ragsdale
thought. *Go home to Virginia, and leave Emma and me to
sort through this terrible time.* He looked at Emma, who was
regarding the carpet as Robert had earlier and chewing on
her lip.

"I think it should be Emma's decision, Robert," he said
finally. "She's the one who has suffered the most from all
this and—"

"I have not suffered," she interrupted quickly. She blushed
and held out her hands to Robert. "I was prepared to, and
maybe I even wanted to, but I have not suffered. And,
Robert, you won't believe what I have learned."

Robert smiled at her. "He's right, Emma. What do you
want me to do?"

Please, Emma, do not leave me, Lord Ragsdale thought. *If
you go, I am sure I will not have the courage to propose to Clarissa and "fix my fate," as you so ingenuously expressed it. I might
not treat my servants right, or keep away from alcohol, or find
anyone half so fine to handle my correspondence.*

"Your decision, Emma," he added, determined not to hold
his breath and appear like a small boy.

She picked up the rosters again and looked at him, then
at Robert. "Take your money and go home, Mr. Claridge,"
she said quietly. "I know your father will be pleased." She
touched Lord Ragsdale's hand. "Lord Ragsdale has promised
to release me when he is engaged, and I think he has almost
reached that point. I want you to go home, Mr. Claridge."

Robert leaped to his feet, pulled Emma up too, and swung
her around until she protested and told him to let her down.
He kissed her on both cheeks and hugged her until Lord
Ragsdale feared for her ribs.

"Emma, you are a game goer!" he said. "I will leave you
enough money to pay your passage back to Virginia, if
you should choose to rejoin us. I am sure Father will find

you a position as a teacher or nursemaid." He went to the door. "And now I want to find Sally and tell her." He leaned against the door. "Thanks, John and Emma. I wonder why I never noticed before what wonderful people you are."

"Perhaps because we were not so wonderful," Lord Ragsdale commented after Robert left the room. He looked at Emma. "My dear, I will release you from your indenture anytime you say."

She took that in and settled herself more comfortably on the sofa, kicking off her shoes. "We have not yet finished the bargain, my lord." She got up suddenly then and went to the desk. "Now I think you should write a note to Miss Partridge and tell her that you will be at her home first thing in the morning, so you can set out for Bath."

He joined her at the desk, sitting down and picking up the quill.

"I know she will do terrible things, like make me propose," he grumbled.

"And it will be good for you," Emma insisted. "When you are finished, I will give it to Lasker and tell him to have the footman deliver it tonight."

He did as she said, pausing here and there for advice on lover-like words. He finished and signed his name with a flourish. "I suppose you realize this means that I will be reformed, rehabilitated, married, and will probably turn into someone so dull that my children will wonder what their mother was thinking."

She smiled at him. "Serves you right, my lord," she replied, with just a touch of her former acidity. She took the note from him and opened the door upon Lasker, who appeared to be waiting outside. "Please have Hanley deliver this to the Partridges on Whitcomb Street," she instructed.

"And bring us some coffee, Lasker," Lord Ragsdale said as he returned to the sofa. "It's going to be a long night."

"I told you to go to bed and rest your eye," Emma said, then blushed and added, "my lord."

He resumed his former position on the couch. "I won't leave, Emma. Sit down right here and let's start looking."

⁓

I am seeing the backside of too many dawns, he reflected several hours later as Emma finally admitted defeat after three readings of the lists. *I would have quit after one reading,* he thought, closing his eye to the smudged, faint lists, weary of looking.

Ever mindful of his eye, Emma had done much of the reading, going slowly through the lists, saying each name aloud and only troubling him when she could not decipher the words before her. He lay with his eye closed, listening to her, holding his breath when she paused, and sitting up once or twice when he heard her sharp intake of breath. But each time was a false alarm. There was no David or Samuel Costello on any of the lists they had searched so hard for.

"Could it be that the political prisoners were not even mentioned?" he speculated at one point. "I mean, if the assizes have no record, why should the ships' manifests?"

It was a discouraging thought, but early morning was a time for discouraging thoughts. Emma considered it a moment, then rejected it. "I cannot see how that would be so," she argued. "A ship would need to know precisely how many were on board, concerning matters of space and food."

"I am sure you are right," he said, happy to agree with her.

And so she had read through the manifests two more times, grumbling the second time about ship captains and bad handwriting. On the third reading, her voice was subdued. Finally, after the clock chimed three, she put down the lists.

"They're not here," she admitted.

She sat on the floor beside the sofa, leaning against it. He reached down and rested his hand on her shoulder. "Emma, do you really think they ever left Ireland?" he asked quietly.

She was silent for a moment as she rested her cheek

against his hand. "Yes," she said finally. "They were in good health, and it was Eamon"—her voice faltered—"Eamon who confessed to everything." She drew up her knees and rested her chin on them. "Do you know, the interrogators pressed him for other names of accomplices, and he recited the whole family graveyard." She turned her head to regard him. "No. Eamon implicated no one else alive. They had no reason to kill Da and Sam too. No reason."

"Well, then, we must find the *Minerva* and the *Hercules*," he said. "Give me a hand up, Emma."

She stood up, rubbed the small of her back, then helped him to his feet. "I suppose it can keep until you return from Bath," she said as she placed the lists on the desk.

"Emma, you have my permission to return to the docks and check some more," he said. "Only please take the footman with you and enough petty cash for bribes. Oh, and return the lists tomorrow."

She nodded. "I'll make sure you have receipts for anything I spend."

"It's not necessary, Emma." He opened the door, surprised how dark the hall was, then remembered that everyone else was long in bed. "I'm so tired," he said, more to himself than to her. *And discouraged, and wondering when this will end for you.*

They walked upstairs together, and she said good night to him on the landing that led to the servants' quarters on the third floor. *Emma, stay with me,* he thought suddenly. *It's only a few hours before dawn, and I'm a little low in spirits.*

He shook his head at the thought and wished it would go away.

But there it was, dancing about in his head like a little shadow puppet. *I would like to hold you in my arms.*

"My lord," Emma said, her hand on the railing.

He looked up expectantly, wondering if by some miracle she could read his mind and was not opposed to the idea.

"Yes, my dear?" he asked, his voice soft.

He could hear her chuckle in the gloom, even though he could not see her. "You should know that I made another confession yesterday morning."

Her tone was playful, but not amorous, so he put away his own roguish thoughts. "Say on, Emma."

She must have sat down on the stairs, because he heard a rustle of skirts, and her voice was lower. "When I went to Fae Moullé, we . . . I encouraged her to cheat you. The receipt we compiled for her milliner's shop was greatly more than she really needed."

"Emma, you're a rascal," he said, amused where a month ago he would have been angry. "You wanted to cost me money."

"I hated you, my lord," she said simply, her voice coming at him so quiet from the darkness of the stairs. "You were just another Englishman."

He felt his way to the landing again and rested his arm on the newel post, not certain of where she was. "Well, what penance did the priest suggest?"

She laughed and got to her feet, and he could tell that she was farther away than he thought. "Remember, I told you he was Irish too! He told me to pray for your soul, but only if I thought I wanted to."

He joined in her laughter. "And do you?" he asked finally.

"I already have," she said quickly, and she seemed almost surprised at his question. "Good night, my lord. I'll be in the book room for your instructions in the morning."

And then she was gone, hurrying up the stairs to her little cubbyhole under the eaves. In another moment he heard a door close quietly.

Chapter 19

*C*OULD IT BE THAT THIS IS WHAT THE
French aristocrats felt like on their way to the guillotine?
Lord Ragsdale thought as the Partridge carriage rumbled
on its sedate way to Bath. He could almost imagine the
cheering, cockaded crowds milling about and ready for a
whiff of blood.

But this is absurd, he thought as he smiled down at Clarissa Partridge, who had captured his hand so possessively
and pressed her thigh against his in a manner that was
faintly pleasant. *When they clamp me to the board, slide me
under the blade, and we are pronounced man and wife, I will be
the envy of my generation. Envious males will probably drink my
health in clubs all over London and marvel at my good fortune.*
The thought sent a shudder through him, which he could
only ascribe to feet of the coldest sort.

See here, John, he told himself, *it is merely that you are afraid
for nothing. Surely every man experiences some little trepidation
at the loss of liberty and at the reality of life with a wife.* He
returned his gaze to Clarissa again, admiring the gold of her
hair and her flawless complexion. *Clarissa, if you happened
to throw out freckles like Emma Costello, you would probably
lock yourself in a dark room and remain there.* But there was
no danger on that head. Clarissa possessed skin that most
women could only dream about.

"Don't you agree, John?"

What? What? Clarissa was gazing at him with something akin to adoration and obviously waiting for an answer. "How could I disagree with you, my dear?" he replied, hoping that would satisfy and wondering to what he had just put his imprimatur.

She appeared satisfied with his response, if he rightly interpreted the little squeeze she gave his arm. *Pay attention, John,* he admonished himself, even as her voice rippled on and he thought about his departure that morning.

Sally Claridge had met him in the breakfast room with the startling announcement that she was returning to Virginia with Robert. He had sputtered into his tea briefly, reminding her that there were several young bucks—chaps he had handpicked, mind you, because they did not require a fortune—who were hovering on the brink of offering for her. She only treated this magnanimity on his part by a smile and a kiss in his general direction as she breezed by.

"I would rather go home," she had insisted when Lady Ragsdale added her admonitions to his. Sally smiled at him, then at Robert. "I am mindful of all you have both done for me, but I want to go home."

His pride piqued, Lord Ragsdale appealed to Robert. "Let me remind you, cousin, that for reasons which you know only too well, Sally will make a much better marriage over here."

Robert was no help. He only shook his head and dug a little deeper into his eggs and ham. "Cousin, you don't really argue with women, do you?"

"Well, I, no . . . ," he stammered.

Clarissa looked at him, her eyes wide, her lips in their ready-made pout, and he realized he was talking out loud. "My dear, I don't think I would be a disappointment to you behind a curricle of my own," she was saying. "Papa taught me to handle the ribbons."

"Oh! I am certain you would not," he agreed. "Whatever

could I have been thinking?" *Pay attention, you cloth wit*, he told himself, then promptly dismissed Clarissa again.

Sally was not about to change her mind. "I will return home to Virginia," she had stated firmly, after he went through a patented catalog of reasons why she should remain in England. "Cousin, I do not care how poor we Claridges are, or how everyone else in Henrico County laughs at us because of Robert's spendthrift ways." She smiled at her brother. "I know he means to change, and besides all that, I want to be with my family. It's where I belong."

Of course she is right, he thought as the carriage traveled through the spring finery of Berkshire. He listened patiently then to Clarissa's description of the rest of this year's Season and the twin delights of a ball and a presentation next month, which, he knew in his bones, would somehow involve him to an unpleasant degree. He nodded where he was supposed to and felt some small relief when Clarissa's eyes closed and her adorable head came to rest against his arm. Lady Partridge smiled indulgently at him and returned to her tatting.

And so he had given his blessing for a happy journey to both of the Claridges, had finished his breakfast, and had adjourned to the book room, where Emma waited with his correspondence to sign. He signed where she indicated and was struck by the fact that if Emma found that her father and brother had indeed been transported, she would probably want to join them in Australia.

The thought was distressing in the extreme. He sat on the sofa and watched her as she finished some last-minute paperwork he had requested. She was young and strong and healthy, but the thought of her going to such a place made him want to rise up in protest. He had heard stories at his club from army officers who had returned from duty in the antipodes, and they had nothing kind to say. It would be the worst exile of all for someone so lovely, vibrant—for someone with such promise—as Emma, he decided. And she would be fifteen thousand miles away. She might as well be on the moon.

It was a melancholy reflection; the idea of losing his secretary pained him. *I could keep her in the indenture*, he told himself as he came closer and looked over her shoulder at the ledger and her careful entries. *But that would be heartless, and if I have discovered anything this spring, it is that I have a heart. It is a dashed nuisance, but there you are.*

But Emma among convicts? Emma condemned to toil for her bread in such an inhospitable climate? Emma so far away? *I will not think about it*, he told himself firmly. *There is no indication that we are any closer to a solution to her mystery, and for all we know, the Costellos went down with the* Lady Penthyn.

He sighed and kissed the top of Clarissa's head, then leaned back, closed his eye, and wondered why on earth he had felt compelled to kiss Emma when he left.

They had just finished the most prosaic of conversations in the book room, like many others during the last few months. She had assured him that she would return to the dock for another look and that she would participate in his banker's upcoming audit. She even promised to go to Norfolk with Lady Ragsdale, if he did not return after two weeks, and check out progress on the construction.

Maybe I shouldn't have put my arm around her shoulder, he considered as the carriage bowled along. He had thought it was a brotherly gesture, perhaps even avuncular. He had not been surprised particularly when her arm went around his waist as they walked together to the book room door. Truth to tell, they had both been through a lot in the past week.

But why had he kissed her? She had done nothing in particular to encourage it, other than look at him when he was raving on about being pitchforked into a visit to Bath that was destined to end in his proposal to Clarissa. It wasn't his fault that she got that twinkle in her eyes when he started to complain about exertion and ill-usage. And truth to tell, probably nothing would have happened if she had not stopped, put her hand on his shoulder and straightened his neckcloth.

It must have been Emma's fault, he decided, because I was only falling back on natural instinct. He thought about the matter, concluding that the experience was inevitable, considering that every time previous to his reformation that he got that close to a woman, he invariably kissed her. *You put water in a streambed, and it will flow,* he reasoned. *If you place Lord Ragsdale in breathless proximity to a female who is not a relative, he will kiss her. It happens ten times out of ten, whether kisses or water.* "Hydraulics," he murmured, then nodded and smiled at Lady Partridge when she looked up from the intricacies of her tatting with a faintly puzzled expression.

A mere few months ago, that would have been enough explanation to satisfy him. He would have promptly dismissed the event from his mind and gone on to other conquests. *Things are different now,* he thought. *I am now blessed with a modicum of sense, and my sense tells me that I enjoy kissing Emma Costello.*

The motion of putting his hand under her chin and his lips on hers had required not an iota of thought, so practiced was his lovemaking. The part that so unsettled him then, and that was breaking out sweat on his forehead now, was the way Emma's lips and then her embrace made him feel.

He eased out his pocket watch, so as not to disturb the sleeping Clarissa, and consulted it. *Up until half past seven this morning, I kissed females with the idea of what I would get out of the exchange,* he thought. *Kissing Emma was the first time ever that I wanted to give more than receive. I wanted to let her know that someone cared what happens to her. I wanted to share my strength, I who have never been strong. That one little kiss—well, perhaps it was not so little—made me better than I ever was before.*

He looked out the window at the glorious spring and wished himself back in the book room. He tried to imagine how he would replay that good-bye again, and he could not envision any other conclusion. As surely as God made sinners and fools to test the world, he would have kissed Emma Costello. The thought shook him to his very soul, and he felt tears starting behind his eye. *Why did I have to do the most stupid thing of all?* he berated himself. *Why did I have to fall in love with Emma?*

At his insistence, they stopped for the night at Market Quavers. "I do not know why we cannot stop at Reading," Clarissa protested, her pout more pronounced than usual. "I mean we usually stop in Reading."

Well, too bad, he wanted to say, *change your blasted routine.* Instead, he kissed his love's forehead. "I have a banking transaction to undertake in the morning, my dear," he explained, tucking his arm through hers as he escorted her to the Quail and Covey.

She suffered him to lead her along, pausing only at the doorway for another attempt to reason with him. When it failed, she gave him a searching look. "This quite cuts up my peace," she assured him.

"I trust you will forgive me," he said with a smile, all the while writhing inside and wondering if he had been so vacuous before his reformation. The realization that he had been that petty and more so did nothing to raise his spirits.

He allowed her to tease him into an explanation, partly to placate her for the disruption to her usual itinerary. "I wish to begin an annuity for Mrs. Mary Roney, the sister of my former secretary. That is all, Clarissa."

He paused, knowing that she would fawn over him for his kindness to the downtrodden and embarrass him with her praise. He waited uneasily for her to laud him for such benevolence to someone who had cheated him. What she said surprised him.

"You cannot be serious," Clarissa said, her voice a trifle flat, the music gone out of it.

"Of course I am," he replied, wondering where this was going.

"You are actually going to help the sister of the man who robbed you?"

He nodded. "It seems about the least I can do for David Breedlow, who only thieved from me to help his sister in her great need."

"John, what do you think prisons are for?" she asked, stamping her foot. "A servant should never steal from his master."

"Not even when the master was a stupid lout who should have cared enough to see to his servant's needs?" He heard his voice rising. "Clarissa, there is a man on his way to exile and possible death in a place I wouldn't wish on a dog because I whined about twenty pounds."

Clarissa, her eyes big at his outburst, yanked her arm from his and hurried to her mother's side. "I can only hope that you do not dole out too much of your income to gutter rats."

There will still be plenty of it left, and then some, for your ribbons, hats, and shoes, he thought. "But I thought you were pleased when I mentioned my work among the prisons?" he asked, reminding her of his fiction of several days ago.

"It is one thing to take Bible tracts and jellies to prisoners, but it is quite another to give them your money and encourage them," she said. "Come, Mother. I feel a headache coming on."

He ate in solitary splendor in the private dining room that night, and the food was excellent. To aid his digestion, he went for a long walk that took him through the village, out into the surrounding farmland, and back again. On the walk out, he had almost convinced himself not to make Clarissa Partridge an offer. On the way back, he realized that was impossible.

She expects me to propose, he thought, *and I would be ungentlemanly not to. My reformation will be complete, and I will free Emma from her indenture. If she ever finds that her father and brother are truly in Australia, she will go to them.* He stood still in the road and watched the lamps lit in houses on the village outskirts. *And even if she never leaves England, she has seen me at my worst and could not possibly want anything to do with me.*

No, he would speak to Clarissa's father tomorrow in Bath, propose, present her with a stupefying diamond, and become an unexceptional husband. No one would ever know that he was in love with his secretary. *How odd it is,* he considered, *that here I am, trying to help Emma find her relatives. If I succeed, she will certainly leave.*

"The old Ragsdale never would have done this," he said out loud to a cow by the fence. "The old Ragsdale would have dragged his feet and whined and not lifted a finger to help, especially if by so doing, he ruined his own chances. I am a fool."

He walked back slowly, trying to figure out at what point he fell in love with Emma. As he stood outside the tavern, he realized that he must have felt something that night she stood beside him with her fate resting on the turn of a card. *Is it possible that what I took for hopeless submissiveness was courage on a scale so great that my own puny resources could not measure it?* he reflected. *Was that when something in me began to understand what Emma Costello meant?*

He couldn't go inside. He stood beside the door, wondering at the workings of fate. *If things had been different, Emma, perhaps you could have loved me too. How tragic for us, this endless war between our people. You have been misunderstood, scotched, lied to, and diddled at every turn. I can only be grateful that at least you do not hate me anymore.*

~

Clarissa was in good spirits in the morning. When he

returned from his errand at the bank, she condescended to take his arm and allow him to walk with her to the waiting carriage. He helped her inside, then climbed in after her.

Lady Partridge was still inside the inn, giving a portion of her mind she could ill spare to the landlord over the damp sheets. He turned to Clarissa. Now was as good a time as any. He took a deep breath.

"Clarissa, I am sure you are aware of my pleasure in your company." *I should take her hand,* he thought, so he did. "I wonder if you would do me the honor, the ineffable honor, of consenting to become my wife."

There. That wasn't so difficult. It was words strung together, and from Clarissa's reaction, they were the right ones. She squeezed his hand, and he returned the pressure.

"I know a lady ought to turn down a first proposal," she said, and his heart rose for a moment. "But I shall not," she continued, "for I fear it would disappoint you, my dear. Yes, I will be your wife. Nothing would make me happier than to put some regularity into your disordered life."

He almost winced at her words and, by the greatest effort, choked back his own indignation. *Regularity? Regularity?* he wanted to shout. *I am so regular now that Greenwich could set its clock by me. You will make me boring, and prosy, and stuffy, and my children will only suffer me. They'll never know there was a time when I was fun and a bit of a scoundrel.*

"I am so pleased," he said and kissed her.

It was a test, really, and not a kiss, and he failed. Her lips were every bit as soft as Emma's, if anything, but he felt nothing beyond the usual stirrings of the healthy male. She wasn't Emma, and he didn't care from his heart.

He was spared from another demonstration by the arrival of his future mother-in-law. Clarissa, all blushes and breathless sentences, told her the good news, and he was rewarded with a beaming smile from Lady Partridge and the assurance that she would devote the remainder of the Season to arranging the most brilliant wedding.

He was content to suffer in silence for the remainder of the trip to Bath. Clarissa and her mother moved with lightning speed from silver patterns to china to damask curtains, and were careening onto the honeymoon itself when Bath appeared like a benediction. He sighed with relief and called their attention to the city before them, using it like raw meat before wolves to distract them. "Now tell me how I should approach your father," he interrupted, not wishing to think about his honeymoon because Emma would not be the last person he saw when his eye closed, and his first sight in the morning.

"Papa will be delighted," Clarissa assured him. "Only do not bump his foot or ask for sherry. The doctor has put Papa on a strict regimen of pump water mixed with vinegar and cloves."

"Heavens," he said. *Is this to be my future as well? Gout and pump water?*

To his dismay, a tidal wave did not roar in from the Bristol Channel and float them out to sea before they arrived at the Partridge home. Sir Clarence was in the library, with his bandaged foot propped on a footstool, looking as though he could chew through masonry. Lord Ragsdale took a deep breath, blew a kiss in the doorway to Clarissa, and closed it behind him.

"Sir Clarence," he heard himself saying, "how nice to see you again. I believe we have a matter of the heart to discuss."

⁓

I refuse to flog myself because I allowed Lord Ragsdale to kiss me, Emma told herself at least one hundred times before noon, laying on the mental lashes as she busied herself with his instructions. That the experience was pleasant beyond all reason only added to her logic that she was getting old now—almost twenty-five—and more susceptible to such things. She considered the matter and resolved that, when this matter of her father and brother was settled one way or the other, she should give some thought to marriage and a family of her own.

Not that her future husband would be anything like Lord Ragsdale, she told herself, suppressing a small shudder. She allowed herself a smile, wondering what he would say if she told him that he had become her measuring stick of what not to look for in a husband.

She frowned, aware of the fiction of that statement. While it may have been true several months ago, it was not true today. Lord Ragsdale showed great potential now. Emma picked up the quill again and dipped it in the ink. *Miss Clarissa,* she thought grimly, *I hope you appreciate the paragon—well, the improved person—that I have helped to fashion. I hope you will have the wit to scold him where he needs it and give him plenty of headroom in matters where he shines.* She sighed. *I should write a manual for the care and upkeep of Lord Ragsdale and give it to you, Miss Clarissa. Why am I afraid that you won't know what to do with him?*

The thought dogged her for several days, but she eventually put it aside as she and the footman made several more trips to Deptford Hard and the shipping offices. No one had ever heard of the *Minerva* or the *Hercules,* not even when she attempted bribery. When she explained it to him, Robert Claridge took her task to heart and traveled to Portsmouth, seeking news of the missing ships. There was no news, not even any scraps of information in the dusty boxes at the Home Office, which she returned to during the remaining days of the week.

"I begin to wonder if they ever existed," she told Robert as he sat in Sally's room, watching her pack.

"You could return to Virginia with us," he offered. "I do not think Lord Ragsdale would mind, and didn't you say he is probably engaged by now?"

She nodded and began to fold the chemise in her hands smaller and smaller. "I am sure you are right." She looked down at the garment in her hands and shook it out to begin again. "Perhaps Lord Ragsdale will have thought of something else. I should wait."

And so she did, although it gave her a pang to stand with Lady Ragsdale and wave good-bye as the Claridges departed for Portsmouth and a ship to America. Robert had kindly left her enough passage money to see her to Virginia, "When you decide you've looked enough," he had told her the night before.

To take Lady Ragsdale's mind off the melancholy of farewell, Emma saw to it that they traveled to Norfolk to look in on the progress of construction and renovation. She took notes on the improvements, pleased to see how well Manwaring and Larch worked together. The sheepherders had already moved into their new quarters, and work would begin on the crofters' cottages as soon as the planting was finished.

"Lady Ragsdale, you can tell your lordship that he has a good instinct where people are concerned," Mrs. Larch told her as they walked around the newly dug foundations on her last evening in Norfolk.

"Mrs. Larch, I am not married to Lord Ragsdale," she said quickly, before she lost her nerve. "I serve him as his secretary. I do not know why he didn't correct you during that first visit, and then I was too embarrassed to say anything."

Mrs. Larch stared at her in amazement. "I never would have believed it!" She looked at her husband, who was chatting with the bailiff. "And didn't my David remark to me that you two looked like you had been married years and years?"

Oh, my, Emma thought to herself. *This is worse than I thought.*

"It was just Lord Ragsdale and his rather demented sense of humor, Mrs. Larch," she apologized. "I trust you will excuse him."

Mrs. Larch allowed as she could. "Well, you may say all that, but I think you would have made a grand Lady Ragsdale."

"Why, thank you," Emma replied. *How curious,* she thought. *A few months ago, I would have pokered up and pro-tested at such a statement. Perhaps I am learning something of toleration.*

And something of patience, she told herself early the next week as she shook her head at Lasker's offer of hackney fare and started walking to the bank for the monthly audit of Lord Ragsdale's accounts. *I will certainly need it if I am to say more than three or four sentences in my life to Clarissa Partridge.*

That morning's interview with Clarissa called for a brisk walk, she decided. They had returned from Norfolk to a letter from Clarissa. Lady Ragsdale read it, then held it out to Emma, a broad smile on her face. "Well, it is about time," she commented.

Emma read the brief note, marveling that Clarissa could write as she spoke, in breathless sentences, little wispy frag-ments that managed to convey her delight at Lord Ragsdale's proposal, and then ping off half a dozen other topics in the brief space of half a page. She looked on the back, but there was nothing more.

And then only days later, the fiancée herself sat drinking tea in Lady Ragsdale's private sitting room, all blonde and lovely and wearing a diamond that Emma thought vulgar. When Lady Ragsdale inquired where her son was, if he had not returned with her, Clarissa only shrugged her shoulders.

"He bolted out of Bath after only three days," she said, her expression somewhere between a pout and a simper. "He said something about business that would not wait. Yes, thank you," she said, selecting a macaroon from the tray that Emma held out to her. "I will have to speak to him about such precipitate behavior."

"He does his best work on impulse, I think," Emma noted.

"Well, it won't do, and so I will tell him," Clarissa con-cluded, speaking with finality. She took a long look at Emma. "And I will also tell him that once he is married, he can find himself a regular male secretary, like all his friends."

Oh, I like that, Emma thought as she quickened her pace to the bank. Of course, as soon as the wedding—and maybe sooner, if today's conversation were any indication—she would find herself an independent woman. *There will be nothing for me here in England. There is nothing in Ireland. I suppose I will return to America.*

The banker's audit was the usual ponderous process of reconciling ledgers and figures, with occasional reminders this time for her to pay attention. "Emma, this is not like you," the senior clerk scolded.

I suppose it is not, she considered as she turned her attention from a perusal of the paneling to the ledger before her. She accepted the Bath receipts, her eyes widening at the cost of the diamond ring that Lord Ragsdale had lavished on his bride-to-be. *He must be dead in love, or monstrously vulgar,* she thought as she added the sum to her entries.

She looked up from the next receipt. "Mary Roney in Market Quavers?" she asked.

The clerk leaned over the ledger, his spectacles far down on his nose. "He has decided to award an annuity to the widowed sister of David Breedlow," he announced, then fixed her with that dry look that clerks reserve for the foolish wealthy.

You dear man, she thought as she finished her accounting and put the ledger under her arm again. *Only marry now, and I will consider your redemption complete.* She started the long walk home, then reconsidered. "No. I will celebrate," she told herself as she stepped into the street to hail a hackney.

"Kensington, if you please," she instructed the jarvey and settled back with a sigh. *I will wander among those paintings I was too frightened to look at when he took me to the gallery. Of course, it would be better if Lord Ragsdale were here, because then he could explain them to me.*

She paid the small entrance fee from the few coins she allowed herself from Robert Claridge's passage to Virginia and strolled slowly through the gallery. The peace of the place made her sleepy, and she found a comfortable bench. *I will sit here and think about my future*, she told herself as her eyes closed.

She couldn't have put her finger on what woke her, except that the sun was slanting across the gallery floor and telling her it was time to go home. She sat up and looked right into Lord Ragsdale's eye. She gasped and let the ledger drop.

"I wondered how long I would have to stare at you before you woke up," he said to her from his seat across the gallery. "And I have only one eye."

Her face red with embarrassment, she fumbled for the ledger and started to rise. He held up a hand to stop her and started across the gallery.

"Stay where you are, my dear. I have such news, and I'd rather you were sitting down.

"Well, did you keep things running smoothly while I was away?" he asked as he reached inside his overcoat.

"Of course," she replied promptly. "Probably better than you would have, my lord," she teased. Her smile deepened as he pulled out a small packet and dropped it in her lap.

"From me to you, Emma. It was easy to find where I've been," he explained.

She unwrapped the package and held up a rosary. "Oh, thank you!"

"You're so welcome, Emma." He reached into his overcoat again. "Here's something else."

The smile left her face when he dropped a bundle of papers in her lap.

He tried to keep his voice casual and offhand, but through his obvious exhaustion, she could almost feel his excitement.

"Emma, you can correct me if I'm wrong, but you might find some familiar names here."

She looked down at the lists in her lap, afraid to touch them. "My dear, it's silly of me, but I must insist that you breathe in and out," she heard Lord Ragsdale saying from what seemed like a great distance. "I found the *Minerva* and the *Hercules*!"

Chapter 20

*I*MPULSIVELY, SHE TOOK HIS FACE IN HER hands and touched her forehead to his. "Somehow, I knew you would," she murmured, and she meant it.

Lord Ragsdale picked up one of the lists and placed it in her hand. "They were on the *Hercules*," he said, unfolding the papers. "Wouldn't you know I would go through the *Minerva's* list first." He scanned the second page and then ran his finger in practiced fashion down the second column. "There."

She looked where he pointed, read the name, and allowed herself to breathe again. "David Upton Costello," she read out loud. "My lord, that is my father."

"I thought as much. And look here," he said, pointing farther down the list. "There were several Costellos. Samuel—I cannot make out the middle name, but it starts with an A."

"Ainsworth," she said, touching the name. She folded the paper carefully, tenderly, then leaned against Lord Ragsdale's shoulder and closed her eyes, unable to say anything.

"They sailed in April of 1804," Lord Ragsdale said as he put his arm around her shoulder. "Now you know, Emma."

She opened her eyes then and sat up, her mind suddenly full of questions. "But where? How? What magic is this?"

He laughed at her and raised his hands as though to fend her off. "For two people who think themselves at least more intelligent than dahlias, we were remarkably thickheaded on this one, Emma."

"Tell me!" she demanded, ready to pluck at his sleeve like a child.

"During my third night in Bath when I was tossing and turning—oh, by the way, you may congratulate me on my forthcoming nuptials," he said, interrupting himself.

"And I do congratulate you," she replied, then looked at him shrewdly. "And why, pray tell me, if you are so happily engaged, were you 'tossing and turning'?"

He was silent a moment, and she almost wished she had not asked. "It is merely that I prefer my own bed here in London." He tugged at her hair under its cap. "That is none of your business and has nothing to do with my narrative!"

"Very well, my lord. Pray continue."

"It suddenly occurred to me that the most logical place to look for a ship bearing Irish convicts was Ireland itself." He smiled at her openmouthed amazement. "Impressive, ain't I?"

You went all the way to Ireland for me, she thought, *even though you have sworn to me how seasick you get in a full bathtub, and I know you really don't care to exert yourself.* "Very impressive," she said quietly. "Lord Ragsdale, you are a wonderful man. Have I ever told you?"

In reply, he took her hand and kissed it. "No, you have not, but it's nice to hear. I made up some fancy lie about business that could not wait, placated Clarissa with an obscene diamond—"

"I've seen it," Emma interrupted, "and you are right."

"—And caught the next ship to Cork." He pressed his hand to his stomach. "I can only marvel how anyone survives a sea voyage. Emma, the things I have done for you . . ."

"I told you I was grateful," she said, twinkling her eyes at him and holding the lists closer.

"I combed the docks for any record of our missing ships but found nothing. It only remained for me to catch the mail coach to Dublin." He looked up as the gallery clerk motioned to them and then tapped his pocket watch. "Emma, we're being ejected. Shall we?"

She put her arm through his and strolled with him into the gardens. She stopped then and looked at him. "How did you know I was here?"

He took her arm again and moved her in the direction of his curricle. "Simple. I went to the bank, and the senior clerk said he thought he heard you tell the hackney driver to take you to Kensington." He looked around him at the flowers. "It's much nicer now than it was the first time I brought you here." He sat her on a bench. "Back to the story."

"But aren't you in a hurry to get home? This morning Miss Partridge mentioned something about a party."

"There will always be a party," he said, dismissing his fiancée somewhat callously, she thought. "I want to tell you here."

"Very well, then," she replied, mystified.

"I went to Dublin." He paused then, as if wondering how much to tell her.

Her hand went to his cheek. "I want you to tell me everything, my lord," she said simply. "You just said that you would, and I have waited so long."

"Of course." He spoke quickly then, as though the news he bore pained him to the quick. "I checked the records at Prevot. Your mother died of typhus, much as you had thought."

She waited for the news to slap her, but she felt instead a peaceful calm. *Mama must not have suffered long then,* she thought. *Ah, well, she is at rest now, and the soldiers cannot touch her.*

"Eamon?" she asked.

He put his arm around her again. "He was hanged in the Prevot Prison courtyard in October, about the same time Robert Emmet was beheaded." He twined his fingers in hers, and she clung to his hand gladly. "Emma, the United Irish dead, or Croppies, or whatever you want to call them, were all tumbled into a common grave. Do you know, it's become a shrine of sorts." He smiled at the memory. "Blamed if the British don't try and try to keep it from happening, but flowers are forever turning up on that mound."

"I wish I could add mine," she said softly.

He kissed her hand again. "Consider it done, Emma. The guards there are really slow, even though I left a regular florist's shop."

The tears came then, and she clung to him as he patted her back and let her cry. They were cleansing tears, and when she finished and blew her nose vigorously on the handkerchief that Lord Ragsdale always seemed to have ready, she knew she would not cry that way again. She would remember Eamon always, but she would not mourn him anymore, now that she knew a nation in the making held him dear too.

Lord Ragsdale looked at the sky. "I think we will continue this as I drive." He stood up and held out his hand for her. "I knew I would find the ships' rosters in Dublin, and I did," he said as he helped her into the curricle. "Both ships had Dublin registries." He spoke to his horse, and they started back to Curzon Street. "I actually spent an evening with the captain of the *Hercules*. He assured me that there was little loss of life on the voyage to Australia." He looked at her. "Of course, you won't know until you get there . . ." His voice trailed off. "Emma, it's a long way."

"I know."

They were both silent for several blocks. "I had to hurry back to Bath," Lord Ragsdale said finally, continuing his narrative. He nudged her shoulder. "By the way, I stopped in to see Fae Moullé's millinery shop, and it is a fine one. How pleased I am that you both cheated me." He laughed out loud at the look she knew was on her face. "She gave me a rather elegant bonnet for you, which I was hard put to explain to Clarissa."

Emma joined in his laughter. "You have my permission to give it to her as a wedding present."

He nodded. "I expect my wife will wear it," he said enigmatically. "But, Emma, I have not finished my Irish tale."

"What more can there be?" she wondered. "Everyone is accounted for now."

"Not everyone, Emma."

What can he mean? she thought as the traffic claimed his attention. *I have no hidden relatives waiting to give me a fortune so I can travel to Australia.*

"I took the mail coach for the return trip to Cork," he continued when the traffic abated.

He looked at her, and she found the expression unsettling. *There is such tenderness in your face,* she thought. *There can be no more bad news, so it must be good news.* "I wish you would tell me," she urged.

"I thought I would stop in Diggtown. I remember you said that was where you left Tim."

She nodded, afraid to speak, allowing herself the tiniest glimmer of hope after years of none.

"I thought to find his grave, so I could give you a complete report, but, Emma, there was no grave for Timothy Costello. I tried all three cemeteries."

She took his arm. "That's all right," she soothed, worrying at the emotion coming into his voice. "It really isn't necessary for you to absorb all my troubles, my lord."

"Oh, Emma." He shook his head. "Well, I tried the better part of the day to remember the name of that family you said you had left him with."

"Holladay," she said automatically.

"Yes. I remembered it just when I was about to climb aboard another mail coach." He chuckled to himself. "I think the other passengers thought me daft when I leaped off that thing and ran back into town."

"Please tell me," she pleaded. "Surely they did not toss him into a common grave with no marker. I could not bear such news."

"Emma, you can bear anything," he murmured. "That is

the wonder of you. I found the house—a nice one, by the way—and knocked on the door." He paused, then covered her hand with his. "Emma, the young lad who answered the door looked a great deal like you."

She stared at him, dumbfounded. "Tim is alive."

Tim is alive, she repeated in her mind as she clutched Lord Ragsdale's hand. She closed her eyes to let the words sink into her brain. *Tim is alive.* She had carried him ten miles through a driving rainstorm, and him burning with fever. She shuddered, remembering all over again the death rattle in his throat, reverberating so close to her ear as she staggered along, one shoe on, the other lost in the mud, her clothes plastered to her, and soldiers everywhere to prod and poke if she slowed down with her burden.

"It cannot be," she whispered.

"Then I can't imagine who it was there at the Holladays who held open the door and asked would I like to come in," Lord Ragsdale said mildly as he pulled up in front of his house. "He has charming freckles, marvelous green eyes, and an appealing way of cocking his head to one side when he listens."

"Tim," she agreed. She folded her hands in her lap, wondering why it was so difficult to absorb such news. "Then I must return to Ireland."

Lord Ragsdale smiled and shook his head as he took her hands in his again. "I wouldn't, Emma. When I told him who I was, and what had happened to his family, he wouldn't settle for less than coming with me."

She looked up at him and swallowed, wishing for words but unable to think of any.

"My dear, he's inside." He tightened his grip on her hands. "I just wanted to break it to you out here before you did something silly like faint or succumb to hysterics." He smiled into her eyes. "Tim said he doesn't like girls to make a scene, and I assured him you would not."

She sat in silence, her senses reeling. *How do I put into*

words my gratitude, she thought as she looked at Lord Ragsdale. *I hated you at first because you are English, and now I have such profound regard for you. I will never be ignorant of your faults, but you have borne mine with uncommon grace. I wonder if I will ever be out of your debt, even if you release me from my indenture and I travel thousands of miles.*

"Emma, I am not handsome enough to stare at for such a length. Is my patch over the wrong eye? Spinach between my teeth?" he teased. "Come, come. You have some reacquaintance to make, and I do believe he is looking out the window right now, wondering about his sister."

She leaped from the curricle, even as he tried to help her down, gathered up her skirts, and ran into the house. Tim stood in the hallway. *How tall you are,* she thought as she just stood there, taking in the sight of him, hugging him in her mind and heart even before she held out her arms.

He walked toward her slowly, as if checking her out with every footstep, looking for the sister he remembered when he was five.

"Emmy?" he asked finally.

Without a word, she grabbed him fiercely into her arms. In a second his arms tightened about her, and she felt his tears on her neck.

"I waited and waited for you to come for me," he sobbed, even as she kissed his neck and clung to him. "I kept hoping."

"Such watering pots," Lord Ragsdale commented as he handed each of them a handkerchief, then pressed a third to his eye. "See here, you have set me a bad example." He grinned at Tim. "But I will practice economy and cry out of only one eye."

Tim laughed and blew his nose, then allowed Lord Ragsdale to give him a hug of his own.

"Good lad," Lord Ragsdale said as he put his arms around both of them and steered them toward the book room. "Do you know, Emma, he does not get seasick." He ruffled Tim's hair with a familiarity that made Emma smile. "He assured me that I would not die and ignored me when I threatened to throw myself overboard and end it all."

"You did not say that!" Tim declared.

"Hush, lad!" Lord Ragsdale said with mock sobriety. "If you and I are to rub along together, you must realize I enjoy giving a tale a good squeeze."

"Like Da," Tim said.

"Why, yes," Emma agreed, wondering why she had never noticed that tendency about Lord Ragsdale before.

In the book room, Lord Ragsdale ceremoniously seated himself at the desk and rummaged about in one of the drawers. "I know it's here, unless you have organized the very marrow out of my bones," he grumbled.

"I would never," she protested as she possessed herself of Tim's hand. "In fact, I think I will advise Clarissa to give you ample room to maneuver, my lord. You do your best work on a spontaneous basis, I believe."

"So glad you finally recognized it," he murmured as he pulled out a document. "Here we have your indenture paper. Tomorrow it goes to the bank to be signed down here and notarized, and then it goes to you, my dear." He folded his hands on the desk. "I think you should frame it, so you can tell your children someday how you reformed a rather dingy member of the peerage because of a card-game wager." He winked at Tim. "It's a story worthy of the Irish, lad."

She accepted the paper from him, looked at it, and returned it to the desk. "I would like to continue working for you for wages, until I earn enough for passage for two to Australia, my lord."

"I fear that is quite impossible. Clarissa has told me on several occasions that she thinks I need a male secretary," he replied.

Emma nodded, remembering her conversation with Clarissa only that morning. "Well, then, can you give me a character reference?"

He smiled at her. "Before I came looking for you, I wrote

this character. Perhaps it will suffice. Take it, Emma, and with my blessings."

She held out her hand for the letter and held it so Tim could read it too. *He can't be serious*, she thought. "My lord, this is addressed to Lachlan Macquarie"—she looked closer—"the governor of Australia . . ."

". . . Who said he would be delighted to provide you with employment in the colony. When I went to the trouble of finding out who he was, I was only too delighted to discover that he is sailing on this next supply convoy. Apparently, the Colonial Office thinks Macquarie is just the man to take over from the unfortunate William Bligh," he said. "It seems that Captain Bligh cannot weather mutiny on sea or land, and there has been trouble in Australia."

"But"—she frowned—"that may be, my lord. Don't think you will scare me off from making the journey."

"I would never!" he exclaimed, his voice shocked. He winked at Tim and quite ruined the effect.

"Lord Ragsdale, do be serious!" she said. "This paper is well and good, but I need employment here to pay for passage there. It is quite simple. I cannot swim there!"

"You probably could," he disagreed. "But to spare Tim any possible embarrassment, I intend to pay your passage and his, if I can't talk him into coming with me to Norfolk."

"You can't, my lord," Tim said.

"You sound just like your sister," Lord Ragsdale said mildly. "I didn't think I could."

"I never asked you to pay our way," she protested, all the while knowing that he was going to do what he wanted.

"I know you did not. I want to do it, and I don't want a lot of argument, and please, no pouts. I am already steeling myself for a lifetime of those from Clarissa. Don't you do it too," he concluded with some finality.

He rose to his feet, as though signifying the end to his audience. *Very well, my lord*, she thought. *Our relationship has changed yet again. Now you are formal and dignified and in control of things. I know this is what I worked for, but I miss the rascal a little.* She held out her hand to him, and they shook hands.

"Thank you."

"It's nothing, Emma." He looked at Tim. "Lad, go tell Lasker not to hold dinner any longer. I want the two of you at my table tonight."

"Oh, that isn't necessary," she said as Tim grinned at Lord Ragsdale.

"I want to, so don't argue. The convoy leaves in a matter of ten days or so. When I visited with the new governor . . ."

"You visited with him?" she interrupted.

"Of course!" he replied, sounding genuinely indignant this time. "You don't seriously think I would just turn you over to the vagaries of life at sea without looking into the matter!"

"Such exertion," she murmured, touched at his interest.

Lord Ragsdale appealed to Tim. "See how she baits me? Was she this way at home?"

"I can't quite remember," Tim said and then brightened. "But my brothers were."

Emma laughed and pulled Tim closer. "Very well! If you must be solicitous, I suppose there is nothing I can do about it. Go on now, Tim, and speak to Lasker."

"There isn't anything you can do about it," Lord Ragsdale agreed after Tim left, his equanimity restored. "I learned from Governor Macquarie that the lord inspector will sail too. You will be in quite distinguished company, so you might brush up on your manners."

"You seem determined that I remain firmly in your debt," she protested with a smile.

"Of course," he agreed cheerfully. "I like to have people owe me."

It is more than I could ever repay, she thought, *but a burden I gladly bear.* She went to the door, then turned back on impulse and kissed him.

Why am I doing this? she thought as his arms went around her and held her close. He was incredibly easy to kiss, and once begun, difficult to leave off. Her hands went to his hair then. She had always admired his thick hair, and she wondered if it felt as good as it looked. It did, to her gratification, and to his pleasure, obviously, because he sighed and continued kissing her.

We simply must stop this kiss, she thought, and then didn't think anymore, finding herself more occupied with the rapidity of her heartbeat and the pleasant feel of him. *I am being kissed by an expert,* she thought. *It was nice before, but this is infinitely better.*

He seemed in no hurry to end the experience, except that someone had the bad timing to knock on the book room door. Lord Ragsdale released her and began to straighten his neckcloth. "Drat!" he muttered, even as she went to the window and stared out, hoping that the intruder did not have intense scrutiny in mind. Her cheeks felt flaming hot, and she stood there, astounded at her own temerity. *This indenture is not ending a moment too soon,* she thought as Lasker opened the door, announced dinner after a quick look around, then took himself off again.

"Dear me," she murmured when the room seemed awfully silent.

"Dear me, indeed," said Lord Ragsdale, sounding quite as out of breath as she felt. "If I had known how you felt about release from your indenture, I'd have signed that blooming document once each day, maybe twice."

The enormity of her indiscretion nearly removed what breath she had left. *I must be losing my reason,* she thought, measuring the distance between the window and the door and wondering why it looked so far away. And there was Lord Ragsdale, his face flushed, his eye decidedly bright.

"I cannot imagine what you think of me," she said, feeling such intense shame that she thought she would melt with it. "Dear me," she said again, her voice more faint this time.

To her acute discomfort, Lord Ragsdale came no closer but continued to regard her, his expression thoughtful. He started to smile then, and her shame deepened. He sat on a corner of his desk.

"How odd, Emma," he commented, not looking at her now but gazing over her shoulder. "You have worked so hard to redeem me, but I wonder if you have succeeded." He grinned at her stupefied silence. "I suppose that would depend on what your aims were. Did you really plan for me to fall in love with you?"

She shook her head, astounded at his words, wishing he had not said them. "I was out of order," she said when she thought she could manage complete sentences.

"Well, no, actually, I thought you followed through in remarkably fine order," he commented as he gave a final tug to his neckcloth.

She edged toward the door. "You simply have to disregard my behavior."

He shook his head. "I am able to forget a considerable number of things, but I don't think my amnesia would extend that far."

"I was improper," she said.

"Decidedly. I wonder why I am not bothered by that?" he asked, more to himself than to her.

What can I say to this man? she thought miserably. *I can only wish that ship were leaving in fifteen minutes.* In another moment there was no need to decide. Someone knocked on the door.

"Cut line, Lasker," Lord Ragsdale snapped, giving her reason to suspect that he was not so calm as he appeared. "We won't perish if the peas are cold."

I will if this conversation continues, she thought. She went to the door and opened it, not turning around when Lord Ragsdale called her name. In another moment, he grabbed her arm.

"Emma, please," he insisted. "We need to talk."

"There is nothing to say, my lord," she replied, retreating behind her formal exterior again. "I will remind you that you are engaged to Clarissa and I am bound for Australia. Good night, my lord. I think I would rather eat belowstairs with Tim. We came somewhat close to forgetting ourselves, didn't we?"

Chapter 21

I AM A COWARD, SHE THOUGHT THAT EVE-
ning as she stayed belowstairs with Timothy and listened to him tell her of his life with the Holladays. She held him close, her arm tight around him, and gradually allowed good sense to reclaim her. After she was sure that Lord Ragsdale had left the house for the evening, she prepared a pallet on the floor of her attic room and took Tim there. They spoke of the coming voyage until she could almost forget what had happened in the book room.

This is the reality of my life, she told herself firmly. *We are sailing to an unknown place, and we do not know what we will find. We will be among soldiers and convicts.* She sighed and looked down at Tim, whose eyes were closing slowly, even as she watched. She touched his shoulder, then pulled his blanket higher, marveling all over again in the pleasure of seeing him. *Am I wrong to take him along to this dreadful place? Lord Ragsdale said he would take him to Norfolk.*

"Emma, I wish you would answer me," he was saying.

"What? What?" she asked, guilty at the thousand directions her mind was taking.

"I want to know if you are afraid," he asked.

"I used to be," she said honestly, knowing that she could not lie to her brother. "But now that you are to come with me, I don't think there is anything that can frighten the two of us."

"But suppose Da and Sam are dead?" he persisted, taking her hand.

"We will decide what to do if it comes to that, Tim. Go to sleep now."

He slept peacefully, quietly, but he would not relinquish her hand. She sat on the floor beside him, knowing that sleep was far from her. *I wish my conscience were as clear as yours, Tim,* she thought as she gazed at his relaxed face. *I have labored so hard to mend a faulty character, not realizing all the while that it was mine.*

She undressed finally and crawled into bed, only to stare at the ceiling and listen to house noises until everyone was asleep. *Oh, well,* she decided as her eyes began to close, *it is better to love foolishly than to hate bitterly. I hope I am wiser than I was and more kind.*

～

Her resolution was firm, and in the morning she dressed quietly and tiptoed out of her room, careful not to waken Tim. She went to the front hall for the mail, dreading that Lord Ragsdale would rise early and demand more conversation.

The mail was gone. She looked around at Lasker.

"Lord Ragsdale has already perused the correspondence and placed it in the book room," he said. "He has gone to Norfolk, taking Miss Partridge and her mother with him."

She sighed with relief and went to the book room. His usual list of instructions was on the desk as well as a folded note. She sat down and opened the note. "Dear Emma," she read, "Clarissa is eager to see the manor and figure out more ways to spend my money constructively. We will return after your ship sails, so let me wish you happy journey and good news at the end of it. Excuse my bad manners. John Staples."

There was no need to read it again and search for hidden meanings, for there were none. She managed a smile and chided herself for being an idiot. *We are talking of Lord*

Ragsdale, she told herself, *he who loves to kiss women. It was that and nothing more. I am only chagrined that I caused such a kind man any embarrassment. I trust he will soon forget it, if he has not already.*

His kindness to her continued through the days of his absence. Her next visit to the bank was more in the way of a command performance, as the custodians of a major portion of Lord Ragsdale's wealth assured her that she was to take the enormous sum of two hundred pounds with her. She could not imagine such largess and told them so, but the senior partners only looked at each other and chuckled.

"He told us you would say that," they assured her. "Lately, he is so well-organized and sensible that we do not argue with him over paltry sums."

I have created a monster, she thought with amusement. "Very well, then, sirs, so it will be. Never let anyone say that I don't know when to save my breath to cool my porridge."

She also knew better than to argue when Lady Ragsdale insisted that they visit the cloth merchants and purchase yards and yards of muslin goods, and silk stockings, and bonnets of a practical nature. "I cannot imagine where you will get these things if we do not buy them now," she said, explaining away her own generosity. She paused in front of a boll of handsome burgundy wool. "Do you suppose . . ."

"No, my lady," Emma said hurriedly. "I fear it is rather hot in the antipodes. Let us confine our enthusiasms to muslin."

"It seems so ordinary," said Lady Ragsdale with a sigh. "Do you not suppose there will be balls there occasionally or even musicales?"

I could never tell this dear lady what I fear I will find, she thought as Lady Ragsdale cast a longing eye on a nearby bolt of pale yellow silk. *We are going to a convict colony, a place of harsh rule and desperate men. She, who had been coddled so gently, would be horrified if she knew how hard it might be. I shall never tell her.*

"Do you know, you may be right, my lady," she said, choosing her words carefully as her own fears returned. "I think that silk would be entirely in order."

"I knew it!" Lady Ragsdale declared in triumph. "With that and a pair of Morocco leather slippers to match, I will pronounce you fit. You may keep my paisley shawl," she added generously.

⁓

"Where can we squeeze it all?" she grumbled to Tim several times in as many days when Lady Ragsdale continued to add to the contents of the sea chest. Her largess spilled over into another trunk and then another, each requiring the strenuous efforts of the footman to close them, with Lasker sitting on top, dignified to the end. "This has to be enough," she said firmly on her last night on Curzon Street as Lady Ragsdale met her on the first-floor landing with another nightgown.

"Certainly, Emma," Lady Ragsdale agreed. "And if I think of anything else, I can send it 'round later."

Emma turned away to hide her smile. *Lady Ragsdale, you have no concept of geography*, she thought. She took the nightgown from Lady Ragsdale, said good night, and went into the book room for one last look around. She could hear Tim and the footman bringing the trunks down two flights of stairs. Lasker had made arrangements with a carter to pick them up at first light.

And we will follow, she reflected. A penny post from the dockyard had informed them of their departure with the tide in the early afternoon. She went to the window to stare down at the street below, rain-slicked from a sudden squall and washed clean of the day's commerce. Soon there would be only months and months of waves and wind and small ships. "And wormy food and sea biscuit," she said out loud as she opened the window for a deep breath of flowers in the window box. "And serious uncertainty, as you would say, Da. I wonder what I will find at the end of my journey."

She tidied the room, hopeful that Lord Ragsdale would be able to discover everything in order when he returned. She was about to turn out the lamp, but suddenly she knew it wasn't right to leave without even a farewell note. *There can be no harm in expressing myself this last time*, she thought, *no harm at all.* She sat down at the desk.

It was easy to tell Lord Ragsdale thank you on paper, to thank him for putting the heart back in her, for making her angry enough at times to keep her from melancholy, for finding her family, for tying up the ragged strings of her life. She labored over the page, wanting to express her whole heart and mind. "I do not know whatever good I may have done you, my lord, but you have given me back my brother," she wrote, then hesitated. *I could tell you I love you*, she considered, the quill poised over the inkwell. *It would be true, probably the most true thing I ever wrote.* She put down the quill and rested her chin on her hands. *There will always be some part of me that longs for you, but should I say that to a man so soon to be tangled in the toils of matrimony?*

"How fortunate I will be so far away," she said, and picked up the quill again. "I can be no possible threat, Clarissa Partridge, bless your pouty hide." She wrote swiftly then, telling him of her love, leaving nothing out, not mincing a single word. Nothing could be safer; she would be in the middle of the Atlantic before he returned from Norfolk. She picked up the letter, still frowning over it, wondering why even that declaration was not enough.

And then she understood and laughed out loud, sticking the quill back in the ink. *Not only do I love you, Lord Ragsdale,* she told herself as she wrote the words, *I also like you.*

It looked silly on the page, like something you would say to a friend from childhood, or a schoolmate. She almost tore up the letter. *He will think I have lost all reason to say something so childish*, she thought. She stared at the note for a long while, then sighed and tucked it in under the paperweight. She blew out the lamp, took another look around the room, and closed the door on her career as a secretary.

~

Leaving the house on Curzon Street was harder than she could have imagined. Lady Ragsdale cried, the footman looked decidedly forlorn, and even Lasker showed a glimmer of some expression besides patient condescension when he helped her into the hackney, nodded to Tim, and told the driver to take them to the docks. When she looked back, she even thought she saw him dab at his eyes. She may have been mistaken; it was a blustery day, and there were cinders in the air.

"We have so much to look forward to," she told Tim, who grinned at her.

"You sound like you're trying to convince yourself," he teased. *I suppose I am*, she thought, struck by the truth of his observation. *Leave it to a little brother to define my own melancholy. If I did not know better, I would accuse him of taking lessons from Lord Ragsdale.*

They arrived at Deptford Hard in plenty of time to catch the tide that even affected the oily swells of the Thames, far upstream from the ocean. The *Atlas* rode low in the water, full of supplies for the seven-month journey, and more victuals for the convict colony that still needed food from home to take the ragged edge off hunger. She looked closer, frowning. There was no bustle of activity on deck to signify a ship about to sail, no one but the captain, who stared at a long list as he paced the deck.

Tim noticed the strange silence too. "Emma, was it today or tomorrow?"

Before she could add her questions to his, the captain

of the *Atlas* spotted them and came to the railing. "Miss Costello!" he shouted to them on the dock. "Go home. Something has happened, and we cannot sail today."

"What?" she shouted back, dreading a return to Curzon Street and another round of farewells tomorrow, or the day after.

"The lord inspector died last night. We won't sail until the end of the week."

Trust the lord inspector to be so thoughtless, she told herself as they returned to Curzon Street in silence. *Now we must go through all this again.* She leaned back and drummed her fingers impatiently on the seat, too irritated for rational conversation with Tim.

By the time they were approaching the turn to Curzon Street, she acknowledged the hand of providence in this event. At least she would have time to reclaim the letter from the book room and replace it with something more dignified. That hope crawled up her throat and then flopped back into her stomach as they turned the corner to see the Ragsdale carriage at the front door.

"Heaven and all the saints help me!" she gasped.

Tim looked at her in surprise. "Don't you want to have a chance to say good-bye to Lord Ragsdale?" he asked. "I know I do."

"I'm not so sure," she wailed, wanting to leap from the hackney, run back to the dock, and hide there.

Tim peered at her. "Don't you like him? After all he's done for us?"

She nodded, kicking herself for her own folly, and hoping that Lord Ragsdale's indolence would lead him to avoid the book room altogether, now that she was no longer there. "Of course I do," she muttered.

"Good," Tim said. "He told me he likes you."

Emma groaned and closed her eyes. *That word has come back to haunt me,* she thought, then stared at her little brother. "He said what?"

"That he liked you," Tim repeated patiently, with that sly look that brothers reserve for especially dense sisters. "I told him of course he did, and he just laughed."

Well, you won't be laughing now, Lord Ragsdale, she thought as she grossly overtipped the jarvey in her confusion. *You will think I am such an idiot.*

She contemplated sneaking around to the servants' entrance, but Lasker flung open the door, an actual smile on his face as she started to tiptoe away.

"Miss Costello! You have changed your mind! Lord Ragsdale, can you imagine who has returned?"

To her everlasting chagrin, Lord Ragsdale stood in the doorway too, his mouth open in amazement. "I thought you would be gone by now . . . ," he began.

"I did not know you would return so soon," she started to tell him at the same time.

Tim laughed and hurried inside. Emma came up the steps slowly. She tried to observe him without being obvious and could see no sign of disgust on his face, or exasperation. There was nothing beyond a deepening of the crease between his eyes, and a certain dullness in his expression she had not noticed when he left. As she watched, he made a visible effort to appear cheerful.

"Change your mind, Emma?" he asked as he held open the door for her. "If it's any consolation, I think I would have." He shuddered. "All that water moving up and down! I would probably get calluses from kneeling over a bucket for seven months. Wise of you to reconsider."

She shook her head. He walked with her down the hall. She glanced at the book-room door, which was closed. His trunk was still at the foot of the stairs.

"Did you just return, my lord?" she asked, her voice hopeful.

"Only just," he agreed. "But you have not answered my question."

Good. He cannot possibly have seen the note yet, she thought with relief. "The lord inspector has died suddenly, apparently. We will sail in a few days, my lord," she explained.

Lord Ragsdale managed a rather mirthless chuckle. "I never thought he was a man for the rigors of Australia, myself. He probably is only pretending until the ship leaves without him."

She laughed because she knew he expected it. *Go upstairs like a good man*, she thought, willing him to move away from the book room, where he stood now with his hand on the doorknob.

"If you do not mind, then, my lord, we will remain here a few more days until we sail," she said, when he continued to just observe her. *And for heaven's sake, don't go in there*, she thought.

"You know I do not mind, Emma," he replied, then opened the door and went in, closing it firmly behind him.

I think I will die of embarrassment, she thought as she stood at the door. She held her breath, expecting any moment for Lord Ragsdale to come bounding out, note in hand, to scold her for being an idiot. Nothing happened. She let out her breath and quietly climbed the stairs.

She spent the rest of the afternoon lying on her bed and staring at the wall, Tim curled up beside her, asleep. She dreaded every sound on the stairs and panicked when darkness came and someone knocked.

"It's only me," said the footman.

"Come in then, Hanley," she said, hoping the relief in her voice was not too obvious. Tim sat up and rubbed his eyes as she opened the door.

"Lady Ragsdale would like you and Tim to have dinner with her," he said, then added, when he noticed the hesitancy on her face. "She does not like to dine alone, Emma."

"But isn't Lord Ragsdale available?" Emma asked.

The footman shook his head. "Oh, my, and didn't he tear out of here like a man with a mission!"

I wonder what that means, she considered as she ushered

Tim out the door. *I only hope he has not returned to his club and his former bad habits.*

She and Tim followed the footman downstairs, and she sent them on ahead as she went to the book room door, listened a moment, opened it quietly, and tiptoed to the desk. Relief washed over her. The note remained exactly where she had left it, tucked under the paperweight. She snatched it up, crumpled it into a tiny ball, and threw the note into the fireplace, where she watched until it flamed and crumbled into ashes.

Her heart ten times lighter, she managed to make herself good company to Lady Ragsdale for the evening, never a difficult task. As much as she disliked cards, she knew she could while away an evening with them, nodding occasionally, making comments here and there as Lady Ragsdale chattered, cheated, and triumphed.

She kept her ears open for Lord Ragsdale's return, but when she finally surrendered her cards at midnight, his candle was still waiting for him on the entrance hall table.

She decided the next day that he must have seen the note, after all, and had chosen to avoid her. It was the only conclusion she could make because he left the house before she woke and had not returned late that evening.

"I do not understand it," Lady Ragsdale commented as she signaled to Lasker to pour the sherry after another interminable night of cards. "Perhaps he is still with Clarissa. The wedding is planned for early June, after all, and these things take careful planning."

"I am certain you are right," Emma agreed, happy to end the discussion by yawning, stretching, then saying good night. *What a sham*, she thought as she climbed the stairs again. *Now I will toss and turn and pretend to sleep, when I am in a perfect agony over Lord Ragsdale. Suppose he has returned to his former bad habits?* she thought again. It seemed unlikely; the footman made no mention of anything out of the ordinary. *I am stewing over nothing*, she decided, but that thought did nothing to hasten sleep.

I cannot manage another day of sleeplessness, she told her-self as she dragged out of bed and sat there until she had the energy to rise. Tim was already gone; in fact, his pallet was neatly folded. She rose, looked at the tangle of her own bed, and shook her head at her folly.

She was straightening the sheets when Tim burst into the room. "Emma, there is a message from the *Atlas*! We are sailing at noon!"

"Thank goodness," she said and meant each word. *The sooner I am gone, the better.*

They arrived at the *Atlas* within the hour, after suffering through another round of farewells. She knew that Lord Ragsdale was in his chambers, because she heard him walk-ing about as she tiptoed down the hall. There were more tears from Lady Ragsdale, and then they were safely inside the hackney. She made the mistake of looking back at the house, where, to her horror, she saw Lord Ragsdale stand-ing at his bedroom window. To her further amazement, he opened it, leaned out, waved, and blew her a kiss.

This is so odd, she thought as she waved back but omitted the kiss. *There have been too many of those to unsettle a rational mind,* she assured herself as she set her heart and mind on the journey ahead.

The *Atlas* was a swarm of activity this time as she and Tim went on board and found their cabin, a tiny cubbyhole crammed 'tweendecks. They drew straws, and Tim won the top berth. She sat on her berth and looked around her. *For six or seven months this will be our home,* she thought, *and then we will be in a most hostile place, from which so few return.* She considered the matter and then realized that it did not make a difference where she was. There was no home anymore in Ireland; Virginia had been a pleasant interlude, but only a place to mark time; England was the enemy still.

She lay back and propped her hands behind her head. *No, that was not true,* she reasoned, thinking of Norfolk and the good people there. *And Lord Ragsdale is in England.* Silent tears rolled down to wet her hair. "Oh, Clarissa, please realize what a gem you have," she whispered. "Do you know that you are the luckiest lady in England?"

She dried her eyes before Tim noticed and assured him that she would join him on deck later. There would be no pleasure taken in watching London recede as they worked their way to the Channel. The familiar numbness that had captured her heart the day after Robert Emmet walked up the lane to her house was returning again. She closed her eyes against it, knowing that she had not the strength to resist anymore.

But I must exert myself for Tim, she thought, sitting up. *Even if we arrive in Sydney and find no trace of Da or Sam, I have Tim to think of.* She straightened her dress and went into the companionway.

It was full of trunks and boxes. She stepped around them and met the apologetic glance of the ship's steward.

"Sorry, mum," he said. "It's the new lord inspector's stuff, and where am I to put it, I ask?"

She shook her head over his dilemma and hurried on deck, minding her steps around more luggage and rope, and casks. Tim had already attached himself to the seamen doing their slow shuffle around the capstan as the great anchor rose. He grinned at her in self-conscious delight, and she smiled back. *This trip will be a boy's paradise,* she thought. *I wonder what I will make of it?*

The captain and first mate were everywhere, bellowing orders to the men balanced on the yardarms. She glanced at the small knot of men standing forward, chatting by the railing, obviously the other passengers. There was a lady with them, well-dressed and standing close to the man who must be the colony's new governor. *Perhaps she will need a servant,* Emma thought. *I should make myself known to her.*

She stayed where she was, shy again. *I have seven months to make her acquaintance,* she excused herself. *It can wait.* She turned to go belowdeck once more but stopped and looked around again. Someone had called her name.

She looked at Tim, who was still pulling up the anchor, his attention concentrated on the sail above him that was slowly filling with air now. *I must be hearing things,* she decided and moved toward the companionway again.

"Emma, I wish you would pay attention," Lord Ragsdale called to her.

She whirled around and stood in dumbfounded amazement as one of the men separated himself from the group by the railing and strolled her way. She stared at him, then sank down on a hatch as he came closer, taking his time, ambling along as though he owned the ship.

"What a lot of clutter," he said with some distaste as he seated himself beside her. "The captain tells me that we will stop in Rio to take on livestock, and then it really becomes interesting."

Her mind was even more cluttered than the deck. *If I look at him, I know he will vanish,* she told herself but could not bring herself to glance his way. She knew quite forcefully that the last thing she wanted was for him to disappear. *I will just sit here and pretend another moment,* she thought.

It would have worked, except that he took her hand then, and she knew he was real. She looked down at his fingers twined through hers and closed her eyes as she sighed and leaned against his shoulder, feeling safe again.

"Emma," he said after a moment, and there was nothing of assurance in his voice now. "I hate to admit it, but I've made a real muddle of your excellent work of redemption."

She smiled but did not open her eyes. "I suppose you will tell me now that there is a ferociously angry lady in London who would probably break you on a rack if she ever catches you."

"Well, yes," he said. "You Irish have such a way with a phrase, did you know?"

She giggled. "What have you done, Lord Ragsdale?"

He raised her fingers to his lips and kissed them. "I think I have made it impossible to return to London anytime soon." He paused a moment. "How fortunate then that I have taken on the job of lord inspector for Australia and Van Dieman's Land."

She gasped and looked at him then. "You can't be telling the truth!"

"Why would anyone lie about that? Really, Emma, you disappoint me."

He kissed her then, and as she let him fold her in his arms, she knew his disappointment did not extend to his lips. Or his heart, obviously; it was pounding as hard as hers was. She would have been happy to continue kissing him until they arrived in Sydney, but he stopped suddenly and looked up at the cheering sailors in the mast overhead.

"We should obviously continue this belowdeck," he commented as he tucked her close under his arm. "I am somewhat squeamish about spectators to my lovemaking. Call me prudish, but there you are."

"I could never call you prudish, Lord Ragsdale," she assured him.

"Yes, well," he said. "Neither are you, my dear. That was quite a note you left on my desk."

She blushed. "I had hoped I was able to retrieve it in time."

"So glad you didn't," he murmured. "It sent me out the door and on my most spontaneous errand ever. Clarissa Partridge—should you ever require this information—does not enjoy tumult, challenge, or change of plans." He kissed her head. "She'd have been a dead bore in a place like Australia, which will probably contain generous parts of all three."

"It was the note?" she asked.

"Well, yes and no," he said. "I had decided several weeks ago that I loved you, but figured that was a lost cause. So I thought it would be less painful all around if I stuck with the original plans and married Clarissa. I did not want to return from Norfolk until I was sure you were gone." He chuckled and shook his head. "I owe such a debt to the defunct lord inspector."

"But I do love you," she assured him. "I didn't think you could ever be serious about me, so I left that note only because I knew you would never see it when I was around."

"Of course; makes perfect sense," he said calmly, with only a hint of a smile, then glanced at Tim, who stood beside Emma. "And you, lad, what does your expression tell me?"

"Only that I do not understand adults," he said honestly.

"Nor I," Lord Ragsdale confessed. He kissed Emma again. "I had to make some arrangements, obviously, to show you what a good fellow I am—hardworking, honest, and all that, and fit to be father to your children. I don't think your da would much approve if I were to arrive unemployed with you in Australia and tell him what a bargain he was getting for a son-in-law."

"And all this because I wrote I love you," she marveled. "I am sure you have heard it before."

"Heavens, yes," he agreed, the picture of serenity. "Fae Moullé used to tell me that on a regular basis, so she couldn't have meant it." His voice turned serious then, and her heart pounded louder. "Actually, Emma, what no one has ever said before was that they liked me."

"I do," she said simply and kissed his cheek.

"Thank you," he said, his voice equally quiet.

"And you are truly lord inspector?" she asked. "How did you manage that?"

"Simple, really. And let me state here how nice it was of the former lord inspector to oblige by dropping down dead during the first course of his farewell dinner."

"You are a rascal," she said with some feeling.

"We know that already," he reminded her. "After leaving Clarissa in strong hysterics and starting to foam, I dashed to the Office of Criminal Business. Emma, I do not understand why our favorite porter gets so excited when I come around. Think how relieved he will be not to see me for a few years."

"Go on, and leave out the dramatics," she warned him.

"He took me right in to see Mr. Capper—imagine that, if you can—who walked, nay, ran me over to the Colonial Office, where they took me to Home Office. Oh, I love bureaucracy, Emma. Think what a politician I will make."

"I warned you . . . ," she began but stopped when he kissed her again.

"A kiss or two, and you are so easy to deal with," he murmured. "Imagine what can happen when we attempt something more strenuous! Well, to my narrative, if you insist."

"I do."

"Someone thought to check my military record at Horse Guard. It must have been sufficiently distinguished—my dearest, lose an eye and gain your country's love—because I waited in a few more anterooms, then was sent back to Home with a recommendation."

"Such exertion," she murmured and held out her arm for Tim, who sat down on her other side. The ship was moving now, the sails filled.

"Actually, it was worth it. Emma, I cannot confirm this, but one of the senior clerks in Home told me that Spencer Perceval—the prime minister, my dear; don't look so blank—even said, 'What a novelty. Did they finally get someone who might actually do the job?'" he concluded modestly.

"They did," she said. "Mrs. Larch always swore that you know how to handle people."

"Let us see if I can deal with felons, murderers, blackguards, assorted lowlife, and touchy Irish. Let me promise you that for every old idea I use, I will think up two new ones," he said and reached into his pocket. "Which brings me to my next bit of effort. Emma, you see before you a special license. It cost me a bundle, and I would hate to waste it."

She took the writ from him and looked it over, then handed it back. "You've become so frugal, my lord."

"Yes. Economy is the key here, my love. Do call me John,

by the way. I think our association is shortly to become somewhat intimate, and I think too much 'my lording' will quite put me off my best conjugal efforts."

"Really, John," she said and blushed.

"Economy, dear. You see, I need a secretary for my new duties—if David Breedlow cannot be found—and I need a wife and mother for my children. As I am only allowed so much poundage for this voyage, I must economize and combine all that in one."

She smiled at Lord Ragsdale and nudged Tim. "Doesn't he carry on?"

Tim nodded. "I think he is asking you to marry him."

"Smart lad," Lord Ragsdale said with approval. "How about it, Emma? Will you marry me? It's an exertion, but I think I can manage."

"Of course I will marry you, John," she said promptly, "but I might remind you that we have left the dock."

"True," he agreed. "Isn't it our good fortune that the Colonial Office decided to send out a vicar to Australia? He's the one over there looking decidedly seasick already. Granted he is not Catholic for you, my dear, but he'll make us legal." He looked at Tim. "Will you mind having your cabin to yourself? I plan to be seasick and a devoted husband, in equal parts, and it won't be a pleasant sight for you. Perhaps Emma will be a loving enough wife to raise my head from the bucket every now and then."

Tim shook his head and grinned. "I won't mind, as long as you treat her well."

Lord Ragsdale stopped smiling then, and his face became so serious that Emma felt tears in her eyes. She brushed at them, then squeezed his hand tighter.

"I promise, laddie," he said softly. "She'll have no cause to regret her decision." He released Emma's hand and reached across her to take Tim by the shoulder. "And if for some reason we cannot find your father, I would beg the raising of you as my own, if that's agreeable."

"Aye," Tim whispered, his face as solemn as Lord Ragsdale's.

"Very well, then!" Lord Ragsdale said and looked at Emma and Tim. "What a couple of long faces!" He slapped his forehead then in theatrical exasperation. "Oh, Emma, I know why you are so solemn right now! Didn't you once tell me that nothing would make you happier than a bed of your own?"

She laughed out loud, wondering how she would manage a lifetime with the quixotic, outrageous Lord Ragsdale. *One lifetime will never be enough,* she decided, loving him with all her heart. "I did say that once."

"You will have to share your bed again, Emma. I'm sorry, but I must insist."

About the Author

Photo by Marie Bryner-Bowles, Bryner Photography

CARLA KELLY IS A VETERAN OF THE NEW York and international publishing world. The author of more than thirty novels and novellas for Donald I. Fine Co., Signet, and Harlequin, Carla is the recipient of two Rita Awards (think Oscars for romance writing) from Romance Writers of America and two Spur Awards (think Oscars for western fiction) from Western Writers of America. She is also a recipient of Whitney Awards for *Borrowed Light* and *My Loving Vigil Keeping*.

Recently, she's been writing Regency romances (think *Pride and Prejudice*) set in the Royal Navy's Channel Fleet during the Napoleonic Wars between England and France. She comes by her love of the ocean from her childhood as a Navy brat.

Carla's history background makes her no stranger to footnote work, either. During her National Park Service days at the Fort Union Trading Post National Historic Site, Carla edited Friedrich Kurz's fur trade journal. She recently completed a short history of Fort Buford, where Sitting Bull surrendered in 1881.

Following the "dumb luck" principle that has guided their lives, the Kellys recently moved to Wellington, Utah, from North Dakota and couldn't be happier in their new location. In her spare time, Carla volunteers at the Western Mining and Railroad Museum in Helper, Utah. She likes to visit her five children, who live here and there around the United States. Her favorite place in Utah is Manti, located after a drive on the scenic byway through Huntington Canyon.

And why is she so happy these days? Carla doesn't have to write in laundry rooms and furnace rooms now, because she has an actual office.